MARY BILLITER

SPIRITED AWAY

For information, contact the publisher, Hot Tree Publishing.

WWW.HOTTREEPUBLISHING.COM

EDITING: Hot Tree Editing

FORMATTER: RMGraphX

COVER DESIGNER: Claire Smith

ARTWORK: JCH Studios

ISBN-10: 1-925655-21-0

ISBN-13: 978-1-925655-21-6

10 9 8 7 6 5 4 3 2 1

DEDICATION

Spirited Away began when one of my writing students, Mareon Stolp, loaned me a book about "Haunted" Cheyenne. I didn't give it much thought until I tucked into bed for the night and read the different hauntings in Wyoming's capital city. I didn't sleep well because my mind imagined the next book in my resort romance series based in a, you guessed it, haunted hotel!

However, I'm a big believer in research. So, I visited the oldest hotel in Cheyenne, which was built in 1911. The staff at The Plains hotel didn't blink an eye when I asked if I could have a tour of suite 444—where supposedly furniture moves and things go bump in the night. If they do, it didn't happen for me. But I left with a real sense of history, which is what makes this western city so great.

Cheyenne, Wyoming is a wonderful town on many levels. It's steeped in tradition, home to myriad historical buildings, but it's the people who make the "Magic City of the Plains" shine. The historical insight I received to write this book was tremendous. (Key individuals are listed in the acknowledgements section.)

So *Spirited Away* is for the community of Cheyenne and it's generous spirit of the west that keeps the legend alive! Go Pokes! #WyomingProud

ALSO BY MARY **BILLITER**

RESORT **ROMANCES**

Do Not Disturb : Book 1
Escape Clause : Book 2
Rule Breakers: Book 3
Spirited Away : Book 4

RESORT
ROMANCES
BY MARY BILLITER
POINT
"SPIRITED AWAY"
Cheyenne WY
"Do Not Disturb" &
"Rule Breakers"
Huntington Beach, CA
"Escape Clause"
Newport OR
"SPIRITED AWAY"
YOUR NEXT BOOK
DESTINATION:
the Historic
Wyoming Point Resort
CHEYENNE, WY

CHAPTER **ONE**

REESE

"What do you mean, it's haunted?"

"The hotel—it's haunted."

The assistant front desk manager and the hotel—hell, even the state—were new to me. Maybe this was how they welcomed a city slicker to town, with a silly yarn right out of a Wild West dime store novel. *Sure, why not. I'll play along.*

"Haunted, huh? As in Casper the Ghost haunted or the twins in *The Shining* haunted? What level of creep factor we got going on here?"

The phone rang and Zavi raised his index finger, as if I'd possibly forget the topic of discussion.

I glanced at the polished marble floors and ornate nineteenth century light sconces that hung on the wall, looking like something a Pony Express rider would suddenly gallop by and grab to deliver the mail past dusk. The crystal chandelier in the lobby cast a subtle hue on the settees upholstered in a rich red velvet. *This place is beautiful. I can't believe I'm the new GM.*

Tiffany banker lamps with amber-cut glass were positioned on vintage card tables. Their rustic copper pull chains added to the charm as western songs from the player piano filled the lobby with a melody that made me want to sing loudly and off-key. But I opted to tame my inner diva and not join the chorus of "Home on the Range."

The musky odor of the old hotel oddly wasn't offensive, but rather a welcome reprieve from the artificial vanilla that was piped into the lobby at my former hotel in California. The vanilla-spiked air was meant to attract and relax travelers, but it tended to have the opposite effect, overpowering guests and staff alike. The only thing this lobby did was transport people back in time. A large bronze coatrack—with a matching hitching post not more than ten feet outside the lobby doors—spoke volumes about what was offered at the Historic Wyoming Point Resort in Cheyenne. Though, at times, it was hard to tell where the saloon ended and the bordello began.

My assistant front desk manager concluded the call with the customary phone etiquette required from any Point Resort employee. The only thing that differed between each property was the hotel's tagline. "Thanks again for calling the Historic Wyoming Point Resort in Cheyenne, where the legend lives," he said.

Where the legend lives? Note to self: change tagline. I returned my focus to Zavi, who typed a reservation into the computer. His diamond stud earrings in each ear shone against his smooth, dark umber skin. His hair had clean edges and a deep side part that offset his black curls and soft brown eyes.

"So, these ghosts—friend or foe?" I asked.

"This isn't some friendly little spirit." His concentration, though, was on the computer screen. I waited while he inputted the necessary data into the FrogKiss registration system. Even if he screwed up, I could find a guest simply by their first initial, or at least a list of potential guests with the same first or last initial. FrogKiss was corporate's answer to reservation issues. They'd hired software designer Hunter Hughes to install a program he created that found exactly who we were looking for on the first try, which was super helpful during busy check-ins. I could tell from Zavi's thoroughness that he'd recently read the memo from corporate emphasizing the need to fill in every data box for each guest.

His eyebrows furrowed, and his full lips flattened into a straight line. His attention to detail was as adorably cute as he was. But Zavi wasn't much older than a recent high school graduate. I was closing in on thirty. The ten-year gap didn't follow my plus-or-minus-four-years gap rule for dating. This way, we would both at least be part of the same generation and have similar cultural references, like life before Facebook. Still, since Olympics and presidential elections were four years apart, my dating rule almost seemed logical.

When he hit the Enter key, he turned toward me.

"So, these ghosts aren't the friendly little things you see in *Ghostbusters* or at the Haunted Mansion at Disneyland. These are straight up"—he leaned toward me—"scary as hell."

"You're not joking," I stated rather than asked.

"No, Reese, I'm not. I won't work the overnight shift, so if that's going to be a problem, let me know now. Because they started me on overnights, which is when I met Campbell."

"As in the soup?"

"No!" Zavi's laughter was a burst that seemed to even surprise him. "As in the first governor of Wyoming." He pointed to the portrait that hung on the mammoth wall behind the front desk. A man with a considerable woolly beard, moustache, and hooded eyes looked grimly into the distance. *Maybe he doesn't like our ghost either. Or maybe he doesn't like playing second fiddle to a phantom that makes his portrait the second most famous entity hanging around the hotel.*

"That's Governor Campbell, but he's not our ghost. Our ghost was probably named after him, but isn't the governor. Legend has it that our ghost, a Mr. Campbell Matthews, was somewhat of an aristocrat, cowboy, and World War II army officer who committed suicide in his honeymoon suite."

I raised my hand. "So hold up, this ghost has a name?"

Zavi's brown eyes narrowed. "He has a name, a legend, and a reputation."

"And his reputation would be…?"

Zavi leaned even closer toward me, as if what he was

about to say couldn't be uttered aloud. "Campbell's wife claimed he killed himself because he couldn't perform his, uh…." He looked around, and when he was certain there weren't any spirits eavesdropping, continued, "Well, apparently the guy couldn't perform his husbandly duties."

"So he shot himself?"

Zavi slowly nodded. "In the head. Room 632."

I rolled my eyes. "I don't doubt that a hotel that's been open since the early 1900s has its history, but ghosts?" I half laughed. "Yeah, just not going with the flow."

"But going with the flow is free." Zavi's tone shifted to playful and light. The boy was trouble—flirty, fun, and too young. Though, it did explain why every female room service attendant we employed constantly checked and refilled the lobby pitcher. In the last two weeks, I'd heard more young women giggle as they passed the front desk than ever before in my life. I'd assumed they were laughing at Governor Campbell's portrait, which made me nervously laugh. The man's far-off stare somehow seemed to follow a person in the room, which sent a cold chill down my back. But until now, no one had muttered a word about any ghost.

"Listen," Zavi said, "people stay here for the legend. Campbell's a big deal around these parts—even if he's spooky as shit."

"That's good to know." I tapped a hotel-branded pen against the front desk blotter. "As the new general manager, this is useful info. But help me understand something. Why would this Campbell guy haunt the hotel? I mean, it makes no sense whatsoever. He committed suicide. Aren't ghosts supposed to be *tormented* or something?"

His laughter was hearty and boisterous. "Uh, didn't you hear my story? The guy *was* tormented. He couldn't take care of business on his honeymoon. Top it off, it was supposed to be a murder-suicide, but he only got it half right. He missed his wife at point-blank range, and piss-poor shooting should be a felony in these parts."

Now I was the one laughing.

"But even the worst shot in the West couldn't miss his own head, so at least he got the suicide part right," Zavi said.

"That's awful. I actually feel sorry for this Campbell guy."

"Great. You can feel sorry for him while he's haunting *you* in the bathroom. Spirits may pass through walls, but damn if there ain't some boundaries they shouldn't cross."

"Is that where you first saw him? In the bathroom?" *Curiosity may kill the cat, but it's catnip to strangers in town.* And Zavi may soon argue that there was nobody stranger in town than his new GM.

"Yeah, we were short-staffed, so I was sent to clean room 632. I was doing my thing when I had to go to the bathroom. But the men's room on the sixth floor was occupied." He paused and I knew why. Staff were not allowed to use a guest bathroom or any public restroom in the hotel. Point Resort staff were required to use the employee locker rooms in the basement, which weren't convenient or close. Plus, the double-ply toilet paper that was reserved for the guests was a far cry better than the wafer-thin, see-through single-ply disintegrate-on-touch toilet paper they expected us to use. When I didn't school him on the minor infraction, he continued. "So, I locked myself in the sixth floor ladies' room, because I just ate a handful of prunes and I was hoping for some relief." He paused. "If you're worried about regularity, I wouldn't eat in the employee cafeteria."

"Got it. So, what happened?" Now I leaned toward Zavi, which probably violated all sorts of manager-employee rules of contact. But he literally had me on the edge of my seat and I didn't want to miss a word of his otherworldly tale, even if it meant sharing his chair.

"I'll tell you one thing. Ghosts are the world's best laxative. I went from constipated to shitless in two seconds flat."

I giggled. At twenty-nine, bathroom humor shouldn't still make me laugh, but it did. I may be old enough to know better, but I was still young enough not to care.

"I was just sitting there getting ready to do my business when I saw something in the mirror."

I whacked his shoulder. "Nuh-uh."

"For shizzle."

"What did he do?"

"His eyes were closed, and then a gaping hole appeared between them and his eyes opened, like he was reliving his last moments on earth or something." Zavi shuddered, and I felt the chill.

"That's pretty…."

"Messed up."

I slowly nodded. "Yeah."

The front desk phone rang and we both jumped. If my older brother, Owen, had been in the hotel, he'd punch me twice and remind me, "Two for flinching." Thankfully, Zavi didn't seem to know that game.

He picked up the phone, but before he could utter the hotel's signature greeting, he nodded.

"Yes, Mr. Nus, your reservation at the rooftop tennis court is secured, as is your poolside massage in our indoor pool area." Zavi wrote *Robert P. Nus* on the pad of paper in front of him.

I stared at the name and blinked. *That can't be right.* Robert *P. Nus*. I pointed my pink-painted fingernail at the name and back to Zavi. "Like penis?" I whispered.

He covered the mouthpiece to conceal his laughter. Then wrote "Patrick" beside the initial.

I smiled.

"Yes, Mr. Nus, we look forward to your stay." Zavi paused and smiled. "Yes, it is Halloween weekend, but that won't interfere with your reservations. No, we haven't been hit with snow yet." Zavi's smile was beginning to look forced. "Yes, we do seem to be having a late winter, but rest assured we've already enclosed the tennis courts so your rooftop game should be in full swing. Excellent. We'll see you soon."

When the call finished, I slightly elbowed Zavi. "Uh, how about we break protocol and put his *entire* name, not just his middle initial in the computer. I know FrogKiss only requires that the first and last name are spelled out for each guest, but… I can just see a room service operator not catching the period between his middle and last name and answering the phone, 'Good morning, Mr. P-nus.' That's *not* a conversation I want to have with either the guest, my staff, *or* corporate."

Zavi grinned. "Good catch on those initials, Reese."

I shrugged. "Yeah, that's why corporate brought me from California to Wyoming, to be on the lookout for penis infractions."

"Excuse me?" A deep male voice made my stomach drop.

Oh, fuck. My body instantly broke into a sweat like I had just run a 10K and not possibly torpedoed my career before it even began. *Great, my first time as GM and I talk about penis infractions?* I carefully turned toward the front counter where a tall, well-built man with a long, black braid stood. Even without the braid, his Native American features were as strong and unwavering as his posture. His face was unlike any man's I'd seen. A dimple appeared on either side of his smile, which briefly surfaced when he arched an eyebrow at me. His striking square jaw and high cheekbones drew me to him. In a denim shirt with the sleeves rolled up, his skin looked kissed by the sun. I wanted to reach out and touch him, but the seriousness that flashed in his eyes prompted me to place my hands behind my back.

He gripped the counter and his forearms bulged with definition. He leaned toward me and the smell of his fresh, minty breath made my mouth water. *Damn, is everyone in Wyoming this fine?* I couldn't stop staring, which made him furrow his eyebrows. I wanted to unbraid his hair and let it fall on his broad shoulders. I quickly shook my head and remembered the line between guest and staff.

"Hello. Good afternoon. Welcome to the… uh.…" I stared into his dark, black eyes and completely forgot the name of the hotel. *WTF, Reese?* "Hello. How may I assist you this afternoon?" I glanced outside. "Or early evening?" I nervously giggled.

"Penis infractions?" His eyes narrowed, becoming penetratingly dark and brooding.

"Uh." I swallowed and felt a sweat moustache form above my lip. Soon I would be in my own personal sauna if I couldn't calm my nerves. "Yes. I, uh.…" I slowly nodded. There was no escape.

"I, well.…" I cleared my throat. "I'd like to apologize for my inappropriate… humor. I was just.…" *What?* Flirting with the eighteen-year-old assistant front desk manager? *Yeah, no.* "I apologize for my crass language. How may I assist you?"

"You can begin by taking a breath and smiling, short stuff."

Now my eyebrows furrowed. I stared at this man, who unlike Zavi had already reached manhood. And how. *Short stuff?* Granted, I wasn't tall, but I wasn't short—not if you included a pair of high heels and if I wore a bouffant updo.

He held out his hand, which felt as sturdy as he appeared.

"I'm Wild Bill Goldstein."

Wild Bill Goldstein? For real? His mother's genetics must be extremely dominant, because it looked like the only thing he got from his father was his last name. I shook his hand and politely smiled. "I'm Reese Pemberton."

"I'm your second in charge." He gently gripped my hand.

"What?" I blinked as if he was a dreamy apparition that would suddenly vanish.

"I'm your number two," he said, still holding my hand. "Your hotel manager."

I tilted my head. "*William Goldstein?*"

"At your service."

I pulled my hand away and swatted his. "Don't *ever* do that to me again! I about had a heart attack."

"Well, a good penis infraction *should* cause a girl's heart to stop."

I felt the heat return to my cheeks. "Listen, William or Wild Bill or whatever you call yourself."

"Wild Bill, if you don't mind," he said, as if the biting tone of my voice hadn't fazed him at all.

I placed my hands on my hips and tilted my chin as I tried to strike a superhero pose to project all the strength and confidence I was sorely lacking. "I'd like you to know that we have a guest named Robert *P*. Nus, and I was trying to ensure that no one called him Mr. *Penis* when they answered his call."

"Sure. Okay." Wild Bill looked at Zavi and then back to me. "I'll buy that. But everyone here already knows **Mr.** Nus. He comes every Halloween weekend for our annual costume party. It's a tradition."

"Great. Swell. *Fan*-tastic." I tried to appear annoyed, but my cheeks hurt too much from smiling to pull it off. Plus, I noticed something. Whenever I grinned, Wild Bill's dimples appeared. Hell, I'd grin like a demented jack-o'-lantern and get lockjaw for life and still consider it a bargain if it yielded even the briefest of appearances of those irresistible double dimples.

He was still smiling when he spoke. "So, you might be wondering why I'm here on my day off?"

"To give me grief?" I said.

His dimples surfaced, and I smiled. "Well, that and the week you arrived I was on an extended vacation. So I wasn't able to meet you, and since this weekend *is* Halloween...."

I slowly nodded. "And...?"

"And it can get pretty, *well*, interesting here at the hotel during our costume party."

"Oh-kay," I said. "I already put in a purchase rec for bulk candy to hand out to trick-or-treaters. The banquet department has the ballroom and the menu lined up, including goblin sliders, which I don't think's the best name, but Chef assures me they're a hit every year. I ordered enough hard spirits to make even the most diehard drinker see ghosts, and aside from my lack of a costume, we're going to have a fabulous costume party tomorrow night." I came up for air. "Oh, and I added two more bellmen to the front drive, which our occupancy rate for the weekend *really* doesn't justify. And trust me, after our Southern California property uncovered some nasty truths about their occupancy rate issues, well, let's just say now we have more eyes on everything."

"It's not the hotel guests I'm concerned about, but all the

extra activity the weekend seems to evoke," Wild Bill said.

"Listen, we're hosting a spooktacular happy hour rate in our lobby lounge for all this extra activity you're so concerned about," I said.

Wild Bill gently smiled. "I'm sure the locals will appreciate that. I'll add that to our costume party announcement on our social media page and website. But that's not who I was referring to."

"Oh, dear God." I slowly shook my head. "You too?"

He raised his broad shoulders. "Once you meet Campbell, you'll have a greater appreciation."

"Sure." I rolled my eyes. "When that happens, I'll welcome him to the property myself."

Wild Bill clapped his hands. "That's the spirit. So… I know you've already met most of the staff, but I thought maybe you'd want the grand tour. Are you ready to meet the rest of your team and perhaps pick up some of the ins and outs of the Historic Point Resort so you'll be ready for our annual costume party?" Wild Bill had what my mother would have referred to as bedroom eyes—dark, dreamy, and extremely seductive. I couldn't think of a better place to discover the meaning of that phrase than at a hotel. I had a selection of bedrooms at my disposal and a sparkle in my eyes.

"Sure, why not." I stepped out from behind the front desk, stood beside him, and smiled. "I'm all yours."

CHAPTER **TWO**

CODY

"What the *hell* is that smell?" I looked around the police station for the offensive odor, but all I saw were fellow detectives sitting at their desks. I glanced at my partner, Dixon, while I loosened my tie and tucked my nose into the collar of my white dress shirt, where I inhaled the new woodsy-scented deodorant I'd bought over the weekend.

"It's called Guard On and it helps purify the air to get rid of all the bad energy we get in this place," Dixon said, holding a small brown opaque bottle.

"It smells like it scared the shit out of the bad energy and it forgot to flush before leaving."

Dixon's brows furrowed, and I knew the look. He was upset. "Sheridan got it for me."

"Well, tell my sister to keep that shit at home." My nose remained in my shirt. "I'd rather inhale the forest and woods than what a bear did in them."

Dixon glanced at the side of the bottle. "Pring, what the hell do you know? It's got wild orange peel, citrus, clove bud, rosemary, tree bark, and eucalyptus leaf." He capped the spray nozzle. "All the essential oils to protect from environmental threats."

"That spray *is* an environmental threat." I waved my hand, hoping to diffuse the air and spread the saturated molecules away from me.

"If you give it a minute, it's supposed to release an uplifting aroma that's warm and spicy," Dixon said.

"Hell no. We don't need warm or spicy up in the police station. The clientele is colorful enough without you spraying that crap around."

"I'm going to tell your sister what you said." Dixon arched an eyebrow like he had just played his best card in our weekly poker game. His tells were so easy to spot.

"Go ahead. Tell my sister. I don't care." I crossed my arms over my chest, which I was sure was my telltale sign when I was angry, annoyed, and had been dealt crap. I spun my chair away from Dixon's constant stare and toward the pile of manila folders that looked like a tidal wave of paperwork that would certainly drown me if I didn't start wading through some of those case files. "Tell my sister," I grumbled, and picked the next case in the stack. "Like I'm scared of my sister."

Dixon purposefully bumped the back of my ergonomic, though highly uncomfortable, department-issued chair with his. The chair, like our county-issued Glocks, were two department mandates that I wasn't crazy about but both apparently protected us from what management called the WCs: wretched criminals and workers' comp. *For fuck's sake.*

I readjusted my numb black ass in the chair, but it did nothing to improve the comfort. *WCs my ass.* Anywhere outside the United States, the letters "WC" stood for "water closet"—more commonly known as a bathroom. So, go figure, the only county-issued WC protection that I did swear by were those thin paper toilet seat covers in the bathroom. I piled those ass gaskets on the toilet seat like a bird building a nest whenever I had to use the filthy bathroom, especially after Dixon had been in there.

"Dixon, Pring, where are we at with the cyberattacks on the county courthouse?"

Chief Wyman stood in the center of the squad room with his right foot back and his right hand resting on the back strap of his Glock. His position was textbook procedural, as if by squaring up with us he'd make himself more of a target. *Hell, that only happens when review time rolls around.*

I swiveled toward my partner. "Dixon got a promising lead from—"

"Good Jesus. Did one of you guys shart yourself?" The chief glanced around the detective division and swiped the air with his hand.

I smiled, and Dixon cringed.

"Yeah, what is that smell?" I leaned back in my chair and fanned the air, mimicking the chief.

"*Dick,*" Dixon muttered under his breath. But to the chief, he spoke loudly and clearly. "Sir, what you're smelling is an essential oil spray."

"I see. And where'd you pick up this little gem?" The chief eyed him.

"Sheridan," Dixon said.

"The city or your wife?" Chief Wyman asked.

"The latter," Dixon said.

I had to give my partner props for being one loyal husband. My sister was a pain in the ass with every new product she *had* to resell.

"Tim," Chief Wyman began, "I respect that you want to support your wife and her exploration into Reiki and other natural practices, but perhaps we can leave the crystals, energy sprays, and healing stones and such at home."

"Sure. Of course, Chief," Dixon said.

I snapped my fingers. "Damn, Chief, I was beginning to enjoy that stench."

The other detectives shook their heads, hiding their smiles and holding their laughter. But a uniformed patrol officer by the coffeepot wasn't as subtle. His chuckle made me grin.

"Okay, that's enough. Detective Pring, why don't you get me up to speed on the cyberattack," Chief Wyman said.

I reached behind me, grabbed the open file off my desk, and tapped my pen at it.

"Sir, what we have from DCI isn't anything we couldn't have read first in the local paper. They're still looking into it, but the general consensus is that the attack was an isolated incident, most likely initiated by a disgruntled employee."

"Where is this employee now?" Chief Wyman asked.

"Rawlins." I knew the mere mention of the town that housed Wyoming's state penitentiary was not going to go over well.

"You mean to tell me the guy who managed to launch a cyberattack on Cheyenne that shut down the state capital conducted the attack from prison?"

I grimly nodded.

"Unbelievable." The chief slid his hand across the top of his head and what was left of his gray hair. "And you got this from the Division of Criminal Investigations?"

"Yes, sir. I contacted DCI directly." I glanced at my notes. "Apparently the attack relied on malware that encrypted data and locked certain government offices from accessing their data. They think the malware was leaked by… uh…." I skimmed the file. "Gene Hanson. He's serving time for a string of B and Es."

"How does a petty crook suddenly acquire the skill set to target the governor's office?" Chief asked.

"According to the warden at Rawlins, Hanson was recently denied parole and blamed Governor Hawthorne," I said. "DCI confirmed motive and have removed Hanson's access to any computers. DCI was able to act quickly with a program to fix the computer issue, but certain offices, like Department of Family Services and Social Security, need to update their systems first before they can get rid of the malware issue."

"How does someone update a system they can't access?" Joe Seitz was a new detective.

"Good question. When Pring and I spoke to DCI, they

explained that's the issue bogging things up. Many of the offices attacked used older operating systems, which DCI's malware fix isn't compatible with," Dixon said.

"And remind me again how a guest of the state's penitentiary was able to lodge this attack?" Chief asked.

"During his allotted library time, he used the prison computer to send a series of emails with a file attached. While all emails are monitored, nothing looked suspicious about it or his attachment. It appeared as though Hanson was writing to every department *he* thought could help him in his request for a new parole hearing—from Social Security to Family Services. None of those departments can help him, but there was no reason to deny his emails. His attached letter was infected with the malware. And from there, it spread. DCI said their investigation would remain ongoing," I said.

"Did DCI have an estimated cost of the impact?" Seitz asked.

I scratched my eyebrow. "All they'd release was that the attack caused phone lines to go down, appointments at Social Security were canceled, but there wasn't any reported evidence that any client data was breached." I paused. "Again, nothing we haven't already read in the Cheyenne Independent."

The chief pursed his lips together, which wasn't a good look for him. His round, bowling-ball-shaped head looked like he was sucking a lemon that doubled as a black hole that caused his entire face to pucker as it imploded on itself. But when he rapped his fingers on the butt of his Glock, no one in our small department spoke. As soon as the chief began playing a silent concerto on the back of his piece, we knew someone had gotten on the wrong side of him. Some poor soul was in his sights, and the chief was figuratively, and perhaps subconsciously, gunning for them.

A slow nod, as if he was agreeing with his internal thoughts, and then he spoke. "I'll reach out to DCI. There may be more to this than they're letting on."

"Like the attack was larger in scope?" Dixon asked.

"Perhaps" was all the chief said before he cocked his head toward the large dry-erase board hung on the back wall of the department. "Okay, so it looks like Dixon and Pring are in the penalty box this weekend."

Has a month already passed?

"Well, this should be fun," Seitz said. "Halloween weekend."

"Halloween?" I squinted toward the calendar and saw our names on the last weekend of the month. "Beautiful. Every crazy in town will be out in full swing."

"Oh, it'll be great," Dixon said. "And if any of you *ladies* want to join us—" Dixon stopped and glanced at the one female detective in the department. "Of course, you too, Maggie. My wife's making a batch of her famous chocolate chip cookies," Dixon said with a stupid, shit-eating grin on his face.

I shook my head. The only thing famous about my sister's chocolate chip cookies was that she didn't use chocolate, but carob, and instead of flour, she opted for rolled oats, which made them taste less like cookies and more like an unholy concoction. If there's such a thing as dessert in hell, my sister's cookies would make the poor damned souls beg for more fire and brimstone. Worse, she handed them out as Halloween treats. It's the only time I've seen trick-or-treaters ask if they could have vegetables instead.

"All right, if there isn't anything else, enjoy your weekend and I'll see you Monday," Chief said and headed toward his office.

"Well, since I have to return early tomorrow morning to begin my weekend in hell, answering every call we get from every kook in town while my partner tries to poison me with my sister's cooking, I think a night of drinking's in order." I tossed my pen on my desk, closed the cyberattack file, tucked my cell into my back pocket, grabbed my jacket off the back of my chair, and glanced at my colleagues. "Come on, gang, first round's on me."

CHAPTER THREE

REESE

"So this is the infamous 632?" I stood in front of a brown-painted door that had about as much personality as my last date. And caused the same reaction—I yawned.

"Sorry my tour's boring you," Wild Bill said, showing off his dimples.

I fanned away his remark. "I'm still working out the time difference between California and Wyoming."

"Aren't we an hour ahead?" He unhooked the radio attached to the belt loop in his jeans and pressed the side button. "Base 365 to Toby 367."

"Uh, yeah, Wyoming's an hour ahead, but somehow I can't seem to get into a groove with my sleep, and it doesn't help that I've had to stay in the hotel until my rental house is ready. Don't you have keys?" I asked, realizing that when Wild Bill invited me to tour the rest of the hotel and meet the staff, I'd arrived empty-handed.

"Oh, I've got keys." He jangled the silver carabiner hooked to his jeans, and a plethora of keys clinked. "But the last member of the hotel's inner circle that I want you to meet is Toby."

"Toby 367 to Base 365." The radio barked. "What's up?"

"Your presence is required at suite 632." Wild Bill held the radio sideways and spoke into it. Somehow I'd imagined that to look sexier than it did. Instead, the way he held the radio just looked odd. Wild Bill was so attractive he looked better suited for the glossy cover of *Cowboys and Indians* magazine that we sold in the gift store. When I'd spotted the magazine, I was horrified, only to discover the politically incorrectly titled magazine was extremely popular among western enthusiasts. Millie, the gift store cashier, provided the 411 on the magazine. As a fellow California transplant to Wyoming, she reminded me that the western lifestyle wasn't anything like the west coast. No argument there. I flipped through an issue and caught a glimpse of former Californian cowboy John Wayne on one page and Native American actor Adam Beach on another. It wasn't a bad magazine, I just wasn't crazy about its masthead. *Cowboys and Indians, really?*

Now, I was in the presence of one of the hottest Native Americans I'd ever met. Hell, Wild Bill was probably the *only* Native American I'd ever met. In his denim shirt, faded Levi's, and black boots, Wild Bill did not blend in behind the scenes of an old hotel, historic or not. Wild Bill was movie-star handsome, and I couldn't seem to take my eyes off him.

"You okay?" he asked.

I swallowed and tucked my long, reddish, wavy hair behind my ear. "Oh, of course. Did I daze off?" I rolled my eyes, trying to play off shamelessly gawking at my second in charge. "Lost in space." I nervously chuckled and brushed my heel against the red and tan carpet. But no matter how many times I swept the carpet with my foot, it didn't improve the taupe weave that looked like random music notes scattered on a red backdrop. The carpet was so busy, it practically caused vertigo. "How old is this stuff?"

Wild Bill's laughter was sweetly rich and deep. "That is the *new* carpet."

"Who chose this design? A manic musician seeing double and having the shakes while weaving?" I said.

"I did." A fortysomething man stood before us with his hands on his hips. His plain brown hair and eyes matched the paint used throughout the hotel. But where his eyes may have lacked in color and pizzazz, the spark of a grin gave his face an abundance of warmth and energy. "What's wrong with this carpet? It'll hide more splotches than a barrel of concealer on high school picture day."

I laughed. "But it has no style, no substance. The carpet just lies there, takes up space and does absolutely nothing for the hotel," I said.

"Sounds like the carpet has an even better union than the staff," Wild Bill said, chuckling.

"Har har," I said. "I just meant the carpet stands out, but for all the wrong reasons."

"Fair enough, but it's not easy finding a carpet that will

match with the rest of the hotel's décor." The man continued to stand with his hands on his hips.

"I believe you. This hotel's historic because it has *a lot* of things going on, from a bordello, which Wild Bill tells me actually existed on the seventh floor, to the saloon in the lobby. I don't know if the architect or interior designer, if they had such a thing in the early 1900s, knew what they were creating." I laughed and held out my hand. "You must be Toby, who like my second in charge just *happened* to be on vacation when I arrived, which I'm trying not to take personally." I giggled.

He grinned. "Ah, it wasn't personal, just a slow time at the hotel, so we took our vacation," he said, accepting my handshake. His hands were thick and weathered, like the lines beneath his eyes. "I'm the chief engineer, head of maintenance, and overall guy Friday."

I smiled. "I've noticed people wear many hats here."

"Or feathers." Toby elbowed Wild Bill.

"We like to say the staff has been effectively cross-trained in various positions so that anybody can step in for anyone and fill a need," Wild Bill said. "We come from a long line of people who have learned not to trust men in hats, no matter how many they wear."

Wild Bill was smart, good-looking, and clearly a leader for the hotel. The staff responded to him because he didn't mince words. But he was also careful with how he phrased things. So, while I didn't doubt his ability to step in and fulfill any need I had, I wasn't about to let my libido lose the hotel its most valuable human resource. I just needed to use a little common sense—and perhaps a long, cold shower.

"So who's going to do the honors?" I patted the door to suite 632.

Wild Bill unhooked his keys and paused before inserting the brass key into the old-fashioned lock that still used keys. "Zavi told you the story about Campbell."

I nodded. "Yup. Apparently, he offed himself on his wedding night." My tact was clearly lacking. My number two slowly nodded, as if to agree with my internal thoughts.

"Legend has it Campbell committed suicide and his spirit hasn't been able to rest since," Wild Bill said.

"Yes. *That's the ghost story.*" I kept my hand on suite 632's door and shook my head. "But, gentlemen, just so you know, I don't believe in Sasquatch, ghosts, or anything else that goes bump in the night. I have a PhD in physics." I glanced from Wild Bill to Toby. "It's a long, complicated story, but suffice to say my resume said Dr. Pemberton, and when the Point Resort needed to transfer someone from one of their California properties to Wyoming, they thought they were getting a GM and a hotel doctor all in one." I half laughed.

"And you didn't correct them," Wild Bill said with a devil-may-care grin and raise of his eyebrow.

"I did not." I raised my hand off the door and held it in the air like I was swearing a solemn oath. "However, my doctorate work in physics will debunk the so-called Campbell ghost once and for all. People may have reported personal experiences, which most likely was unexplained phenomena to them, but not science." I took a deep breath before continuing. "So, what usually happens in these situations is that, since these phenomena were experienced by a layperson who couldn't identify what they encountered, it's easy to become convinced that the unconventional image was a ghost. Personal experience is flawed, but scientific evidence is not."

"Science? What science can disprove ghosts?" Toby said, and crossed his arms over his chest. His skepticism was all but a challenge.

Game on, bubba.

"In physics, the law of conservation of matter states that matter cannot be created or destroyed, so a ghost cannot possibly exist because it was not created and has no mass or volume. So all these mysterious or eerie Campbell sightings"—I widened my eyes and cut the air with my hands as if I were a magician and could magically make this nonsense disappear—"aren't real."

"Well, since Campbell only reveals himself to females, you may just be able to set the record straight," Toby said, with a grin that made me smile.

"What do you *mean* only reveals himself to females?" I wagged my finger. "Nope. Zavi saw him. Or supposedly saw him right here in the women's restroom." I pointed down the hall toward the guest bathroom on the sixth floor.

"The key here is that Zavi was *in* the women's restroom," Wild Bill said.

I rolled my eyes. "Oh, brother. Are you telling me our ghost can't differentiate between a man and a woman?"

"Well, Zavi is pretty," Toby said.

I laughed along with Wild Bill. "Great," I said, "that's all I need, a sexist, nearsighted, voyeuristic spirit. Can you imagine the legal mess and the bad press we'd get if a guest filed a sexual harassment complaint against a ghost?"

"Not sexist," Wild Bill said. "Campbell's spirit shows himself to women or who he perceives are women, I believe, because the last woman he was with betrayed him."

"Betrayed? How do you figure that?" I backed away from the door to let Wild Bill access it. He opened it, and I got a hallway view of the suite. Seemed standard to me: king-sized bed covered with a drab gold-colored quilt, walk-in closet, bathroom, and two large picture windows overlooking Cheyenne's depot plaza. "No, there's no betrayal. From what I've heard, Campbell's the one who couldn't follow through on his wedding night. The only betrayal I see is that, instead of confronting the problem with his new wife, he killed himself. Granted, I've never been married, but that'd make for one lousy honeymoon memory." I shook my head. "No, Campbell wasn't betrayed. He was weak."

Wild Bill's dark eyes seemed to absorb me with one glance in my direction. "The energy I've always felt isn't weak, but sorrowful."

There was something about Wild Bill that made me pause. I'd only known the man for a handful of hours, but he just didn't come across as the bullshitting type. In fact, he was such a straight shooter, I feared I wouldn't be able to measure up to his standards.

"Okay, I'll open my mind to the possibilities and allow

myself to *feel* this energy," I said. "Physics is, after all, concerned with observing and understanding the natural universe. So, I might as well study the subject that seems to be of such interest to the staff and guests alike in our corner of the Twilight Zone."

Wild Bill stood beside the door, and the only thing I felt was his magnetic energy when I brushed past him and into suite 632.

CHAPTER **FOUR**

CODY

The mahogany bar at the Wyoming Steakhouse Saloon was positioned in the center of the historic tavern with high-top tables and stools strategically placed around it. There wasn't a bad table at the Steakhouse Saloon or a bad drink, because there weren't any ugly servers. The attractive waitstaff was the great equalizer, drawing everyone from the conservative black suits that worked in the state's capital to the rowdy roughnecks on the oil patches. I liked to think Cheyenne's finest was the happy medium. Detectives were required to dress well, so even on casual Friday jean days, our shirts and ties blended with the capital clique, and we could throw down if we needed to like the drilling crew. And if one of the servers didn't get a guy's attention, the women who gathered at the bar did. From soccer moms to CEOs, when women came to the Steakhouse Saloon, they dressed to be noticed.

I eyed a cute brunette bundled in an oversized white parka and blue knit hat that made her look like a cross between the Michelin man and Stay Puft Marshmallow Man. But the legs that stretched out beneath the parka in white fishnet stockings were anything but round and puffy.

"If she'd just take off the damn jacket and stay a while," I said.

Joe Seitz glanced in her direction and shook his head. "Dude, she's *way* out of your league." He grabbed his beer and took a hearty swig.

"Pring, I have to agree with Seitz on that one. She's hot *and* she looks normal," Dixon said.

I glanced at the hottie who kept eyeing me. "If she wasn't sitting near the end of the bar where the side door blows nothing but cold wind, I might actually get to see more of her." I casually smiled in her direction. "And what do you mean? I can get normal."

Somehow my comment made everyone at our table laugh.

"What the hell do you guys know anyway?" I raised my empty pint glass toward Millie, our server. "How was I to know the last woman I dated had daddy issues?"

"I don't know, Pring, maybe the decade age difference?" Maggie's pragmatism was sobering.

"I've got to defend my partner on that one. It's not his fault he's so damn young looking," Dixon said.

"It's one thing to look like you're in your mid-twenties and another thing to act like you're in your mid-twenties," Maggie said.

"Well, it's not like I'm too far past my twenties, but yeah, that last woman was a bit younger than me." Who was I fooling? I veered toward younger women so I didn't have to deal with the demons from my past. My childhood was marred by one's man selfish decision. But it was my general disinterest in starting a family that kept me at a safe distance from a woman my age. So I couldn't help but watch Millie's long, blonde ponytail bounce behind her when she approached our table.

"You still working two jobs?" I handed her my mug.

"Yup. Until I pay down my student loans, I'll be hotel gift store cashier by day and barkeep by night." She giggled and everyone, including Maggie, smiled. Millie was prime for the picking, but something kept me at a safe distance. I think she reminded me too much of my sister, Sheridan, and that just creeped me out. Both were brown-eyed blondes, which just wasn't something you saw every day. I shuddered at the thought.

"How you liking the amber lager?" Millie waved my mug, and I grinned.

"You were right. The red ales don't disappoint." My mouth practically watered waiting for Dean, the bartender, to refill my pint with the caramel sweetness that arrived in a handsome crimson color. Millie grabbed Dixon's pint glass.

"Another pale ale?" she asked, though she didn't need to.

"Dixon always orders the same thing." I shook my head. "Millie, you know this. He never mixes things up. Dixon's Mr. Predictable."

"I like my beer as blonde as my women," he said with a sly grin, and I rolled my eyes.

"I guess I deserved that," I said. "But any more talk about my sister and you're picking up the tab."

"Talk about predictable. I *always* pick up the tab," Dixon said, and we all laughed.

I grinned. "But, see that? That was some good deductive reasoning. You're figuring this out all by yourself. I'll make a detective out of you yet."

The table's laughter caught the attention of the brunette, who smiled.

"Yeah, we'll see who the real detectives are after this weekend," Seitz said.

I glanced at Joe. "Why, because tomorrow night's Halloween?" I fanned my hand through the air like I was waving a wand. "Look at this place. The party's already started, and so far my cell phone hasn't gone off once." I patted my back pocket.

A man dressed as a lobster walked past us, waving his tail. A mermaid shimmering in silver wasn't far behind him. And neither was Millie, who set two new pints on the table just as the brunette at the end of the bar peeled away her parka to reveal a naughty nurse's uniform. *Oh, yeah!* Suddenly, I wasn't feeling so well. I grinned and she winked.

"See"—I leaned into the table—"everyone's happy. In fact"—I slid my thumb across the lip of the frosted mug—"I bet this Halloween's going to be uneventful."

Dixon closed his eyes and shook his head. "Why did you

just jinx us?"

"Jinx? I didn't jinx anything. I mean it. Look at everyone." I glanced over my shoulder at the nurse in fishnet stockings and white heels. "Damn, everyone's happy and looking mighty good. Granted, the half-price IPAs aren't hurting the mood, but you know Dean, he's not going to let anyone be served who's already well past their limit," I said with a head nod to the bartender.

"Pring, the Steakhouse Saloon is *one* bar in town. One," Dixon said. "There's a handful of others, like the Crow Bar, that doesn't give two shits how much someone's drank. If they can pour another shot and be paid, they're going to do just that."

"Sure, that happens, but I actually have a good vibe about Halloween this year." I leaned back on my barstool until I teetered on two legs.

"Keep whistling in the dark, Pring, that always helps." Maggie raised her pint toward her partner, Joe, who laughed as their mugs clashed.

"Yuck it up, but mark my word, nothing out of the ordinary is going to happen this Halloween. It'll be business as usual," I said.

Dixon buried his hands in his dirty-blond hair. He looked more like my sister's brother than I did. I was as dark as she was light. Same mother, vastly different fathers.

"Just shut up. You've already hexed us with your talk about 'no big deals.' Don't make it worse by taunting the universe," Dixon said.

"Tim, you used to be normal, so I don't blame you for

your sudden lack of balls. I blame my hippie-dippie sister and all the mystical crap she feeds you," I said.

"Yeah, it's amazing what a guy will do for a piece of ass," Joe said.

"Whoa, whoa, whoa, too far." My hands cut through the air. "My sister may be a lot of things, but she's not a piece of ass."

Joe raised his hands. "Totally out of line."

"*Yeah*, you were," Dixon said.

Maggie elbowed Joe. "Listen, partner, you can't talk that kind of smack until the dynamic duo's got at least three pints under their belts."

Joe smiled. "What are we?"

She looked puzzled.

"If they're the dynamic duo, what are we?" Joe asked like the naïve rookie detective he was.

"You're the two who'll be picking up the tab for our steak dinner when Halloween proves to be an uneventful weekend," I said.

"I'll take that bet," Maggie said.

"Me too," Joe said.

"Fuck me," Dixon said.

I heartily patted my partner's back. "Now come on, when I get one of those feelings, when have I ever been wrong? Hell, it's why I set you up with my sister. Now look at you—you're married and whipped."

Dixon's blue eyes honed in on me. "Do you have one of those feelings?"

I slowly nodded. "Actually, I do. I just don't see this

weekend being that busy—aside from the normal drunk and disorderly, but we assist patrol on those calls every weekend."

"So, if your weekend is simply routine *like any other weekend* in the number of calls and activity, then we owe you and Dixon a steak dinner with all the trimmings," Maggie said. "*But,* if your Saturday and Sunday shift during Halloween weekend ends up like *Nightmare on Elm Street,* then you and Dixon owe Seitz and me steak and all the works." She held out her hand.

"Agreed." I shook.

Dixon reluctantly shook Seitz's hand, who grinned. "Let the haunting begin."

We raised our pints, and I drained the last of my amber ale. It was my only night of freedom before a weekend in the office. So when the crowd began to increase in volume and drunkenness, I knew it was time to make toward the door. Dean was a good bartender, but I didn't want the tap on the shoulder to escort someone out, or worse, lecture them about the ills of drinking. *No thanks. Not tonight.* Maybe tomorrow when I was on the clock. Besides, it was crowded and hot, and that sweet little brunette in the nurse uniform looked like the perfect person to check my temperature.

CHAPTER **FIVE**

REESE

"Thank you, gentlemen, for the wonderful tour of suite 632, and Wild Bill for the grand tour." I leaned against the doorframe while Wild Bill locked the suite.

"So, does our new GM have plans for tonight?" Toby asked.

I raised my eyebrows. "Well, as exciting as the nightlife looks in Cheyenne, I think I'm going to stick to my nightly ritual of running, reading, and calling it an early evening."

"It's pretty foggy." Toby's concern was sweet in a brotherly kind of way. And like my brother, a slew of nicknames filled my head.

"Thank you, Toby-Wan Kenobi," I said and burst out laughing.

"Like I haven't heard *that* one before." The apple of his cheeks tinged red.

I elbowed him and smiled. "To me all the time, it happens.

Yoda, get it?"

Toby's laughter was raspy like a seasoned smoker's. I glanced at the pocket of his uniform shirt, but it didn't bulge with a pack of smokes.

Wild Bill twisted the doorknob, and when he was convinced it was secure, he turned toward me. "Reese, I'm sure the fog in…."

He paused for me to fill in the blank, when I'm sure he already knew which Point Resort property I had transferred from. "San Francisco," I said.

"Well, I'm sure the fog in San Francisco is no joke. But the fog in Wyoming likes to settle on the oil on the road, which makes it slippery as shit… so just be careful," Wild Bill said.

I gently nodded toward my hotel manager, who didn't appear to be in a joking kind of mood. No smile. No dimples. No nonsense.

"Thanks," I said. "Duly noted. But if I don't get out of this hotel and have a change of scenery, I'm going to end up like Jack Nicholson in *The Shining*. You know, all work and no play, and the new GM winds up with an axe…."

Neither Toby nor Wild Bill smiled.

"Guys, that was a joke. You're still not stuck on the hotel being haunted?"

They headed toward the elevator that was located at the opposite end of the sixth floor. I quickly followed. "Listen, I appreciate a fun little legend to entertain tourists, but there's no such thing as ghosts."

Wild Bill pressed the key to the main elevator and

neither of them spoke. *This isn't good.* The only way I could accomplish what corporate sent me to Wyoming to do would require their help. And if playing along with their ghost stories ensured an allegiance, I'd acquiesce.

"Okay, just because I'm not a believer, doesn't mean I'm not willing to be proven wrong," I said. It was as far as my science would stretch.

They glanced at each other and then to me.

"Since the gatehouse I've rented isn't available yet, I've been staying in the hotel. Tonight, I'll stay in suite 632," I said.

They both shook their heads.

"On Halloween weekend?" Toby's brown eyes got as large as quarters. "That's *not* a good idea."

"I agree," Wild Bill said.

"I don't agree, because it's an *awesome* idea! I'll stay in suite 632 tonight and all weekend if it'll bridge the distance between us. I don't want something as silly as a—" I stopped when their expressions shifted from open back to closed. "I mean, I'd like to experience this Campbell fellow once and for all."

They slowly nodded.

"You know, make peace with the man who haunts our hotel," I said.

Toby's face lit with a smile. "Actually, this could work. I'll set up a tape recorder in the suite, and if you hear something, you can press the button."

"Sure," I said. "Why not."

His face grew solemn. "Just make sure you bring a two-way radio with you. The cell reception on the sixth floor is crap," Toby said.

I glanced at my phone. There was one bar of service. "Good call. I'll have a bellman move my bags from the second floor to the sixth, and grab a radio."

"Excellent, I'll put a recorder in there before I clock off," Toby said.

The elevator door opened, and we stepped inside. Wild Bill pressed the L button for the lobby, and an English-sounding voice announced, "Going down."

I tilted my head. "Is that new?"

"Floyd? No, he's always been the programmed voice for the elevator," Toby said.

"Floyd?" I glanced at the meshed intercom on the elevator panel that looked like a small, flat waffle pressed into the chrome.

"That's what we call him because he sounds British," Toby said.

I bit the inside of my cheek.

"It was either Floyd or Gunther," Wild Bill said.

"Oh" was all I could muster. They both laughed.

"Gotcha," Toby said with a nudge to my ribs. "Besides, everyone knows Floyd isn't a British name. It's Australian."

"Hardy har har," I said. "But seriously, is he new? I don't remember hearing the elevator talk to me before."

"Sometimes the volume isn't turned to the maximum setting. We're still working out the kinks," Toby said. "But when we modernized the elevator to make it ADA and code compliant, we didn't want to lose touch with the elevator history."

"Elevator history?" I had to ask.

"Reese, this is an *Otis* elevator." Toby patted the chrome siding. "It's been here since the hotel first opened in 1901. It was one of the first electric elevators in Wyoming, made by the legendary elevator manufacturer, Otis."

"Otis, huh?" I said.

"Yes, Otis. Otis elevators are in the Eiffel Tower, the Empire State Building, and even the Kremlin," Toby said.

"I did not know," I said.

"Toby's big on Otis," Wild Bill muttered under his breath.

I smiled, and his dimples shined back. "And this is an Otis elevator?" I asked Toby.

"It is. We worked hard to maintain this ride into elevator history by keeping the original cab and expanding it to be accessible for wheelchairs and the like," Toby said.

"And the voice?" I asked.

"That was an upgrade, same with the emergency call phone that's now linked to our security office *and* the police department. The emergency phone link is an extra security measure in case our system fails. The local PD's won't. They record all the calls that come into the station, so it's a great backup security system."

"That was a great idea," I said.

Toby smiled proudly. "And, of course, you have your master key that will allow you to access the lower levels— should you ever need to. Just remember you place your key into this keyhole." Toby pointed his grease-stained fingernail toward the older-shaped keyhole. An engineer with grease-stained hands was like a certificate of authenticity. Same with a mechanic. There were just some things expected in certain lines of work. "Turn clockwise, and then you can press this button for the lower level." The button was identified by BR, which I assumed was for the boiler room because the basement level, which was one floor above the boiler room, was actually spelled out for the employees to access.

"Got it. Clockwise. And the staff uses this lower slot with their card key to access the basement, locker rooms, time clock, and cafeteria," I stated more than asked.

"Exactly." Again, Toby smiled. "You're getting the hang of things quickly. It's easier to replace a card key than an actual key like we have."

I smiled. "Thank you, Tobias, but you know this isn't my first hotel elevator."

"Yes, but the Wyoming Point Resort doesn't function like other hotels." I couldn't tell if Wild Bill was serious or not.

"Sure, traditions are important. I get it." The faster I could table this nonsense about ghosts, the quicker I could work on bringing the Cheyenne property into the twenty-first century. "So, the elevator, his name really isn't Floyd?"

"It is now," Wild Bill said with a laugh.

"No," Toby said sternly. "It's Otis after the manufacturer. I wasn't crazy about a talking elevator at first, but the guests seem to like him. So, his name is Otis. You can't argue with history."

"Sure." I shrugged. "Talking elevators, resident ghost, why not."

"That's the spirit! We'll make a believer out of you yet," Toby said.

CHAPTER SIX

CODY

"Daisy Collins, huh? That's a pretty name," I said. "Were either of your parents a fan of Fitzgerald?"

"No, they're a bunch of bilingual alcoholics. I was named after a drink. The English translation of margarita is Daisy."

It was rare when a woman left me speechless, especially in my line of work, but Daisy did. It also proved that most people wanted to tell the truth if asked the right question. Still, the night was young and Daisy was even younger.

"So, let me guess, your brother's name is Tomas, or Tom for short?" I flashed her my best smile, which quickly turned upside down when she answered.

"Oh my gosh! How'd you know?"

Despite how good she looked in the naughty nurse costume—and she did look good—there was a disconnect I could no longer ignore.

"Well, Daisy Collins, it was a pleasure meeting you." I placed a twenty on the bar and nodded toward Dean. "Next round's on me."

"You're leaving?" She crossed her legs and gently pulled on the seam of her fishnet stockings.

Kryptonite. Legs. Stockings. I felt like Superman in the presence of my greatest weakness.

"Cody, I was having fun talking to you. You kind of remind me of my dad—only, you know, he's white and all. But you remind me of him," she said.

Well, that's what every guy wants to hear. I politely smiled, and for some reason, patted her hand. Suddenly, I became a full generation older. Now I was more like a grandfather figure. I might as well offer her a hard candy while reminiscing from a rocking chair.

"Be safe, Daisy."

Thankfully, the side exit was no more than a foot away, which I covered in one step. The sooner I got out of the saloon, the better. My sister's voice rose in my head: *"Find 'em in a bar, leave 'em in a bar."* As much as I hated to admit it, Sheridan was right. Nothing good ever happened after happy hour ended. I picked up women so I wouldn't go home alone, yet the year was almost over and there was no one waiting for me in my home in the Avenues. Something had to change. *I want to meet the one who will always be next to me in the morning and not someone I just met that night.* I wasn't in any rush to find love, but I sure would like the search to pick up the pace.

CHAPTER **SEVEN**

REESE

Everything will look different after a run. A little music blasting in my ears would hopefully drown out the late evening email from the corporate office that resonated in my mind like a bad song on repeat. I stood in the alley between the buff-colored brick backside of the hotel and the red-brick theater, where I began and ended my nightly runs. There wasn't any alley in California where I'd feel as safe. But in two weeks' time, I'd discovered a lot about Wyoming—the first state to grant suffrage to women, the last in total population, and neither would ever change, unlike the weather, which always changed. In the early morning, I froze to the core and needed to defrost the windshield on my rental car and crank up the heater. But by midafternoon, I was drenched in sweat and seriously wondered why the Nobel Prize never went to the guy who invented air conditioning. The one constant since I relocated to Wyoming was this alley, whose corner slab bore a date stamp of 1901. The bricks and mortar felt like the only things grounding me. I didn't need to glance at the email on my phone, yet I did one more time.

> *Reese,*
>
> *Hopefully you've acclimated well to Wyoming's climate! I checked the weather and was surprised to find there still isn't snow. Enjoy it while it lasts!*
>
> *As we discussed during the interview and subsequent transfer process, your role as the new general manager is to help shape and streamline the Historic Wyoming Point Resort in Cheyenne. We are looking to you to find cost-saving measures to lessen the operating and payroll expenses.*
>
> *However, since we last spoke, the board convened and decided to maximize the Point Resort portfolio by relinquishing those resorts that aren't operating to their full potential. This will enable the corporation to focus on a select number of properties to maximize our brand in the industry.*
>
> *To that end, the Historic Wyoming Point Resort is slated to be listed on the real estate market in the spring. At this point, this development is not for public or staff disclosure. There are many balls in the air at this time, and we certainly don't want to upset anyone before the holidays.*
>
> *I look forward to visiting you in the spring. In the meantime, please forward a current profit and*

> *loss statement, indicating where you project to streamline the budget.*
>
> *Best,*
> *Angus Thurman*
> *CEO Point Resorts*

"*Sonuvabitch.*" I felt my jaw tighten again. "I only took the job because it was a smaller hotel and I could learn from the ground up without making too many mistakes. I knew I'd have to make some cuts, but I never thought I was brought in to prep the hotel for the slaughter." I bent down, tucked my master hotel key into the side of my left sock, tightened the laces on my running shoes, and stood.

"So basically, unless this property suddenly turns into a moneymaker, it's all but gone." I liked the alley. It never spoke back, argued, or commented on my nightly rant. *Yup, this alley was my first friend, and probably my only after that email.* I tucked my iPhone into the pocket of the black armband and fished the earbuds from my jacket.

"I mean, it's one thing to cut seasonal staff, shit, that's expected," I mumbled as I plugged the earbuds into the side of my iPhone. "But to cut into the operating staff?" Wild Bill, Zavi, and even Millie from the gift shop surfaced in my mind like bobbleheads that bounced back and forth, taunting me. "It's bullshit. They don't know I was sent here to bring the hotel into the twenty-first century. They'll probably think I knew corporate's plans all along. *Sonuvabitch.*"

I scrolled to the music app on my phone, and my playlists surfaced. I hit "Power Mix" followed by the Shuffle button.

My music was as essential to my daily run as my sneakers, sports bra, and the black armband I strapped around my bicep beneath my jacket. I zipped my jacket and the sleek neoprene band hugged my arm. If only there was some kind of neoprene to protect me from the heat and weathering that was bound to happen when the staff discovered corporate's end game. If there was one thing I'd quickly learned about Wyoming, it was that towns were small, and the worse the news, the faster it traveled.

I tucked the buds into my ears, felt through my jacket for the side button on my phone, and cranked up the volume. His voice yelled above the cries of the concert crowd, "Remember in the end, nobody wins unless everybody wins."

The Boss. Finally, a boss I liked. The guitar and heavy beat of the drums kicked me into high gear when I needed it the most. I was tired, hungry, and lonely. There wasn't anyone here who I could confide in. I was alone in an alley in Wyoming's capital city, and after tonight's email, I felt even more isolated. The only thing I knew to do was hit the back streets and hit them hard. I jumped over puddles, sidestepped potholes, and pumped my arms and legs like every corner I took led to the finish line.

The music beat in my ears with a tempo I had to keep. Bruce Springsteen's lyrics lifted me up, reminding me that life was about taking chances, that unfamiliar roads led to new frontiers, and no matter how crappy and desperate things seemed, the romance of escape and running away was always within reach. *Shit, that's what I'll do. I'll just quit and let corporate find another henchman. I won't be anyone's scapegoat.* I knew I'd never quit, but the Boss's tempo and voice hit the sweet spot. I picked up the pace and ran faster, farther, and more fluidly than I had all week. After all, tramps like me were born to run.

As I passed the Wyoming Steakhouse Saloon, I unzipped my jacket, peeled it off, glanced down to wrap it around my waist—and either ran into the side door to the bar or it slammed into me. Dazed, I took a step back to get my bearings and slipped on something greasy. I quickly pivoted away from whatever it was, but it was too late. The left side of my foot caught the edge of a pothole and turned out, causing the inside of my knee to bear all my weight. My knee buckled, and I came crashing down. My palms skidded across the pavement that was rough, patchy, and cold. The pain cut through me instantly. I rolled to my side, slowly sat up against the dumpster, and grabbed my knee.

"Fuck!" I yanked out the earbuds and let them hang on my chest. I pulled my knee toward me, and thankfully it didn't pop like it had when I'd torn a ligament. However, the pain went from a dull ache to a hot, searing, kill-me-now intense throbbing. It wasn't a tear, but a strain that left me wishing I was inside the bar drinking instead of outside it.

When the bar door continued to push against my right foot, I realized that I may have run into it, but whatever idiot held it open was oblivious to the fact they'd slammed into me. I leaned forward and banged on the door with my bloody palm.

"Hey! Hey! I'm back here!" I sounded like a kid from

New York and not a sunny, smiling Cali girl.

The satiny sheen from his bald head was the first thing I saw. The second was his eyes, which magnified in size when his face popped around the side of the door. "What the…?" But instead of closing the door, he continued to push it against me. The guy was easy to look at, but every man I'd met in Wyoming seemed to be a stereotype or a cliché of the west. In jeans, black boots, and a white shirt with sleeves rolled and open at the collar, the only thing this guy was missing was a cowboy hat to shield his enticing distinctive green eyes. Those eyes shone like rare gems that were impossible to ignore. Yet there was something else. In his eyes, I saw a glimmer of something startlingly beautiful and tragically sad. I didn't know what haunted this guy, but it wasn't ghosts. He pushed the door further into me.

"Hey, how 'bout shutting the *damn door*?" My knee had ballooned to the size of an orange, the Boss was all but silent, and this very tall, broadly built, extremely dark-skinned man with annoyingly smiling eyes stared at me like I'd magically materialized from a mystical portal.

"Seriously? This is Wyoming, not Narnia, you moron. Stop staring at me and shut the damn door!" I clenched my jaw to redirect my knee pain and wiped my skinned palms on my neon-green running tights. Two handprints marked my thigh. "Perfect. Just perfect."

***

CODY

The golden tones in her red hair shone beneath the moonlight. Long, bouncy curls pulled away from her face revealed shades of red that reminded me of the moon during a total eclipse. And like an eclipse, I couldn't stop staring— even if it was bad for me. The fog wrapped around her fair face and delicate dancer's body. I stared at green eyes that suddenly flashed with anger.

"Hello?"

"Oh, right." I stepped outside, closed the door behind me, and instantly wished I hadn't. From the looks of her knee, she needed ice, which would have been easy to get from Dean if the side door wasn't shut and locked behind me. "Uh, hi."

She shook her head, but didn't even flinch at the sight of a black man. Most white women backed away or suddenly clutched their purses when I passed, as if the mere color of my skin was threatening. All she did was raise a reddish eyebrow my way.

"*Hi?* Are you kidding me? That's all you got?" She tried to stand, but her knee collapsed beneath her.

I rushed to her side. "Here, lean on me."

She looked up at me. "Uh, that would be swell if I could stand!" She gnashed her teeth, and her red hair looked like it was on fire.

"Right." *Right? I sound like an idiot. Come on, Cody, man, kick into gear.* I glanced at her, her knee, and where we were. All the different methods to carry an injured person by myself during first aid surfaced. *Do it by the book and no one gets hurt.* I crouched with my knees bent and my back straight and positioned myself next to the side of her injured leg. She sat up as straight as she could, and I wrapped my arm around her tiny waist.

"*What* are you doing?" Her body stiffened, but not from fear. This girl was way too angry to be scared.

"I'm picking you up," I said with a smile while I slowly released her. "You're outside a bar, after all."

"You're an idiot."

I slowly nodded. "So I've been told. But right now, I look like your best option...." I glanced toward the trash dumpster she leaned against. "Of course, unless you'd like to wait until morning for the trashman. Cheyenne's sanitation crews are friendly folk, and I think tomorrow is pickup day, so...." I shrugged. "Or perhaps you'd rather hop to safety by yourself." I slowly stroked the stubble on my chin, never breaking eye contact with her. "Either way, Red, it's entirely up to you."

If I thought the hazel in her eyes was intense before, the color shifted to extreme, along with the tone of her voice.

"You can call me Reese or *Ms.* Pemberton, but I do not answer to 'Red' or 'Sugar' or 'Honey,' and if you ever say the last two, you better be asking me to pass those sweeteners for your tea. Otherwise, your tea won't be the only thing in hot water."

"Right," I said, after again making all the wrong moves. There was something about this headstrong, assertive, downright willful woman that turned me into a bumbling idiot, and I'd just met her. I slowly exhaled. "So, what will it be? Do you want my help or not?"

"Fine. Whatever. Just don't hurt me."

"Wouldn't think of it." But before I secured my arm around her again, I paused. "May I?"

"*Yes!*"

Damn, she's pissed *off.* What's that expression? You catch more flies with honey than vinegar. And this girl was straight-up vinegar. Maybe she's scared. "So," I lightened the tone of my voice, "how'd you fall?"

"Are you kidding me?"

I shook my head and gently placed one hand around her waist. She wrapped her arm over my shoulder. My other arm went under her knees.

She drew a sharp breath. "Don't hurt me."

I stopped. "Never."

Her eyebrows furrowed. "Says the guy who slammed the door into me."

"What?" I took a staggered step and almost lost my balance.

Her arms wrapped around my neck to the point of suffocation.

"If you drop me, so help me God, I will hurt you."

She was small, but mighty. "Yes, ma'am." I regained my balance and slowly stood. Her entire weight hung on my arms. She felt like air and smelled like heaven—or what I imagined heaven would smell like—lavender, rose, and jasmine. Sure, it was a weird combination, but hey, it was my vision. And it was pretty sweet. Heaven was an endless field of Wyoming wildflowers, and this woman smelled like an orchard of the best the Rocky Mountain West offered. Shit, she brought the fragrance to life.

I kept my back straight as I stood with her in my arms. If I injured myself in the process, I wouldn't be any help to her or anyone. When I was firmly standing, I realized there was no way she could lean on me as a human crutch. I was too tall and she was too injured. I'd have to carry her to my truck, which was two blocks away. Normally I'd place her on my back and carry her like a backpack, but her knee was in no condition to extend any further than it already had.

For a shorter gal, she was all legs, which draped over my arm like eye candy. Sexy legs left me weak in the knees, and hers made me feel like I'd run a marathon uphill in combat boots.

The chilly autumn Wyoming wind whirled around us and brought her closer to me. She tucked her head beneath my chin. The woman fit perfectly in my arms.

"So, Reese, is it?" I said while I carried her away from the alley and toward my truck.

"Yes."

"Hello, Reese." I paused. *Ah, what the hell.* "I'm *Detective* Cody Pring."

No reaction. She either didn't hear me or didn't give a shit. My gut resonated with the latter.

"So crazy that's it's almost Halloween, right? It seems like yesterday it was spring." She remained mute in my arms. "You have any fun plans for tomorrow night?"

"Let's not," she said.

"Let's not, what?" I glanced down at her.

"Let's not do this." Her eyes were as cold and unwelcoming as the wind. "I appreciate the assist, but now that we're on the main street, I can take it from here."

She released her hands from around my neck, but I didn't let go.

"Reese, I hate to break it to you, but you can't stand. I can safely drive you to the emergency room, your house, or wherever it is you call home, even if it's a castle with flying monkeys. I'm sure you also have a deathly fear of water, too."

I thought a slight smile lit her face, but I wouldn't bet on it. Instead, she reached for her jacket tied around her waist and wiggled in my arms. "I have my phone. I'll call the hotel. They'll come get me."

"If that's what you'd prefer…."

"It is," she said sharply.

"Hold up," I said with her in my arms. "You'd rather hobble along alone than accept help from me?"

"Who knew you were smarter than you looked?"

I mentally started counting to ten and barely got to two when I blew out a mouthful of hot air. "*Sure*, lady, *whatever* you want."

I bent to set her down, and she carefully, slowly slid out of my arms. But as soon as she tried to retrieve her phone and balance on one leg, she leaned like a lightweight drinker at an Irish pub on St. Patrick's Day. Or Halloween.

Instinctively, I reached for her, and she just as quickly turned her shoulder. "I've got it." She tucked her injured left leg behind her right to prop herself up. When she didn't fall over, she tipped her chin toward me.

"Thank you, *Detective* Pring, but I'm not someone who needs rescuing. Not me." She stabbed her chest with her finger. "Nope. I'm the new general manager for the Historic Point Resort in Wyoming or whatever the blast it's called." She shook her head, and her green eyes flashed as she pointed at me. "I don't need rescuing because *I'm* the one corporate brings in to…." She paused. "I've got it from here." When she exhaled, I could have sworn her nostrils flared.

"In fact," she said, "thank you. You've helped me realize that whatever happens, including getting *smacked* by a door or straining my knee, it's up to me to pull myself up. I *will not* and *cannot* rely on you or anyone else."

There was headstrong, and then there was stupid. *When was the last time this woman laughed, let go, or got laid? Good God.* Still, I had learned in my profession it was better to keep people off the defensive.

"So, you *did* hear my title," I said with a wry grin.

"If you're Cheyenne's finest, then we may as well cut out the middleman and just send me straight to the morgue." Her eyebrows rose, and the curve of her lips turned into a smile that was nothing short of bewitching. "To protect and serve? More like maim and cripple." She pulled back her narrow shoulders like a bull ready to attack. "Thanks again, but I'm going to be okay." She glanced down at her knee. "I've injured my knee a helluva lot worse. This doesn't feel like a torn ligament. Probably sprained it. Nothing ice won't heal.

Yup, I'm just fine." I wasn't sure if she was convincing me or herself. She turned and limped toward the street lamp.

I must be a sucker for pain. But there was something about her jagged edge that drew me to her like a bear to a beehive. Most likely I'd get stung by the feisty little critter, but the chance for sweetness was worth the risk.

"Well, good night," I said as I walked past her.

"Uh-huh." She slightly tilted her head and returned her focus to her phone.

I walked in the direction of my truck, but when I was out of her line of sight, I ducked into an alley and watched. Whether she wanted to be rescued or not, I wouldn't leave until I made sure someone came for her.

CHAPTER **EIGHT**

"Good evening, Historic Wyoming Point Resort."

I knew the men at the hotel wore many hats, but having my chief engineer answer the hotel phone after hours was seriously cramping my plans to drink the rest of the night away. I needed a bag of crushed ice for my knee and cubed ice for my bourbon. It had seriously been a day that required a multidrink night.

"Toby or not to Toby," I said, and giggled. He really reminded me of my older brother, Owen, so I had to mock him.

A gravelly laugh followed. "I wondered when you'd call."

Huh? I pressed my ear against my cell phone. "What? Why? What happened?" It was hard to hear with the wind that whipped my hair like a blender. The Wyoming wind was no joke. There was a cloudless sky, full moon, and all would be picturesque if it weren't for robust winds that blew down from the Rocky Mountains and across the never-ending sea of sagebrush that seemed to be everywhere.

Either his raspy voice increased in volume or I had learned to hear through wind. "I figured it was only a matter of time until you called."

"Why?"

"Because you've been gone for a while. Plus, it's cold, rainy, and I just started a fire in the lobby." He paused. "You saw the smoke signals, didn't you?"

I shook my head and smiled. "No, Tobias, I'm too far from the hotel to see any signal other than the one blinking in the window of the Steakhouse Saloon. Beer on tap. Beer on tap." I slowly nodded. "I think I need many beers on tap."

"Doc, what are you doing all the way over there?"

"Doc?"

"Yeah, you said you had your PhD in physics, right?"

"Yes, I did, but that doesn't make me…." I raised my shoulders. *Doc?* "Hey, would you please send the shuttle over?"

"Sure. I still don't know why you're so far away."

"Toby! I was running."

"Doc, there's no need to get upset. Sheesh."

I stared at the sky that twinkled with stars. Even with the cold, bitter wind, Wyoming remained untouched. Hell, it was probably the wind that kept it that way. Still, for a state that had more cattle than people, the locals preserved and protected the past. And God help the outsider who tried to change it. Everything I was sent to do for the hotel went against what Wyoming stood for. My chest felt heavy and my stomach ached.

"Doc?"

"Yes, Tobias."

His laughter was husky like his build. "You okay?"

I slowly shook my head, but instead said, "Of course. I'm fine. In fact...." I drew a breath. "Would you mind making sure the bellman moved my things to suite 632? It may be a mess in my suite, so no judging."

"Already taken care of. And we don't judge around these parts."

"I sure hope so." I paused.

"Doc?"

"Yeah, I'm here. I was just lost in thought. I'm envisioning a long, hot soak in one of the oldest bathtubs still in existence." I half laughed. "What's better than that?"

I could practically hear my chief engineer and self-proclaimed guy Friday smile. "That's great, Doc. I have a tape recorder set up in case Campbell comes and visits. Maybe he'll talk to you."

I rolled my eyes, if only for my own sake. "Perfect. Can't wait."

Toby laughed.

"Okay, well, I'll just wait here for the hotel shuttle outside the Steakhouse Saloon." I ended the call and tucked my iPhone into my armband protector.

I untied my jacket and slid it on, but it didn't lessen the chill that ran through me. I looked around, but other than the cars that passed and people inside the bar, I was alone. Still, it felt like someone was watching me.

CHAPTER **NINE**

CODY

"So, who's your knight in shining armor?" I crossed my arms over my chest, leaned against the brick side of the local thrift store, and kept my sights on the difficult redhead who repeatedly shifted her weight off her injured knee. Even from a distance, it was clear her knee was jacked up. *She could be in the ER right now if not for being such a she-devil.*

My cell phone vibrated in my back pocket. I walked into the alley before answering the call. I knew the station would keep calling until they either got through or received an email reply.

"This is Pring," I said.

"Hey, Cody, it's Connie in dispatch. There's a 10-16 on the corner of Carey and 30th Street."

I hate domestic calls. As soon as the police arrived, warring spouses suddenly found a common enemy.

"Hey, Connie, I'm not on call until tomorrow. It's either Greenman and Garring or Wolfe and Cragin in the penalty box."

"Greenman and Garring were investigating something and got the call about the domestic. They called in for assistance," she said. "Dixon is en route from his home residence."

I glanced at my watch. It was only nearing ten, but it felt later. The sky was darker, the moon fuller, and the vibe in the air was no longer promising me an uneventful weekend. *Fuck.* "Ten-four, I'm on my way."

I jogged to the edge of the alley and glanced in Reese's direction, but she was gone. All that remained behind was the memory of her red hair, catlike hazel eyes, and a sharp tongue.

I jumped in my steel-blue truck and headed north. Cheyenne wasn't a big city by most standards. Sandwiched between Colorado and the wide-open spaces to Canada, the Magic City of the Plains was magical because the crime rate was low. When something significant happened, like the recent cyberattack, it required real police work, which none of us shied away from. I preferred Cheyenne to other Wyoming towns where the biggest crimes committed involved cattle rustling, claim jumping, or horse-hair theft. Horse owners wanted justice, and I understood. When horses were hit multiple times, it left the animals with little hair on their tails. The crimes in the capital city were typically petty misdemeanors and usually didn't involve rounding up a posse, which suited me just fine.

My beat consisted of more than 300 miles of city streets and alleys. Patrol units ensured safety for most it. However, when events stretched beyond the scope of a patrolman's purview, or they were short-staffed due to a holiday, like Halloween, detectives were dispatched. I was within walking distance to Carey and 30th Avenue if time wasn't an issue. But when a team of detectives requested backup, time was of the essence. I cut my lights and pulled behind Greenman's white, four-door civic and parked at an angle to create a barrier if one was needed. I grabbed my sidearm holster and magazine from beneath the seat and clipped them to my belt. My Kevlar vest was beside my tie on the passenger seat. I strapped the vest around my chest and cinched it tight.

I quickly surveyed the scene. Two-story, brick corner house. Side yard. Gated backyard. Garage or guest house hard to tell. No visible dogs or dog signs posted. Two women, one in their fifties and one in their thirties, and a teenage boy stood on the sidewalk at the corner of 30th Street and Carey. They were separated by detectives Andy Greenman and Grant Garring. Most likely a mother-daughter dispute with the poor kid caught in the middle of their mayhem. I wasn't sure if they occupied the corner house or if the occupants of the corner house had called to report them. I was reaching for the handle of my car door when something flickered from the corner house. It wasn't much, but enough that I waited and watched. The curtain on one of the street-level windows moved, and the person behind was lit. I couldn't make out if it was a man or woman, only that they wielded something that gleamed in the evening light like chrome. I leaned toward the dash, and stainless steel popped light from the house back to me. *Fuck. Handgun.*

I bolted from my truck, crouching low as I approached the side of the house, where I carefully made my way through the shrubs. Greenman spotted me, but no one else had, so he quickly ushered the trio further down the street out of harm's way. Garring followed cue and placed himself between the threesome and the house. I didn't see Dixon or his car. He lived outside of town in a rural area. Even without traffic, he was easily fifteen minutes out depending on when he left. I'd have to do this without him. *Fuck.*

I drew the Glock from the holster and checked my hip: one magazine on my belt. I leaned against the house sideways and ducked beneath the window. Adrenaline pumped through me and magnified my surroundings. Everything and everyone was a threat to me and my fellow detectives, who had their weapons drawn and stood in the line of fire to protect three morons who'd decided they had nothing better to do than fight on a Friday night.

I glanced at Garring and slightly nodded. When I was close enough to the right side of the window, I carefully slid up the brick wall, drew a deep, steady breath, and stole a glance into the house. The screen was open, and a breeze blew the curtain back. She looked at me just as I made eye contact with her. The pistol didn't concern me as much as the sinister look in her eyes. It was like staring into evil.

"Police!" I flattened against the side of the house. "Put down the weapon and open the door."

The only sound I heard was a "tisk, tisk" followed by the window slamming shut.

Motherfucker.

I retreated to the side yard where there weren't any windows. Dixon darted low across the street and positioned himself beside me.

"What we got?" For being a little thick in the middle, Dixon barely drew a breath. And damn if I wasn't glad to see my partner.

"Elderly woman with a handgun. Looks like an older piece—maybe a pistol? And she's old." I wiped the sweat from my forehead with the sleeve of my shirt. "As soon as she saw me, she shut the window and any further conversation."

"I flanked the back, and there's a screen door open," Dixon said.

"Probably not anymore," I said. "But the gun gives us probable cause to enter."

"And so did the call into dispatch. Greenman and Gerring called in after interviewing those three." Dixon cocked his head toward the two women and teen who were now being escorted into a squad car that had arrived on the scene. The squad car would keep them safe.

"What did they say?" I glanced from the women back to Dixon.

"Apparently the woman you spotted with the gun owns

the house and rents out rooms. The renters estimate she's in her eighties, but she's still kicking and kicking hard. She got pretty verbal with the tenants and started demanding they pay more rent. The three decided to leave and get something to eat and let her cool down, but when they returned, she had put something to block the front door or did something to jam the lock. Not sure, but besides not being able to access the rooms they rent, they say they haven't seen the boy's dog in a week. A German shepherd mix. When they asked her about the dog, she threatened to hurt him if they tried to reenter the home. That's why they called."

"She's got a gun, and I didn't hear any dog. Did you?"

Dixon shook his head.

"What about the back? Is there a guest house or garage she could have gone into?"

"Guest house, and negative. It was locked," Dixon said.

I glanced toward Carey Avenue. We were beginning to draw a crowd. One squad car was no big deal. But when three patrol cars arrived on the scene to assist, it signaled to the community that things were definitely not all right. The only thing helping was that Carey was a one-way street. "We've got a 10-0 hinky."

"Copy that."

My partner knew our unofficial code—10-0 hinky meant "be careful, this doesn't feel right." In other words, something about the call made me nervous, concerned, or stand-the-hairs-on-my-neck-up freaked. We used code in case anyone was listening to our conversation.

"We got to get Unit thirty-two and thirty-three and patrol

to clear the street. We'll enter through the back," I said.

"Copy that." Dixon spoke into the two-way radio attached to the shoulder of his vest. Mine was in my desk at the station. "Delta, Unit thirty."

"Unit thirty, advise code." Connie was still on her shift in dispatch. Dispatch was referred to by every officer as "Delta," and every officer was referred to by Dispatch as "Unit" followed by their badge number. The detectives were numbered thirty through thirty-eight, which was easy to remember because Dixon was thirty and the rest of us followed suit. I was thirty-one; Greenman and Garring were thirty-two and thirty-three.

"Delta, code 10-32," Dixon said. "Unit thirty-one made contact and individual refused to surrender. Advise Unit thirty-two and Unit thirty-three to clear Carey. We're going to approach house from back entrance."

There were four police codes universal to any police officer in Wyoming: 10-69 officer in danger, 10-4 okay, 10-0 use caution, and 10-32 gun/weapon involved—subject armed. I knew once other officers heard 10-32 on the scanner, they'd dump whatever they were doing to assist. When a weapon was involved and the subject was armed, Cheyenne's finest came out to protect their own.

"Ten-four, Unit thirty, copy code 10-32 at twenty-three hundred."

I glanced at Dixon, who lowered the volume on his radio speaker, tightened the straps on his Kevlar vest, and tucked his wedding band into the top pocket. He didn't have to remove his wedding band, but he always did. It was almost as if the gesture symbolically separated Dixon's personal life from his job. I did the same in how I viewed him. Dixon wasn't a husband, my brother-in-law, or a future father, he was my partner. We'd worked together before he married my sister, and we remained partners afterward because we separated our personal lives from the job. Besides, there wasn't anyone I trusted more than him.

We stayed low to the ground as we made our way toward the rear of the house. The gate was unlatched. Gun drawn, I went through first, followed closely by Dixon. We quietly approached the back screen, which remained open. The radio speaker on Dixon's left shoulder murmured.

"Unit thirty, home at 632 Carey Avenue owned by Ames Reed."

"Any priors?" Dixon whispered into the mic.

"No known."

"Ten-four, Delta," Dixon responded, and gave the nod.

I kicked in the screen and came through the door with my Glock up and my finger on the trigger. "Police!" The enclosed patio was small, dank, and smelled like cat piss. The patio was connected to the house by a narrow hallway. I made my way toward the hallway, and a figure moved in the shadows.

"Drop the gun!" I shouted.

Dixon was behind me, scanning the enclosed patio, which was full of overgrown plants.

"Who are you?" An elderly voice spoke in the dark.

"Police! Drop the gun and—"

A bright light suddenly shone overhead. She could see

us, but the blinding light prevented me from seeing her. I moved forward, charging toward the front of the house and where I thought she stood. Dixon had my six. If I went down in the line of fire, he'd finish her.

The long, constricting hallway ended at the front door that had a kitchen chair propped beneath the door handle. I kicked out the bottom legs, and it tumbled to the floor. Rooms were on either side of the front door. I quickly turned right, and Dixon left. The light in the hallway illuminated each room, and she wasn't in either of them. Suddenly, a sleek black cat popped out from the side of the couch and casually strolled on the armrest. I about shot the fucking overgrown hairball. *I hate cats.*

"Why are you here?" Her voice echoed overhead.

I glanced at Dixon and pointed toward the ceiling. The stairs were tucked in a corner of the house off the front room. Didn't surprise me. The houses in the Avenues dated back to the early 1900s, before ergonomics. Or common sense.

"Ma'am." I carefully approached the staircase that was as tight and confining as the hallway. *Fucking house doesn't provide one ounce of protection.* "I need you to drop the gun."

"What gun? Leave me alone."

"All right. Then let's talk." When she didn't respond, I took the next step on the stairs, and the hardwood creaked beneath my boots. *Fuck.*

"Go away. I don't want to talk."

She moved across the hardwood floors above us, and we both stood still, our weapons pointed toward the top of the stairs. There was no other way to reach her, save using a ladder against the side of the house, and we didn't have time. The sound of her voice unraveled along with her resolve.

"I hate the police. You always think I've done something wrong. You always point your finger at me. I haven't done anything wrong."

"Okay." I softened my tone. "Then talk to me."

"Nothing to talk about. Those ingrates called you because I wouldn't allow them to take advantage of me. *No one takes advantage of Estelle.*"

"Uh…" I was so focused on the pistol in her hand, that while I knew she just introduced herself, my brain faded to black. *Fuck.* "Ester, I understand."

"It's not *Ester.*" Her voice was strong. "It's *Estelle. Not some woman from the Bible! Do I look like a Bible character?*"

"Of course not, *Estelle.*" It was a name I'd never forget. I paused and carefully took another step on the staircase.

"No use coming up here," she said. "'Less you have some news about those bastard renters. You know that boy's a bastard, don't ya? He got no daddy."

"Okay. Well, they're all in a squad car as we speak," I said.

"Really?" It was the first time I detected a shift in her tone.

"Yes, ma'am. Detectives placed them in a patrol car." I nodded toward the top of the stairs, which was dark. All I saw were shadows. "Estelle, you don't have to worry about them anymore."

Suddenly, she appeared at the top of the stairs, and it felt like my heart jumped to my throat. Dixon quickly took two steps back, creating the necessary distance to drop this motherfucker. The only thing that stood between me and her and the revolver was six stairs. She had me in her sights, and we both knew it. But I'd go down shooting.

"I'm Cody." My voice remained calm, cool, and collected when internally my mind was on overload. My finger remained locked on the trigger, and I shifted to the right to make myself less of a target. Although it wouldn't matter. If she pulled the trigger, unless she was the worst shot in the west, she'd hit me. I didn't want to find out. "Estelle, I need you to drop the gun."

Her hair was grayish-white, but her eyebrows were as dark as my skin. She raised one and cold, steely eyes looked at me. "This isn't just a gun. It's a custom-made, single-action revolving-cylinder Colt revolver. It was a gift from my first husband for our wedding."

I slowly nodded. "Thought maybe it was a Walther." I didn't care who the fuck made the piece while it remained pointed at my head. The bitch wasn't messing around. My vest wouldn't protect me from a head shot.

"A Walther, really?" This seemed to make the old woman smile. She sure didn't look almost ninety, and she certainly didn't act her age. "No, it's not a Walther. Is that what Negroes prefer?"

Now, with her racist remark, she seemed ninety. "Walthers are solid firearms," I said.

"Nothing's as good as a Colt. My first husband had it custom-made for me. He firmly believed in the best, and Colt is the gold standard."

"It's very impressive. But, Estelle, I need for you to set it down."

"Do you think Buffalo Bill Cody, Wyatt Earp, or Billy the Kid ever set down their Colt in the middle of gunfight?"

I swallowed hard. *Gunfight?*

"The American West was created from their legends. And legends never surrender." Estelle probably didn't weigh more than a buck ten, and under normal conditions, I'd tackle her to the ground. But there wasn't anything normal about her or her acclaimed Colt. The single-action army "Peacemaker" revolver she wielded with her shaky hands and unstable mind could easily make pieces of me. The famed revolver may be known as "The Gun That Won the West," but I hoped to hell her Colt wouldn't see any more victories. Gunned down by a little old lady would be a humiliating end of watch for any lawman.

I knew Dixon was within shooting distance. Hell, I was too. But neither of us wanted to drop a granny, no matter how batshit crazy she was.

She didn't want to surrender, nor did I expect she would voluntarily, so I did the one thing she didn't expect. Neither did my partner when I laid my Glock on the stairs between me and crazy. My Glock was within reaching distance, but setting it down placed me and Dixon at greater risk.

I raised my hands in surrender. "I'm a Wyoming boy. I'd never want to disrespect the west, it's legends or traditions."

If I'd had my cowboy hat on, I'd have tipped it at her for good measure. But I think from the cut of my boots, the rodeo buckle poking out beneath my vest, and the serious tone in my voice, she knew I was the real deal. You can't fake Wyoming. And I stood cowboy proud.

Her body may be frail-looking, but her graying eyes were alive and danced with malevolence. When she smiled, yellow, crooked teeth made my blood turn cold.

"That's a good boy," she said, and I wasn't sure if she was talking to me or her Colt that she placed on the top stair.

I never took my eyes off the Colt or Estelle. My feet moved with lightning speed. I breached the distance between us and grabbed the pistol.

"Weapon secured." I tucked it into the back of my jeans, then reached back and grabbed my Glock, which I aimed at Estelle.

Dixon flanked my left, cuffs out and gun aimed. Crazy bitch was going down.

"Hands. Behind your back." Dixon's tone matched his demeanor, which remained on high alert. Until we had her cuffed, she remained a threat. She could have a concealed weapon, knife, or knitting needle she intended to use against us.

Dixon slapped a cuff around her right wrist and reached for her left arm.

"I'm not going to hurt you," he said.

Dixon was much kinder than me. I would have tightened the cuffs and then cinched the middle to intensify the grip as I dragged her down the stairs. There was something about this woman that just didn't sit right with me. Call it instinct, but Estelle's evil ran deep. When Dixon clicked the cuffs into place, he spoke into his two-way radio. "Individual contained."

No sooner had Dixon spoken than I heard the front door burst open.

"Up here. Corner stairs," I yelled to our backup. Then I turned to crazy. "Estelle, who else is in the house?"

Her gray eyes spoke volumes, even though she said nothing. She was hiding something or someone. I glanced at Dixon, whose expression conveyed agreement.

Greenman and Gerring rushed to the bottom of the staircase.

"Clear the house and the guest house," I said, and they dispatched to the lower level to ensure that no accomplice was hidden anywhere.

To Dixon, "Take her outside. I'll clear upstairs."

"Copy that," he said, and carefully guided the woman downstairs. The last thing either of us wanted was a police misconduct violation for the old bat twisting her ankle, or worse, the appearance of mistreatment. And all it took was one cell phone video to create the wrong impression. Fucking cell phones. *Where are the videos of crazy pointing a gun at my fucking head?* No one ever saw that shit.

When Dixon and Estelle were downstairs, I crouched against the wall and took the first corner. Clear. I searched the hallway wall for the light switch that I flipped on, lighting both the hallway and master bedroom. I cautiously approached the bedroom, and the smell hit me before I set foot into the room. It was worse than the enclosed patio. *What the fuck?* I tucked my chin, but the stench overpowered the room, sucking up all the oxygen and hurling out a strong smell like something had rotted. *What is that?*

The bedroom closet and master bath were clear. There wasn't anything behind the dresser or in the drawers. The only other place was the bed. I lifted the bedspread with the tip of my boot and glanced beneath the bed.

I wished I hadn't. My muscles tensed, I began breathing heavily, and my mouth went dry. *Oh, God.*

I holstered my weapon, dropped to my knees, and quickly surveyed the situation. The dog was lying on his back. His hind legs were sprawled out, and it looked like he was cut, but I couldn't be sure. I carefully reached for him. His eyes shot open, and I about shat myself.

"Hey there, fella. It's okay. I'm here to help." I gently placed my hand toward his nose to familiarize him with me. His dark eyes bored into me. *Help.*

"Okay, so we're going to do this together. All right?" My voice softened and my throat tightened. *Who would do this?*

I slowly rubbed the top of his nose, finding it wet. He whined.

"I know, buddy. I got you." When I brought my hand out, it was covered in blood. The German shepherd was captive beneath the bed by some kind of wire that stretched from his hind legs to the box springs. He looked like meat ready for processing. And from the blood on my hand, I wasn't too far off the mark.

"Okay, buddy, I'm just getting my Leatherman tool."

I slowly reached into my jean pocket for my knife, opened it, and lay on my back to get a better view of the maze of wires. Someone had bound this poor dog to the bed.

I didn't have a radio, which was probably good because I would have sounded like a wuss. This dog was breaking my heart. His hind legs looked broken from the taut trap. No matter what I did, it was going to hurt him. I cut the wire closest to me, and his leg fell limp to the floor. I quickly crawled to the other side of bed and cut the other wire. When the dog was free, he remained motionless. The bed was making the rescue difficult. If I dragged him out, I could cause more harm. I stood, grabbed the bottom edge of the top mattress, and lifted it until I could topple it to the other side of the room and let it fall to the floor. I did the same with the box springs. The dog lay beneath the frame with a jagged knife wound down his belly. The fact that he was still alive was a miracle.

"Hey, buddy." I lay beside him. "I'm so sorry this happened to you." I swallowed hard. The bedframe needed to go, but it was attached to a behemoth, solid oak headboard that I couldn't lift alone.

"So, my buddies are downstairs making sure the house is secure. I'm sure they'll be here any minute." If the dog's brown eyes conveyed anything to me, it was that he didn't have another minute. God only knew how long he had held on. The pungent smell of decay and death hung in the air.

"Okay, we'll do this together." The slatted bedframe made it impossible for me to lift him through it. There was no other way than to slide him toward me. At least with the mattresses off, I could see what I was doing. Still, I knew it wouldn't be comfortable for him or easy for me. He might bite, and I wouldn't blame the poor guy.

I placed my hand beneath his neck and my other hand under his body. Fresh blood gushed from the wound, and he whined.

"Oh, buddy, I'm so sorry." I cradled him on my forearms as best I could in the tight space between the frame and the floor, and pulled him toward me.

When he was out from beneath the bed, I scooped him in my arms. He was a good-sized German shepherd, but I felt his ribs through his fur. "I got you." I embraced him against my chest, and he barely made a sound. "Okay, we've got a few stairs, but we got this."

The narrow staircase required me to turn sideways so he wouldn't be banged against the walls. I took each step slowly and carefully.

"Clear!" I heard Greenman shout from the maze of the first floor.

Garring appeared at the bottom of the stairs. "Fuck."

I nodded. "Find a blanket and call Farmer. Let them know to expect us."

"Copy that," Garring said.

"I'll bring the patrol car around." Greenman stood behind Garring.

"No, get my truck. Keys are inside." Patrol cars smelled about as foul as this house. This dog deserved better. I wasn't letting go of him until I placed him in Cal Farmer's capable hands. He was the best vet in town and a friend to our department.

Greenman and Garring left as quickly as they appeared. When I reached the front door, Garring carefully draped a tan-colored blanket over the dog. The blanket instantly turned crimson, soaking up his blood.

"It's okay, boy. I got you." I carried him outside, where a crowd of neighbors and spectators stood behind the barrier Greenman and Garring had put into place and patrolmen now guarded. A shocked silence filled the air as I carried the dog toward my truck that Greenman pulled onto the curb. Garring ran ahead and opened the passenger door.

"Is he going to be okay?" It was the teen boy's voice. He stepped out of the patrol car where he had been placed for safety and ran toward me.

I nodded, but signaled to the nearby patrolman with a stern glance to have him keep the boy at a distance. I still didn't know for certain who had done this to the dog. My gut told me crazy had, but until every suspect was interviewed, I wasn't about to subject this dog to any more trauma.

The teen's mother or aunt or sister or whoever the hell she was popped her head from the patrol car. "We aren't paying any vet bills," she yelled toward me. "I can't afford it. Besides, it's that bitch's fault."

Tears fell from the boy's eyes, but he quickly wiped them away. I looked at him and gently smiled. I turned to Garring, and before I could speak, he did.

"I'll handle it."

"Thanks." I cocked my head toward my shoulder. "The weapon's at my back."

He reached into his vest pocket, put on a pair of evidence gloves, and opened an evidence bag. When he withdrew the Colt pistol from my waistband, he carefully placed it in the bag.

"Run it through ballistics. I want to know if it's connected to any priors." I scanned the crowd for Dixon, but he wasn't anywhere to be seen. He must have taken Estelle into custody himself.

I carefully got into my truck with the dog tucked in my arms. Greenman pulled away from the curb. I glanced over my shoulder to the corner house. It appeared like all the other houses in the neighborhood, which made it all the more frightening. There were no discernible features that hinted at the horrors within. A Halloween haunted house could be seen a mile away, but the true terrors that nightmares were made of could be just next door.

CHAPTER **TEN**

REESE

"Doc, what'd you do?" Toby was instantly at my side as I hobbled from the hotel foyer toward the elevator.

"Ah, this?" I slightly shook my left leg and instantly regretted the move. Pain shot to my heel. I must have winced because Toby put a protective arm around me.

"Maybe tonight's not the best time to stay in Campbell's honeymoon lair."

"Lair?" I shook my head, and his arm off me. I liked Toby, but the closer I got, the harder it would be when corporate sold the property. I pressed the call button for the elevator and glanced at him. Concern reflected in his eyes.

"Oh, Tobyson, I'll be fine, and so will my knee. Thank you though."

He slowly nodded. "But it's Halloween weekend, and you've already hurt yourself. Maybe it's a sign."

"No." I sliced the air with my finger. "It's no sign.

Besides, do you really think I'm going to let a little thing like a sprained knee keep me away from the biggest party of the year? Before I even relocated here, all I heard about was the infamous costume party at the Point Resort. I'm switching suites, and suite 632 is simply a suite—Halloween weekend or not. Everything else is rumor, urban legend, or hype based on false assumptions. There are no such things as ghosts, spirits, or lost souls trapped on earth."

Toby's brown eyes dulled as if I had revealed the identity of Santa Claus.

"Ah, don't do that." I gently gripped his shoulder. Selling a property would suck regardless of any connections I made—personal or otherwise. It wasn't for nothing that many in our industry called the hotel their mistress. The hotel took all our time, attention, money, and affection. "Toby, I'm a doctor of physics. That means I'm grounded in science—tangible, tested, proven results. And all I've heard is conjecture."

"And all you have is theory." He crossed his arms over his chest, but my hand remained on his shoulder.

I slightly smiled. "Ironically, while I was working toward this degree, I learned to be highly proficient at problem solving, in and out of the lab—theory and practicum. The college wouldn't have bestowed their highest degree on me if I hadn't demonstrated an ability to solve tough challenges by thinking creatively *and* out of the box." I released my hand from his shoulder. "I gave you and Wild Bill my word that I'd be open to this Campbell fellow and that I'd think outside the box—and I will. I just don't want you to be disappointed if nothing happens, *or* if it does and I'm able to explain the phenomena."

The elevator arrived, and Toby held the door open. "We'll see, Doc. We'll see." He pressed the button labeled six.

I hopped inside.

"Doc, do you need anything?"

"I'd love a bottle of the hotel's best bourbon, but my expense account won't justify it, so I'm going to open those little bottles I was given on the airplane when I was bumped to first class." I laughed. "It's not as good, but it'll do the trick."

Toby held up a finger. "Hold Otis, and I'll be right back." He darted away.

Otis? "Oh right, the elevator." I pressed the doors open button. It was nearing midnight, and we didn't have any late arrivals scheduled, so I wasn't concerned about holding up Otis. Besides, the lobby bartender had two hours left on his shift, and from the looks of it when I walked past, Friday night had wrapped up an hour ago.

Otis spoke. "Going down."

"What?" Before I could figure out what was happening, the elevator door shut so quickly I almost lost my fingers. The elevator descended past the basement level. I'd thought the lowest floor could only be accessed with a master key inserted into the elevator control panel that only Toby, Wild Bill, and I had.

The door opened on the floor labeled BR, yet Otis announced, "Lower deck."

"Lower deck? What? This is the boiler room." I pressed the L button for the lobby, but nothing happened. The door remained open.

"Seriously, Otis?"

I pressed the button for the sixth floor, but nothing happened. I tried the lobby again. Nothing. The sixth floor. Nothing.

"Listen, Otis, I've had just about enough. My knee is killing me, and I just want to soak in a tub with my airline bottles of bourbon!" The shrill sound of my voice echoed in the dimly lit lower level. I repeatedly pressed the buttons for the lobby and the sixth floor, but nothing changed. I wiped my hand down the row of buttons and lit the entire switchboard like a Christmas tree. It stung my raw palms, but it was worth it.

"Whatcha think about that? Huh, Otis?"

With every button lit on the switchboard, the doors remained open, and I remained stuck.

"Dammit, Otis! Get me out of here."

Zilch. I opened the silver door on the operating panel labeled Phone and picked up the receiver. There wasn't a dial tone or anyone on the receiving end.

"Hello? Anyone there?" No response.

I glanced into the phone box. There wasn't a button to call or activate. It seemed to operate by picking up the receiver, which I put back and then picked up again. It remained silent.

What else can go wrong tonight?

I pressed the phone against my ear and spoke loudly

into the receiver. "Okay, well in case *anyone* is looking for me—that'd be Reese Pemberton, general manager of the Historic Wyoming Point Resort in Cheyenne." I smiled. "That's right, I actually *remembered* the full name of the hotel I've been placed in charge of! Go, me. So anyway, if anyone is looking for me, hell, if anyone even realizes I'm gone, I'm stuck in the boiler room or lower level or whatever you want to call it." I paused. "I actually prefer to call it hell because I can't go down any farther and it's the hottest place—ever." I giggled. "So, if you're looking for a very hot redhead, figuratively and literally, you'll find one in the boiler room. Or the elevator. Basically, head to the depths of hell and you're likely to find me."

I slammed the receiver back in its box. *One more thing to have fixed.*

I reached for my iPhone from my jacket pocket, but the most loyal battery had finally succumbed to my neglect of not juicing it. I hung my head and stared at my running shoes. *My master key!* I reached into the side of my shoe and retrieved my master key that would open every room and fit perfectly into the keyhole in the elevator. I placed my key in the keyhole and turned the brass end, but nothing.

"Huh? Okay, Toby said to put it in the keyhole and turn clockwise." I looked at the position of the key and imagined the face of a clock. I turned it right, but nothing happened.

"What the hell?" I scratched my head, which was itchy from dried sweat. I grabbed the ponytail holder in my hair, pulled it out, and held it in my mouth while I twisted my hair into a knot. I wrapped the ponytail holder around the knot of hair. It wasn't the best look, but it'd work. I tried my key again, but it remained stuck in one position. I carefully pulled it out lest I get it stuck, or worse, broken in the keyhole. Then I banged on the elevator cab with my fist. "Otis!"

Not surprisingly, yelling didn't advance my cause and only made me more aware of my hunger. My hands shook, and I knew my blood sugar was low. The last time I ate was at breakfast when I grabbed a yogurt cup from the continental breakfast buffet. I was beyond tired, and if I didn't get off my knee pretty soon, I risked injuring it further. I glanced at the dimly lit lower-ground floor, which Wild Bill had presented during the tour, along with the boiler. I also remembered that, due to safety issues, there was a separate staircase for the boiler room that led to the basement level, which connected onto the main emergency stairwell.

"Okay." I slowly exhaled. "Looks like I'm walking." I gingerly stepped from the elevator into the boiler room. No sooner had I set foot onto the lower level cement than the elevator door shut. I whipped my head toward the door and stood in shocked disbelief. The arrow on the elevator was lit and pointed up. "Are you kidding me?"

I pressed the lit call button, hoping I could catch Otis before he ascended, but nothing happened. When I pressed my ear against the outside of the elevator, there wasn't any sound. The elevator was shut, but it wasn't moving. I elbowed the closed elevator shaft, hard.

"Otis! Historical elevator or not, when this is over, God

help me you're getting replaced."

I limped toward the Exit sign that burned bright red and reminded me of the glowing mummy eyes in a Scooby-Doo cartoon. The staircase was located in the corner of the building where I thought there was a light switch.

"Sure, why not? What's another hundred yards? And a flight of stairs." I limped my way to the staircase and felt vindicated when I reached for the door handle. I grabbed it, but it wouldn't turn.

"No. No. No. No." I shook my head, and my eyes brimmed with tears. "This *can't* be happening."

I tried my master key, but it didn't fit the lock. "Now why the fuck would I have a master key if it's not truly a master?" There were so many things I needed to address, from why my thirty-dollar-an-hour chief engineer answered the phone after hours, to this master key situation, but nothing was going to be accomplished if I couldn't get out of this level of hell I had descended into.

I was stuck and physically tapped. All my reserves were gone. I had no energy and a hunger that our bottomless Sunday buffet and room service combined couldn't satisfy. *That's it. I surrender. Toby will eventually find me. Right?*

I slid down the wall next to the staircase door and remembered why I hadn't spent much time with Wild Bill on this level. The heat. Every radiator throughout the hotel was hooked to the boiler. Instead of running water through the pipes, the hotel used steam through large pipes that routed to this level. The intricate maze of thick, white-painted pipes zigzagged across the ceiling and funneled into the boiler located in the far corner of the floor. I understood why boilers were always featured in scary movies. Even at a distance, it looked menacing. A very stout, short beast. I remembered the measurements because it consisted of one number: five. The boiler was five feet high, five feet wide, and five feet deep.

The cube-shaped contraption would be a monster to a small child, but an expensive upgrade to an adult who only slightly towered over the five-foot monstrosity. The layers of soot and dust almost made the boiler two inches taller. Time and neglect had not been kind to it either. The true monster was the cost of replacing the relic that dated back to the opening of the hotel.

Wild Bill was the first to remind me that the eyesore was tucked away, still functioned well, and provided ample heat to the floors, rooms, and lobby. In short, there was no reason to justify the cost to upgrade the system. Besides, in the short time I'd been at the property, guests often commented that the historic heating system was charming.

What wasn't charming was being locked in the boiler room with a dead cell phone, nonfunctioning master key, and dysfunctional elevator. The heat was oppressive, and it felt like I was in a steam room. I was already dehydrated from my run; I didn't need to lose any more fluids. I kicked off my shoes, peeled off my running jacket, shirt, and tights, and when I leaned against the wall, the bricks were cool. But in a pair of holey granny panties that practically went to my belly button and a sports bra that flattened my healthy C cup to an A, I was a sight. Since I hadn't done laundry in two weeks or sent any to our laundry department, I was lucky to be wearing anything. Besides, as soon as I heard the elevator ding or the door handle twist, announcing someone, I'd grab my jacket to cover me. I slid off my socks and wiggled my toes, freeing them. About the only thing that was in good shape was my pedicure. I rolled my jacket into a ball that I placed beneath my knee, and found a comfortable position against the wall. *How appropriate, I've officially hit rock bottom in sex appeal at the very bottom of the hotel. And if I don't make it out alive, all they'll find is an incredibly unsexy skeleton.*

I closed my eyes and listened to the pipes talk. Wild Bill had mentioned that, when the radiators relieved pressure to let steam into the air, they clanged and banged. But I didn't hear clanging, banging, or whining. All I heard was whistling. A beautiful melody in my ear like someone was serenading me to sleep.

CHAPTER **ELEVEN**

CODY

"That was some solid police work." Chief Wyman stood in the men's locker room as I stepped from the shower with a towel wrapped around my waist, and Dixon walked past me in a towel toward his locker.

"Thanks, Chief." We spoke in tandem. It happened after working together for more than a decade.

As I walked toward him, the chief patted me on the back. His back slaps were legendary. A guy could feel the praise the next day. The chief was robust, and his atta boys were hearty and heartfelt.

"How's the dog?" he asked.

I pressed my lips together and shook my head. "He's with Farmer. Cal gave him about a 40 percent chance of surviving." It was like a punch to the gut, and I clenched my jaw. "The dog was pinned beneath the bed so forcibly it broke both his hind legs. He was just left to die." The anger welled inside me.

"Keep me updated on his condition."

"Will do, Chief." I wiped the water out of my ears with the edge of my towel. "Where are we at with charging Estelle?"

The chief had one tell that always foreshadowed bad news. No matter the hour, the chief always wore a tie, and as soon as he straightened his tie and adjusted its knot, it was like a hangman preparing his noose. I knew what followed wouldn't be good.

"Estelle Reed's attorney already contacted me."

"What?" I glanced behind me at the wall clock mounted above the row of sinks. "It's almost two in the morning. What attorney in Cheyenne does that crazy bitch have on speed dial?"

"David Benjamin," Chief said.

Dixon slammed his locker. "David Benjamin? How the hell can she afford him?"

The mere mention of the attorney left a bad taste in my mouth. David Benjamin was as well-known an attorney in Wyoming as Gerry Spence, and both had reputations for doggedly defending their clients and bordering the line of decency and legality.

"What do you mean, how can she afford it?" Chief's voice sounded as puzzled as he looked. "It's Estelle Reed."

I glanced from Dixon, who shrugged, back to the chief. "So?"

"Ames Oil? Ring any bells?" Chief said.

I ran my hand over my cleanly washed head, and yet it

still felt like the stench of death clung to me. "Fuck. Ames Reed is Ames Oil?"

"The one and the same," Chief said.

"So that old woman who pointed her Colt at my head is the widow to the largest oil producer in Wyoming?" I said.

The chief solemnly nodded.

"Wouldn't know it by her house," I said. "I mean, it wasn't bad, but it wasn't a mansion. And why would someone that rich need to rent rooms?"

"Oh, man." Dixon leaned his head back. "I knew she looked familiar. She was recently featured on *Wake Up and Smell the Coffee* with Scott Willis during his senior birthday shout-out." Dixon said. "She just turned ninety-one."

"What?" I stared at Dixon. "When did you start watching morning talk shows? Have you taken up knitting too?"

"Fuck you. Sheridan likes Scott Willis. He's a good guy. And funny too."

"He's a poor man's copy of Al Roker, and *Wake Up and Smell the Coffee* is a weak take-off of *Good Morning America*," I said.

"Doesn't change the fact that Estelle Reed is well-connected and recently given a huge shout-out for turning ninety-one," Dixon said. "Her birthday was spotlighted *all* week. She was interviewed and said she rents rooms in her house so she's not all alone and to give those less fortunate a hand up. At the time, I thought it was sweet. But I've got to say, the woman I saw on TV looked a lot different than the woman I handcuffed and booked into the system. The woman on TV was a sweet-looking ninetysomethingyear-old. The woman we encountered tonight was scary and demented."

"Scary, perhaps, but let's not throw around demented. As you pointed out, Estelle is well-connected," Chief said. "The mayor awarded her with a key to the city. She's a descendant of one of the first homesteaders to Cheyenne."

"Well, I don't care if she founded the city walking beside the Plains Indians. The bitch is going down for what she did to that dog." I walked toward my locker, and the chief gently reached for my arm.

"Pring, it's not going to happen."

"What the fuck?" I stood with my hands on my hips. "She tortured that dog."

"Until we have substantial evidence that Estelle Reed played any part in what happened to that dog, we can't charge her."

"The dog was in her room—under her bed!" I slammed my locker.

"Her attorney claims Ms. Reed knew nothing about the dog because she can barely use the stairs anymore and sleeps downstairs. She rents out the entire second floor," Chief said.

"Well, that's bullshit because the old bat was on the top of the stairs when we found her," Dixon said.

"Yeah, '*barely use the stairs anymore*' my black ass. Then we charge her with a felony firearm assault offense. She aimed her pistol at an armed officer, and the bitch is lucky I didn't use lethal force to stop the threat. And let me tell you, Chief, ninety-one or nothing, she posed a very real threat to Dixon and me." I kept my stance.

"Cody." The chief rarely addressed us by our first names, and my chest deflated. "Her attorney's arguing imminent danger."

"You've got to be fucking kidding me." I glanced at my partner, whose fair skin reddened.

"That's bullshit," Dixon said. "She posed the imminent danger. If there was anyone posing a threat, it was her. Not us."

"That's right." I high-fived Dixon.

"Guys, I'm not arguing how it went down, but we know that all it takes is for her attorney to present the appearance of a threat and impending injury to create reasonable doubt for self-defense," Chief said. "And God only knows we don't want the mayor brought into this after he just awarded her the key to the city."

I opened my hands in disbelief. "It's bullshit, Chief, and you know it."

He slowly nodded. "I'm thankful as hell this didn't turn sideways for my men or her. This could have had a different outcome."

"So she walks," Dixon said.

"She already has." It was the only time the chief broke eye contact, and I knew he didn't agree with how things panned out. Estelle's attorney didn't skirt the charges because his client was ninety-one or awarded a key to the city. No, Estelle Reed's attorney was known as a walker. He walked his client out of tonight's mayhem because he got paid the big bucks. And when the heir to the biggest oil producer in the state was on retainer, shit happened. Didn't matter. Her attorney may be good, but I was better.

"What about the pistol?" I studied the chief's face, and when it remained neutral, I continued. "Can we at least run a ballistics test on the Colt to see if it was used in any priors?"

"Her attorney arranged for her personal belongings to be returned Monday, but"—Chief slowly nodded—"it's Halloween weekend and sometimes shit gets misplaced."

I took the subtle cue that Chief would have the Colt processed.

"I know you're on call this weekend," he said. "Grab some sleep, and I'll see you later." The chief's eyes were bloodshot from being awoken in the middle of the night, and decades on the job had left deep lines across his forehead. "Good job, guys."

We both nodded as he left the locker room.

"I'd say a beer was in order, but we're due back in a matter of hours," Dixon said. "How about some coffee at the house."

I laughed. "No, thanks. After making it out safe from crazy, I'm not about to risk it with my sister's coffee." I shuddered. "She's the only woman I know who can foul up a simple cup of coffee."

"Suit yourself. I'm heading home for a few hours of sleep."

CHAPTER **TWELVE**

The whistling slowly faded, and a hauntingly light voice sang in my ear, "The very thought of you." He carried a familiar tune that reminded me of my grandparents and their music.

The music, though, and his voice sounded far away, as if in a dream. *Am I dreaming?* My eyes felt heavy, and I leaned my head against the wall next to the stairwell that felt cool to the touch. In the distance, I heard an orchestra of strings accompany his voice. It was a beautiful sound. Then he appeared.

He was dressed in a single-breasted khaki jacket that cut at his waist and accentuated his build. Gold braids and epaulets adorned his shoulder, signifying his higher rank. He wore an officer's uniform well. The crisp, tailor-made army jacket offset his dark eyes and hair that shone when he removed his hat and tucked it beneath his arm. He was staring at someone. I glanced over and saw her.

In a soft, pastel-yellow chiffon dress that hugged her slender body, she was a vision. Spaghetti straps cupped her slight shoulders and revealed skin that looked like it had never seen the sun. It contrasted with her hair, which was as dark as his. Her eyes looked violet, but that couldn't be right. I was staring at the woman when he suddenly approached her. It felt like I floated to the side of the room, I saw so vividly. And as I floated to the corner of the dance hall, I could hear, see, and feel everything that happened between them. Their internal thoughts were mine to know.

"May I have this dance?"

He knew she was the only woman at the Officers' Club worth noticing. And at seventeen, she was also one of the youngest. But her yellow dress brightened the dour look on her face. Why was she so sour? She was younger than him, but his gaze followed her in the room.

I continued to watch their story unfold, not able to open my eyes. I knew I was dreaming, but it was a deep, restful sleep that was like watching a classic, romantic movie. I stared at the officer and young woman.

"Yes, you may." She took his hand as he led her to the dance floor. Bing Crosby's voice filled the room.

"My name's Campbell. Campbell Matthews," he said in her ear. He inhaled the scent on her neck, and his senses were spiked with hints of jasmine, rose, and violet—like her eyes.

"Nice to meet you. I'm—"

"Estelle Simone," he said before she could introduce herself. "I already know who you are."

She pulled away and looked at him. He was tall and thin,

but his officer's jacket added ten pounds to his lean frame. He brushed his hand across his black hair that he slicked with some kind of pomade that added a rich shine, which definitely caught her eye.

Bing Crosby crooned, filling the silence between them.

I swayed to the music.

He lowered his head, leaning toward her floral-scented shoulders, and her violet eyes widened. He knew she was the prettiest, most eligible girl in Cheyenne, but she was no one's fool.

I smiled. *Neither am I.*

"Last summer," he said, inches from her pink lips. He watched her eyes, which focused on his mouth.

Oh, she likes him.

"I did some work with your father."

"Oh."

The energy instantly drained from her voice, and her violet eyes dulled. He knew her father was the owner of the lumber mill and one of the richest men in Wyoming. Her reaction made sense. She thought it was a courtesy dance.

She doesn't think he's interested in her.

"You're all your father spoke about," he said.

"Oh," she repeated. Her focus was no longer locked on him. She seemed to look past him to the other men in uniform.

I glanced but couldn't see anyone else. The room had a haze about it that looked fuzzy, but inviting. I did spot a calendar that hung from the wall in the dance hall. 1943.

He broke eye contact with Estelle to look at me. His dark

eyes focused on me intently. I knew he had something to tell me. I leaned forward, and his voice was in my ear. The entire room paused. Estelle was frozen in time, and the music stopped. My dream broke while he whispered in my ear.

It was 1943. World War II raged like an inferno that sucked the air out of the room. The officers' club at Fort Francis E. Warren in Cheyenne was the only source of light in this wretched assignment. I was a cowboy, not a training officer. But with war raging in Europe and between Japan and China, any man between twenty-one and thirty-five was required to register with local draft boards. The draft began in October 1940 and required twelve months of service. Draftees were selected by lottery. My number was one of the first pulled. Enough younger men enlisted voluntarily that I wasn't called until March 1942. I had just turned twenty-eight, and was one of the oldest drafted with other able-bodied male Wyomingites. Those few men with college degrees were stationed at Fort Warren, which served as training grounds for the US Army Quartermaster Corps. Add to it, the fort had one of the few prisoner of war camps constructed on site. I proudly served my country, but it wasn't where my heart was. My heart belonged in the open plains of Wyoming with someone I loved beside me, someone that wanted to build a future with me—not for my family money, but for me. This was our story, and if you listen, you'll understand why it ended so tragically.

I slowly nodded and drifted further into sleep. The movie continued, and their love story unfolded before me.

Estelle looked over Campbell's shoulder at the other men. Men who weren't right for her.

"I was surprised," he continued, "when I saw your picture."

"Hmm," she said.

He glanced toward a young officer standing by the door who seemed to hold her interest, but Campbell wouldn't let her go that easily.

"It's not often when a father's pride equals, or even comes close to matching, the subject in question."

"Uh-huh," she said. Her gaze remained fixed on the younger officer.

As the beat of the music increased, his feet loosened up and he relaxed. He suddenly pulled her into him, placing his hand on the small of her back, and moved them around the dance floor.

"Your picture," he said in a soft murmur in her ear, "revealed something your father hadn't mentioned."

This got her attention. She looked at him.

"You're a real doll."

"Am I?" She tried to hide her smile, but when he looked at her, she didn't turn away.

"Yes, Estelle, you are." Now that he had her interest, he raised an eyebrow and snapped his fingers. "Let's get this thing hopping." He spun her away from him.

She smiled and giggled as he pulled her back toward him.

"There's my girl," he said, bobbing his head. "You just needed a little pick-me-up, and there's no one better than

Bing Crosby."

"*True.*" *She was polished, refined, and polite. Her upbringing would have demanded it, but there was a spark in her violet eyes that he knew he had to ignite.*

I could tell from the heat in Campbell's eyes, he wanted to know what Estelle was like when she wasn't perfected for her role in high society.

He wanted to scratch beneath the surface to the unreserved woman whose violet eyes held promises of liberation, release from the war, and his dream for eternal love.

Brass accompanied Bing Crosby as the song ended.

"*Let's get out of here.*" *Before she could protest, he grabbed her hand.*

CHAPTER THIRTEEN

CODY

"I can't believe you're still here." I gently cupped Connie's shoulder. She looked up from her dispatch cubicle and smiled.

"Only those lucky enough to pull Halloween weekend duty are here."

I chuckled. "I feel your pain."

"Speaking of pain, I heard your night was pretty eventful. How's the dog?"

I rubbed the stubble that would be a beard by morning, if I didn't get a razor to it. "I'm not sure. Farmer hasn't called, so I'm hoping that's a good sign?"

Connie was about my mom's age, and when she slowly nodded, it felt like the assurance I needed. "I think so. Cal wouldn't call unless it was dire. He's good that way."

"Agreed. I'm headed to Mickey's for either an early breakfast or late dinner. Can I bring you back anything?"

"No, but could you watch the desk for a minute?"

I nodded. "No problem."

She unclipped her headset from the computer terminal. "I haven't been able to break since this whole ordeal started."

"Take your time. Mickey's is open all night." I sat in her seat, which was warm and worn to her plump body shape. Connie was like a second mom to all of us. Or probably more like a grandma, if I thought about it. Even her perfume smelled like my grandma, with a heavy floral scent like a thousand flowers, which would overpower anyone else, but Connie wore it well. I basked in the scent of flowers that started to erase the stench of death that seemed to cling to me after carrying that tortured dog. I shook my head, but it didn't dislodge the anger that built inside me anytime I thought about that dog. There were some images I'd never be able to erase, and finding that dog was one of them.

The switchboard lit, and I plugged the earphones into the terminal jack and placed them over my bald head.

"911, state your emergency." My fingers were at the ready to begin typing the contents of the call.

"I was told to ask for Connie." A thickly accented voice was on the other end of the line.

"This is Detective Pring, please state your emergency."

"This is Hector in maintenance. I was cleaning Chief Wyman's office when a call came through, and I was thinking it was my wife, so I picked it up. But it wasn't my wife. It was the answering service for the hotel's elevator."

My fingers remained poised above the keyboard, but so far, I didn't know what the fuck was going on, only that

Hector knew he was in deep shit for answering the chief's phone.

"Hector, was the answering service reporting an emergency?"

"I don't think so. I asked them to call back, and it went into the chief's message. His phone is lit now."

I slowly nodded. "Okay, thank you, Hector. Do you remember which hotel in Cheyenne?"

"The call came from the Ghost Host."

I couldn't help but laugh. Spotty cell reception was common in wide-open Wyoming, so dead zones were to be expected. But the only place in Cheyenne where the longest-staying guest happened to be dead, and treated as a minor celebrity, was one hotel. "Would that be the Historic Wyoming Point Resort?"

"Si."

"Gracias, Hector. I'll contact their engineering department."

The call ended, and all I typed into the computer was *Probable elevator issue at Historic Wyoming Point Resort.*

When Connie returned from her break, I swirled around in her chair. "Would you happen to know what answering service is assigned to the Point? There's a message on the chief's phone—I'm not sure how it got routed there, but I might as well look into it and save him the hassle."

Connie nodded toward her Rolodex. She was the only person I knew who still kept her contacts on colored mini index cards that spun with a twist of the knob. I often wondered how she color-coded the contraption, but never asked. She reached over me, and a floral fragrance bombarded me.

"Toby Baker is the chief engineer and head of maintenance, but I doubt he's still on property at this hour." She plucked a card from the center of the spindle. "Hmmm. Have you heard the recording?"

I shook my head. "No. It's on the chief's line."

"Move over."

I slid out of Connie's seat, and she resumed command, unplugging the headphones from the jack and turning the volume on the computer terminal to its maximum setting. "I'll have you listen in." Her fingers rapidly moved across the keyboard, and suddenly I heard a voice that made me smile.

"Okay, well in case *anyone* is looking for me—that'd be Reese Pemberton, general manager of the Historic Wyoming Point Resort in Cheyenne."

Her recording paused for a minute then resumed.

"That's right, I actually *remembered* the full name of the hotel I've been placed in charge of! Go, me. So anyway, if anyone is looking for me, hell, if anyone even realizes I'm gone, I'm stuck in the boiler room or lower level or whatever you want to call it."

The message paused again.

"I actually prefer to call it hell because I can't go down any further and it's the hottest place—ever."

I'd never heard her laugh, but it was the cutest giggle. *What I wouldn't give to see her face when she's happy.* Her recording continued.

"So, if you're looking for a very hot redhead, figuratively and literally, you'll find one in the boiler room. Or the elevator. Basically, head to the depths of hell and you're likely to find me."

"Can I get a copy of that?" There was no hesitation, and none on Connie's part either.

Her fingers moved documents around on the screen, she hit Enter a few times, and then my work cell phone vibrated with an incoming email.

"That's why you're the best." I almost kissed the top of her hair-sprayed updo, but remembered that she may remind me of my granny and mom rolled into one, but she wasn't. Instead, I shook her hand. It was the safest bet. "Thanks, Connie."

"Anytime. Should I log that you're going to handle this?"

I nodded. "There weren't any new calls that came in, were there?"

She shook her head. "Nope. This was time-stamped zero, zero thirty."

The corner of the computer screen read the current time in military time: 0230. "Two hours? Is that right?" The adrenaline that had kicked in earlier in the night had finally worn off.

Connie nodded. "Yes, sir. Call came in at twelve thirty, and it's two thirty now."

"God, I hope she hasn't been stuck in the boiler room for two hours." After finding that dog, I was keenly aware the importance of being found. "Connie, will you call Dixon and then the hotel? Tell Dixon I'm heading over there now and I'll wait for him in the lobby." I reached into my duffel bag for my vest and radio. I strapped on my Kevlar vest, then attached the metal clip for the radio mic strap to the front of my vest. I placed the earpiece in my ear and cinched the distance between the earpiece and the mic. I preferred the mic strap to the shoulder strap, because I never had to worry about my radio slipping off my shoulder or falling forward. My radio had to be there when I needed to call in. The strap was worn diagonally across my vest and held my mic securely to my chest. My Glock was loaded, and now I had two full magazines on my hip. I highly doubted a redhead stuck in an elevator or boiler room would require any of this, but after tonight, I wasn't about to question the value of protection.

CHAPTER **FOURTEEN**

REESE

Where are they going? I tried to make sense of what was happening. The music faded, the dance hall disappeared, and loneliness took its place. *Come back. The story's not over, is it?* Suddenly, Campbell appeared. He pointed toward Estelle and whispered to me, *"The best is yet to come."* I smiled. I liked this story. I wanted this beautiful dream to last forever. Campbell led Estelle to the parking lot, and I watched with rapt interest.

A small American flag on the hood of his military Jeep flapped in the night air.

"How 'bout we take a spin?" He opened the passenger side door and tossed his hat on the dash.

She hesitated.

I imagined her thoughts, because I would have them too. "Don't go into dark places with someone you don't know," a warning from her mother. Or perhaps, "Keep a dime with you at all times. Call if you get into trouble. Your father will come get you." I had a cell phone, but in 1943, she wouldn't. I knew my granny had kept a dime with her for emergencies. Still, despite her brief pause, Estelle got into his car.

"Where are we going?" she asked.

Campbell replied by raising an eyebrow and smiling before closing her door. Estelle opened her black satin purse. A tube of lipstick, a comb, and a set of house keys barely fit in the small evening bag. She quickly searched.

She's looking for a dime, but somehow, I knew she used it earlier on a crème soda.

"Where are we going?" she asked again. I felt her uncertainty. This was a woman who was used to being in control and knowing exactly how her day was going to unfold.

"Oh, I don't know." He swiftly maneuvered the Jeep out of the parking lot with the palm of his hand on the steering wheel.

"You don't know where you're going?" Her voice rose.

"I'll know it when I see it." Campbell saluted the guard as they left the base.

She stared at his hands as they gripped the steering wheel. They were large and tanned from the sun. A thick gold band with a center signet circled his left wedding finger.

"You're married?" she asked, her voice noticeably raised.

He turned his head toward her and slightly smiled. "No. Not married. It's my family crest. My hands take a beating working on gunnery equipment. It's the only finger that it'll fit."

"Family crest?" Her pale face colored.

He leaned forward, and she scooted toward the car door, hugging the handle.

"It's okay. I'm not coming after you," he said, winking at her. "Not yet." He smiled. "I just want to hear some music."

He turned the silver knob on the car radio and punched one of the black buttons on the row beneath it.

The music rose from the speakers.

"Hey, what do you know?" He hit his palm against the steering wheel. "More Bing."

"I think I should get back," Estelle said.

"Shh. Just listen. This is our music."

Estelle sat back and released her grip on the door handle. She listened to Campbell sing along with Bing Crosby.

"Where is your family?" Estelle asked in between lyrics.

"What?"

"Your family."

"You still on that?"

"Yes, I'm still on that."

"Casper. My family place is along the banks of the North Platte."

"A river view."

He smiled. "That stretches for miles and miles."

"What do you do on base?"

"Since I'm one of the few officers with actual flight time, I train the men on simulated aircraft."

This made her laugh. "I thought the war effort was

well-funded. Can't Fort Warren afford actual airplanes?"

"Fort Warren has nothing but a single dirt strip for light fixed-wing aircraft. We don't have any aircraft assigned to us. The real action is at Fort Casper, where I was first assigned after Officer Candidate School."

"You had to go to school to become an officer?" Estelle's tone was relaxed and downright playful.

"Unless you're a West Point graduate, everyone who wants to be an officer in the army must graduate from OCS." His tone was dry.

"I see." She slowly inched toward him. "And after officer school, you went to Fort Casper?"

"Casper Army Airfield. I returned home to Casper for flight training."

"Do you like to fly?"

"I do." He placed his arm across the seat while he drove. "And when we danced tonight, it's the closest I've gotten to feeling like my feet weren't touching the ground since the world exploded around us."

He spoke a language she seemed to understand. "I've seen families ripped apart by the arrival of a telegram. It's awful. The whole world has changed. I can't imagine what the war has been like for you."

"I haven't seen any of it yet, but I can fly, and I'm becoming a pretty good tail gunner. If things go as planned, I'll have additional training with the Combat Crew as a B-17 tail gunner. Working on the base isn't my idea of serving my country."

She slowly nodded. "You want to be a war hero."

He smiled. "Would that be so bad? My wife could be married to a war hero."

It was as if she was trying the title on for size, and when it fit, she smiled. "It does have a nice ring to it."

Campbell veered the Jeep to the side of an isolated road. Gravel crunched beneath the tires. He cut the engine, leaned toward her, and their lips met in a tender, long kiss that spoke of the days when kissing meant more than a means to an end. Their kiss was passionate, yet reserved, as if they both knew that was as far as their desire could stretch.

He pulled back and sang along with Bing Crosby, looking at her and only her. No one else existed. He snapped his fingers to the melody, and Estelle watched and smiled like she had just met the most wonderful man in the world.

I knew the look. Though every instinct told her otherwise, she was falling for a man she barely knew. By today's standards, we'd call it a fast hookup, but in 1943, it was a whirlwind romance. Either way, it was the most wonderful, yet frightening feeling when the right man took a woman's breath away. And there was no denying the body's reaction when a man's mere presence kick-started the heart. It was what I felt when that tall, dark, and delicious detective scooped me into his arms and carried me to safety. And it scared me shitless. Wasn't that why I ran—or limped—away?

I watched Estelle try to do the same thing, but no matter how far she distanced herself from him, her attraction to Campbell and his to her was palpable. I felt their heat. I sensed their burning passion, and I longed for my neck to be caressed the way Estelle's was by Campbell.

He drove a little further along the side of the road with one hand on the steering wheel and his other hand gently stroking the side of her slender neck. His hand seemed to be learning her, memorizing every detail. She responded to his touch by closing her eyes. Their attraction moved at a pace that would seem quick if not for the war that simmered beneath every thought and every unspoken word. For one enchanted spring evening, the uncertainty of war didn't consume them. The only thing that seemed to pull on them was desire.

"Here we are." Campbell cut the engine and extended his left arm toward the windshield.

"Where are we?" Estelle opened her eyes.

"Not sure. But I like it." He reached behind the seat for something while she rolled down her window. Spring greeted both of them: humid night air and the pulsating cadence of crickets that kept beat in the tall grass.

"You coming?" He peered his head inside the Jeep. A blue-and-white-striped serape was draped over his arm, and he cradled a bottle of wine and a corkscrew. Even in a khaki uniform, he looked like a sommelier.

"You certainly are confident," she said. "And prepared."

He replied with a flashy grin. "Why wouldn't I be?"

She opened her door and crossed her arms over her chest, slowly walking behind him. It was picturesque. The grass was tall and would chill her ankles as she trespassed on the untouched landscape. She looked up. A handful of stars adorned the evening sky. "There's a full moon."

"No, actually, it's not," he said, studying the sky. "Close, but it won't reach its full cycle until later in the month. That's a penny moon."

"Penny moon?"

"Didn't you ever play penny moon when you were little?" He slightly tilted his head. "Ella, were you ever young?"

She didn't correct his nickname for her. "I was young like everyone else."

"Then certainly you played penny moon."

Her dark hair brushed her bare shoulders when she shook her head. "Never heard of it."

"Penny moon is where you take a penny, nickel, and quarter and hold each one toward the sky. If you hold a penny and the moon can still be seen, but with a nickel it's covered, you've got a nickel moon."

"And I suppose a quarter moon is just that?"

He raised a single eyebrow. "I knew you were a smart girl."

She gazed into the sky. "So tonight's moon would be covered by a penny."

"Exactly." He spread the serape on the grass.

Estelle looked at Campbell. Sideburns the color of ash and small creases near the corner of his eyes sparked something, because her demeanor changed. She smiled, and her body language softened. Her hard edges weren't so jagged.

Did he remind her of her father? He had to be ten years older than her.

Campbell gripped the neck of the wine bottle and opened

the dark vintage. A sweet woodsy smell released with the pop of the cork.

"Try this." He handed her a plastic glass.

"You are quite prepared." She sat on the serape and accepted the wine. "How often do you do this?"

He shrugged. "First time."

"No." She shook her head. "You're much too rehearsed."

I smiled. I liked this woman. She was a straight shooter.

"Ella, it is. The boys in my squadron got me the wine and taped the glasses to the bottle."

"The boys?"

"Excuse me, the men in my squadron."

"What was the occasion?"

"I don't want to talk shop anymore, not with this moonlight and stars." He tilted his head back. "Look at it. It's amazing."

Estelle focused on him.

And I knew why. She wondered if this night was real, or if she was simply swept up in the moonlight moment. She took a sip of wine, and I longed for a taste. There was truth in wine, and I wanted to know all their truths.

"How'd you meet my father?"

"While I was stationed at Casper, your dad had the only civil contract with the base, so we worked together on a project."

"Daddy never mentioned you or going to Casper."

"No, he probably didn't, and I shouldn't have, but you see," he said, moving toward her, "I didn't want to scare you. I figured, if I mentioned that I had worked with your

father, it might improve my chances."

She laughed. "Sounds calculated."

"It was."

"What picture did he show you, anyway?"

"The one of you and some mangy dog."

"Chippy? That's no mangy dog. That was a great dog. Wait," she said, "my daddy showed you a picture of me and Chippy? We haven't had him in years. How old was I?"

Campbell shook his head. "Don't know? Twelve or thirteen?"

"And you wanted to meet me?"

He blushed in the moonlight. "What can I say? The dog made you look good."

Estelle shrieked and gently brushed his shoulder. "Oh, brother."

"Saw a picture of him too, but"—Campbell shook his head—"wasn't my type."

"Oh my," she said, laughing.

I laughed too. They were perfect for each other. I didn't know why, only that they were.

"More wine?" Campbell asked.

"No! I think I've had enough."

"Oh, doll, we haven't even begun," he said, standing up. "What we need is some music."

Within moments, the sound of the car radio gently merged with nature as the rhythm of the night unfolded on the blanket between them.

"Ella, I've got a crush on you." He leaned her back on the blanket, and she didn't resist.

Campbell glanced at me, and they blurred from view like a movie from that era that faded to black. But I knew. Their love affair began beneath a penny moon with Bing Crosby serenading them. It was 1943, the spring before Estelle's freshman year in college.

CHAPTER FIFTEEN

CODY

"The elevator appears to be working, but I'd rather not risk it," I said to Dixon, who nodded.

"Connie relayed that Toby, the engineer, was indeed where we expected him to be at three in the morning—at home. He assumed Reese had gone to her suite. But after talking with Bob…." I cocked my head toward the man who stood quietly to the side. "Bob, you checked the suite and it was vacant, correct?"

"That's correct," he said. "But we have a master key left on property for emergencies, and I spoke to the hotel manager, Wild Bill, who told me to give it to you."

"Wild Bill Goldstein?" Dixon asked.

Bob nodded.

"I didn't know he worked here." Dixon elbowed me. "You know Wild Bill—he's the guy who's sweet on Millie. He's always at the Steakhouse Saloon when she works.

Cheyenne native with long ponytail. Sometimes he wears it in a braid."

"Millie?" I raised an eyebrow. "She works at the gift shop. Why would he come to the bar when she works here?"

Dixon shook his head. "Because that's what men do when they like someone."

Bob laughed, and while I wanted to silence him with a look, I knew if the joke wasn't at my expense I'd find it funny too.

"Whatever. The bottom line is we have a master key." I glanced at Bob. "And this key will lead us where?"

Bob directed us to the stairwell. "This stairwell will lead you to the basement. There's a separate entrance to the boiler room that's located on the basement level. It's the only door on that floor that's locked. Turn the key clockwise to enter, and then there's a door at the bottom of that stairwell that leads directly to the boiler room."

"Copy that," I said to Bob. I turned to my partner. "You ready?"

Dixon rechecked the straps on his Kevlar vest, the magazines on his hip, and put his wedding ring in the top pocket of his vest. He smiled.

"What?" I asked.

"Sheridan tucked her spray against bad energy vibes in my pocket."

"Keep that shit in your pocket where it belongs. You ready?" I asked.

"Ten-four."

I took the lead down the staircase with Dixon on my six.

The key allowed us access to the separate stairwell that led to the boiler room where I expected to find a very angry redhead.

***

REESE

Campbell appeared to me by himself. He was still in his officer's uniform, but blood stained the front of his jacket.

"What happened?" I tried to walk toward him, but I couldn't. My legs were fast asleep.

"That's for you to piece together. Ella and I waited a year until she was eighteen to marry. It was May 1944, and we had a small civil ceremony." His eyes no longer shone like they had just moments before when he was with her. Now, there was something sad, something tragic about his eyes that reminded me of that detective. They were beautifully sorrowful. *What happened?*

"You didn't have a big wedding?" I asked. Campbell was easily the romantic one of the two. Maybe a civil ceremony saddened him.

"Ella's father wasn't too keen on his youngest daughter marrying a man twelve years her senior. But, my God, we were in love. Ella was the most beautiful bride I'd ever seen." He paused. Sadness clung to him. "Our honeymoon had to be delayed. I wouldn't meet my wife again until mid-June 1944, at this very hotel. *Your* hotel."

"I don't understand," I said. "Zavi told me you shot

yourself on your honeymoon because you couldn't… well, things didn't go as planned."

"Things didn't go as planned."

"But you and Ella—weren't you together before you got married?"

He didn't respond.

"I don't understand. What happened? Why would you kill yourself if you were so in love?"

Blood began to spout from the center of his head, and I screamed.

***

CODY

I drew my gun and charged down the dimly lit stairs that ended with a locked door. Her screams intensified, and I heard her yell.

"Go away! Leave me alone!" Her screams turned to pleas. "Stop, you're hurting me."

I placed the key in the lock, but it wouldn't open. I tried again, but it remained deadlocked. I glanced back at Dixon. "It's a fireproof door. This thing's steel. There's no getting through it without something stronger than what we got on us."

"Copy that. What about the elevator?"

"Only option."

"No! Leave me alone! Go away!" she cried.

I banged on the door, but her shouting drowned my

attempt to reach her. Dixon turned, and we darted up the flight of stairs, assuming the door at the top had remained unlocked. But it hadn't. Dixon reached for the handle, and when it wouldn't turn, he shone his flashlight on the knob.

"Cody, we've got a situation."

I stood on the top stair next to him and tried to twist the doorknob, even aiming my flashlight on it as well, but there wasn't a keyhole.

"What the fuck?" Again, I tried to turn the knob, but it wouldn't twist. It appeared that the only way to exit the stairwell and access the basement level was if someone opened the door from the basement. "How the hell did this pass building code?" We cut our flashlights and holstered them back on our belts.

"Let's try the key again," Dixon said.

We were headed back toward the locked door at the bottom of the stairwell when a man in an officer's uniform suddenly appeared.

Dixon and I stopped and aimed our guns at him.

"Police!" we yelled.

He slowly shook his head, and it looked like he was bleeding, but I couldn't be sure. The stairwell was poorly lit. I pulled out my flashlight, but it didn't fully illuminate the bottom of the staircase where he stood. I holstered my flashlight when Dixon yelled, "Drop your weapon!" His voice echoed in the stairwell.

I squinted, but I didn't see a gun. It didn't matter. When a man in full uniform suddenly appeared out of nowhere, my partner and I were going to assume the worst—especially after the night we'd been through.

"Drop your weapon and turn around!" I yelled.

The man remained stationary, but when he appeared to float up the stairs or take two at a time toward us, I lost my grip on the situation and reverted to my high school football days, because I charged right at him—or more like right through him, because even though he was as unprotected as a blindsided quarterback, I tackled nothing but air.

"Is that a…?" Dixon's voice trembled.

The man in his dress uniform seemed to linger in the middle of the stairwell. The bottom of the stairs remained too dark to take a clear shot. Reese could be behind him. Besides, after tackling nothing but air, I wasn't about to shoot.

"Where's your spray?" I yelled over my shoulder to Dixon.

"What spray?"

"That crap my sister gave you. The shit that stinks." He tossed it to me, and by pure luck I caught it. The only other weapon I had at my disposal was the oil spray, so I let him have it. But the so-called essential oils were essentially useless, because the malodorous mist had absolutely no effect, other than a boomerang one. The mist hung in the air like a cloud of doom, and since I had the only set of working lungs, I was the one who began to choke. So, after two failed attempts—the blitz and the spritz—I called it quits.

"So, what's your name?" At this point, with two strikes against me, building rapport was about the only option I had left.

When the man that appeared to float before me didn't respond, I did. "I'm Cody." Hell, it worked on Estelle, maybe it'd work on him. I nodded behind me. "That's Dixon."

But just as suddenly as the man appeared, he instantly vanished.

"Where'd he go?" Dixon asked.

I looked around, but he was nowhere to be seen. "Fuck!" I aimed my gun toward the bottom of the stairwell and had cautiously begun down the stairs when the door opened. A crack of light surfaced, and Dixon and I both yelled, "Police!"

Her red hair appeared before she did. "Don't shoot!" She emerged with her arms raised.

I sidestepped, keeping my back against the wall until I reached her. She was in next-to-nothing—except panties that looked like something even my granny wouldn't wear. *Damn, those are some big britches.*

"Hands!" Dixon yelled behind me.

My focus returned to the situation at hand and off her dingy drawers.

Her arms remained raised, and Dixon brought them down behind her back, where he cuffed her. We still didn't know what was going on. Had she yelled? Who was the man? What the fuck was happening?

Dixon led her into the boiler room. Her face looked burnt, her hair was damp, and the frightened, anguished expression in her green eyes told me she didn't belong in cuffs.

"Are you all right?" I glanced at the pile of running clothes and shoes on the cement floor.

"I must've fallen asleep," she said, sidestepping my question.

"You're Reese Pemberton, general manager?" Dixon asked.

She nodded, and her moist hair clung to her face. I gently reached to brush it aside, and she flinched. Things were definitely not all right. I took off my jacket and placed it around her while Dixon removed the cuffs. She wasn't the threat. But something or someone had been, and until we got her to safety, I wasn't about to let down my guard.

CHAPTER **SIXTEEN**

CODY

The elevator dinged, and I glanced from Dixon to Reese. I had to get her to safety. "Reese, I need you to sit tight in the stairwell for a minute."

Even though her face looked sunburnt, it drained of color, and she shook her head.

"I'm not shutting you in the stairwell, my flashlight is propping it open." I pointed to the butt of my flashlight stuck between the door and the doorframe. "I just want to know you're somewhere safe."

"Okay." The vacancy in her voice let me know she wouldn't feel safe until we got her the hell out of this boiler room, which we'd been working on when the elevator announced itself. She tucked behind the door on the first stair.

"That's perfect," I said to her with a gentle smile, and then shot Dixon a look. "Cover me."

"Ten-four."

Gun drawn, I approached the elevator, which was located in the middle of the lower level and stood off to the side.

The door opened, and the light in the elevator lit the man in shadows. My gun emerged along with my deep voice. "Hands!"

His arms shot into the air. "I'm the hotel manager."

Dixon flanked my right side. "Walk forward slowly."

A man about my height with a helluva lot more hair appeared in a pair of jeans, boots, and a T-shirt.

"Wild Bill, right?" Dixon kept his Glock aimed.

"Yes, William Goldstein. I'm the hotel manager." His hands remained in the air.

Dixon spoke to me without breaking contact with Wild Bill. "It's him."

I nodded.

"You can lower your arms," Dixon said.

"What's going on? Where's Reese? Bob, my overnight manager, called when you hadn't returned right away."

"Well, maybe if the stairwell had a door that actually exited, we would have returned sooner." My tone was as on edge as I was. I still didn't know what had happened to Reese, but I wouldn't stop until I did.

"What do you mean?" Wild Bill nodded toward the corner of the room and looked at me for permission to proceed.

I nodded and escorted him toward the stairwell door, but stopped twenty yards shy of the actual door. He didn't know Reese was behind it, and I intended for it to stay that way. I still didn't know where this Wild Bill fella was when Reese was locked in here, and God only knew what was done to her. Or by whom.

"Bob gave you a master key," Wild Bill said. "That would have gotten you into the boiler room."

"Well, it didn't work, and the door at the top of the stairs was locked with no way out." My jaw tightened, and I narrowed my focus on him like a suspect. "It's a real safety issue you've got there, Wild Bill."

I was pissed, and for some reason, this guy was getting the brunt of my anger.

"I don't know what to say. It worked yesterday when I gave Reese a tour." Wild Bill looked around like a trapped animal searching for an escape. "Where is Reese?"

I was about to answer when she appeared in my jacket that was zipped to her chin. It was two times too large for her, but she seemed to find comfort with its oversize.

"Oh my God, Reese, are you okay?" Wild Bill rushed to her, and she lowered her head.

What the fuck? "Let's not crowd her," I said.

But my words seemed as hollow as the mysterious man we'd encountered in the stairwell. Wild Bill tilted Reese's chin toward him and tears streamed down her reddened cheeks. He tucked a protective arm around her.

"I'm so sorry this happened to you," he said, and she nodded against him.

Are you kidding me?

"We need to ask Reese some questions," I said.

"Can't it wait until later in the morning?" Wild Bill asked.

He wasn't trying to be a dick, but the guy was pissing me off.

"Actually, it can't." Dixon crouched to become eye level with Reese. "Ms. Pemberton, I'm sorry, but we still don't know what happened, and I'd like to have you checked out at Cheyenne Medical Center."

I knew instantly my partner's thinking. Rape kit. *Fuck.* Maybe she needed Wild Bill. Maybe they were a thing? Or maybe…. Fear paralyzed me. I couldn't help her, but he could.

"Wild Bill, if you'd like to accompany us to the hospital, I don't have any issue with that," I said, and my partner did a double take in my direction. I looked at him, and he knew. My past was something I'd never be free from.

CHAPTER **SEVENTEEN**

REESE

I feel lost. Tucked beneath Wild Bill's arm, I looked to the detective for direction.

"Hey there, Reese, how you doing?" His voice was calm and reassuring. "You remember me from earlier tonight? I'm Cody. And that's my partner, Tim Dixon."

Tim and Wild Bill looked at him oddly. He must not have told them how we met. It was about the only thing that made me feel something lighter than horror.

"I remember you," I said.

"How's your knee?" His iridescent green eyes broke contact with mine when he glanced at my knee. "That looks like it hurts."

I had forgotten about my knee or any pain. I stared at my bulbous knee like it didn't belong to me. My mind was a battlefield between what was happening and what had happened. *Why did he scare me? Why did he grab me?*

Why would he do that? I tucked in my shoulders like an injured bird and tried to disappear from view. It was just a dream. I was tired, and everyone was looking at me. They wanted to know what happened, but no one asked. If they'd only ask.

"That's okay," Cody said when I remained silent. "We can have the doctor take a look at that, too."

"Why are we going to the hospital?" I finally spoke more than a few words. Even though Wild Bill had me wrapped beneath his protective arm, it was Cody who assumed the role of protector.

"Reese, we just want to make sure you're okay. You were stuck in this boiler room for a few hours, and your face is a little red."

I reached and touched my cheek, which instantly stung like I was sunburnt.

"I need my phone." I stared at my phone that was on the cement beside my running stuff.

"No problem." Cody reached for it carefully without disturbing the rest of my things. He handed it to me, and I tucked it into a pocket in his large and roomy jacket.

"Reese, we want a medical professional to check you out for dehydration and make sure everything's okay," Cody said.

I stared at him. *He's hiding something. What isn't he telling me? Did I do something?*

He held the door open for me, and I stared at the flight of stairs that led to freedom. "I...." *Can't do it.* But the words remained stuck. *I'm so tired. I can't do anything else. I just want to go home, but I don't know where that is anymore.* My eyes brimmed with tears.

"The sooner we get you out of here, the faster I can get you to the medical center," Cody said when I didn't move.

"What about the elevator?" his partner asked. "Wild Bill came down in it. Why don't we go up the same way?"

I shook my head. "I'm not getting back in there. I don't trust Otis."

"Otis is the elevator," Wild Bill said.

Cody and his partner nodded as if they understood.

Cody was a good foot taller than me. He crouched, and I looked into his eyes. I leaned forward until our noses almost touched. My voice was barely a whisper. *"I can't do this."*

He slowly nodded. "That's okay, I can." He glanced to Wild Bill, who seemed to understand their unspoken exchange because then Cody looked at me again. "You trusted me once to carry you to safety, and I don't know about you, but that was fun."

His smile was broad and inviting. Campbell had smiled like that at Ella.

"Carrying you was the highlight of my Friday night. So, I was thinking, maybe I could do it again?"

I nodded, and Wild Bill gently removed his arm. Cody bent and wrapped his arm gently beneath my legs. I wound my arms around his neck, and he carefully stood.

"Don't hurt me." It was the only thing I said before I laid my head on his shoulder and closed my eyes. The sooner I got out of this hellhole, the better.

"My truck's a little dirty from earlier...." His voice trailed off. "But it's clean." He laughed. "Well, that's a contradiction."

I opened my eyes and looked into his. "Why are you *really* taking me to the medical center?"

His Adam's apple moved like he was swallowing a hard truth. "From the condition we found you and, uh, from the cries we heard, the hospital can check you out thoroughly and collect any evidence."

"Evidence? What are you talking about?" I was still in his arms, but I pushed back. I would have jumped down and run to Wild Bill, but he was in the hotel securing the stairwell.

"The hospital has a kit that can collect DNA, a blood sample, and other samples," he said.

"DNA? Blood? Why would they want that?"

His eyes seemed to answer for him when he broke eye contact with me. "Reese, it's for your protection. DNA evidence from a crime like sexual assault can be collected from your body, clothes, and other personal belongings. That's why we left your clothes in the boiler room. We'll have our forensics team collect them. But the hospital can perform a sexual assault forensic exam to preserve possible DNA evidence while giving you medical treatment."

"Oh my God." The truth sank into me like a lead weight. I was glad I was in his arms, because I wouldn't have been able to hold myself up. "You think I was raped?"

"A sexual assault kit can be sent to a lab for testing," he said, bypassing the word rape.

Tears stung my eyes. "I wasn't raped."

He slowly nodded, but I could tell he wasn't convinced.

"There was this man," I said, and his eyes widened. "But it was just a dream." I paused. "Actually, it was a nightmare, and when I yelled, he grabbed and shook me. But it was just a dream."

"The hospital can check your knee," he said.

I half smiled. "You don't believe me."

He shook his head. "No, I just know women who regret not getting tested—especially when it's an acquaintance or someone they trusted." The gravity in his voice was grounding, even though I wasn't standing. "Reese, you don't have to report the crime to have an exam, but the exam gives you the chance to store evidence should you decide to make a report at a later time."

"Cody, I wasn't raped. I had a really bad dream, and that's what you heard." The tone in my voice must have been convincing, but not convincing enough.

"Let me take you to the hospital," he said. "No one will force you to be tested, but I think a trip to the medical center, if only to check your face and knee, would be well worth the time."

It was a dream, right? I couldn't think straight.

"Okay." I shrugged. "I'll go."

"You're going to be okay," he said, gently placing me in his truck. He glanced behind him to his partner, who was talking on his cell phone in the distance. His partner was shorter, thinner, and with his white-blond hair, blue eyes, and perfectly tanned skin, he looked rich and preppy. I never would have thought he was a cop. But what did I know? I never thought I'd be stuck in a boiler room.

"Dixon," Cody called. His partner held his cell against his chest. "We're headed to the hospital."

"Copy that."

"Dixon's going to stay at the hotel and wait for our forensics team." Cody returned his focus to me. By contrast, Cody was tall, broad-shouldered, and well built. He had a high forehead that led to a shorn, shiny, satiny head. He had clear green eyes, a stubborn jaw, and full lips that looked kissable. Cody was as dark as Dixon was light.

The contrast between the two was as striking on the outside as their similarities within. I'd only seen them operate together in the boiler room, but their sense of integrity, dedication, and service to others was what truly defined them both. So, while they differed in style, they were nearly identical in the substance of their character. And if I had to be rescued, I couldn't think of two better men.

"Okay, let's get you buckled up." He pulled the seat belt over me and locked me in. When I was secured, he gently held my hand. "You're going to be okay."

That's what he kept saying. *You're going to be okay.* But I wasn't as sure.

CHAPTER **EIGHTEEN**

CODY

"There's no evidence of sexual assault, so there wasn't any DNA to collect," the sexual assault nurse examiner said in the hallway outside Reese's room. The relief I felt was instant. Reese wouldn't have to live with the never-ending trauma and stigma of rape. As far as we'd advanced as a civilization, rape remained one of the most misunderstood crimes. Women often carried the shame for the violence perpetrated against them. I rolled my shoulders, but the heaviness from my job wasn't that easy to shake.

"Her forearms have bruising," the nurse said.

"Like someone grabbed her?" I pulled my notebook and pen out of my vest pocket. "It could be from someone grabbing her, or...." She shook her head. "You said you found her in a boiler room?"

"Yes. She was in the boiler room for at least two hours."

The nurse slowly nodded, like she was trying to piece

something together. "Well, the marks on her forearms could be the start of first-degree burns. Her face is severely burnt. I usually don't see these kind of burns unless there's been an explosion."

"There wasn't any explosion," I said. "But the hotel uses steam heat. I spoke to the engineer, and that boiler dates back to the early 1900s."

She slightly smiled. "That would make sense. Steam showers and steam boilers can cause catastrophic injuries. Thankfully, her injuries aren't life-threatening, but the exposure to her face caused second-degree burns."

"Will that cause permanent damage to her face?"

"No. There're three levels of burns, and while second-degree burns affect both the outer and underlying layer of skin, if treated properly, they can heal without scarring. I'm surprised she lasted two hours. The exposure to wet steam can't be pleasant."

"She was locked inside the boiler room, and all I can think is that the boiler must have had a leak" was all I knew to say. "Is she in pain?"

"The redness and swelling can be painful, but the blistering can be worse."

I ran my hand over my bald head. "Damn."

The nurse nodded. "Facial burns are not pleasant. The ER doctor's wound assessment was to send her home with Silvadine, which is a cream that prevents bacterial infections for second- and third-degree burns. He also prescribed a low-dose anti-anxiety sedative. The goal of treatment is to control pain, and with facial burns, there's often an emotional component."

"She's had a rough night," I said.

"She's shaken and she saw a glimpse of her face, but we didn't want to alarm her. Every day her face will look better, and it may not blister. I've seen Silvadine work wonders. She needs rest, relaxation, and fluids. Plenty of fluids. She mentioned she just moved to Wyoming and didn't have any family here?"

"Oh, I didn't know that." I tapped my pen against my notepad. "I can look after her."

The nurse slightly smiled. "I'm sure you'll ensure she gets home safely and that the boiler is checked. Thankfully, steam boiler accidents don't happen often because there aren't many steam boilers still in operation."

"Copy that." I closed my notebook. "I'd like to see her."

The nurse gently touched my arm. "She's badly shaken by this nightmare she said she had, but I think being trapped scared her more than anything."

"Copy that," I repeated, before entering her room.

She was dressed in a pair of blue hospital scrubs, with one leg dangling from the side of the bed and a black knee brace hugging her other leg, which was extended across the bed. My jacket was beside her.

"Hey." I slowly walked toward her.

She weakly smiled.

"The nurse gave the thumbs-up to discharge you. I'm sure you're exhausted. I thought I'd get you back to your suite and make sure you're secure."

Panic flashed in her green eyes, and she shook her head. "I'm never going into that hotel again."

CHAPTER **NINETEEN**

REESE

"Okay, no hotel. Got it. Where can I take you?" Cody stood with his hands on his hips in front of my hospital bed that I refused to get comfortable and make my own, even though it looked warm and inviting.

"May I borrow your phone?"

"Sure." He reached into his back pocket and handed me his iPhone. "Hit three and one to unlock the screen, that's my badge number."

Within seconds, his voice was on the other end of the phone. "This is Wild Bill."

"Hey, it's me."

"Reese, how are you?"

I raised my shoulders to my ears. "I've had better nights. Or mornings." I exhaled. "I don't even know what time it is."

"It's almost five," he said.

"Can you come get me?"

Cody waved a hand. "I can take you anywhere you need."

I avoided his eyes and his help.

"Where are you?" Wild Bill spoke into my ear.

"The hospital, but I'll wait for you at the front."

Cody waved his hands. "I can take you anywhere." He paused. "Please. I'd like to ensure you get home safely."

I finally made eye contact with Cody while I spoke to Wild Bill. "Actually, forget it. I've got a ride. But can I stay at your place tonight?"

Hurt flashed across Cody's face, like I had slapped him. I turned away.

"Of course. I'll text you the address."

"Thanks." I handed Cody his phone. "Wild Bill's going to text you his address."

"Copy that." His demeanor changed, and he spoke into the mic on his vest. "Delta, Unit thirty-one."

"Unit thirty-one, advise code."

For a moment, his face softened at the sound of the operator's voice.

"Delta, I'm a ten-four at Cheyenne Medical with Ms. Pemberton, who I'm taking to, uh...." He cleared his throat. "She's requested transport to William Goldstein's residence."

"Unit thirty-one, copy that, zero five hundred."

He placed his mic back on the strap across his vest. "Okay." He clapped his hands. "Let's get you to Wild Bill's."

Before I took the hand he extended toward me, I carefully

brought both legs to the front of the bed. "I can stand on my own."

"Of course." He took a measured step back, but stayed within reaching distance.

I carefully placed both feet on the hospital floor and stood. "Listen, two rescues in one night is more than any man should have to deal with." I tried to laugh, but it sounded as flat as I felt.

"Didn't you know I'm all about the rescue?" A slight smile lit his face, and he leaned toward me. "Damsels in distress are kind of my thing."

"You don't have to do that," I said, putting on his jacket that I wasn't sure he'd ever get back.

He leaned back. "Do what?"

"Try to lighten the mood."

He nodded. "Okay, but just so you know, if I was trying to lighten the mood, I would've led with the obvious."

"The obvious?" Now, I took a step toward him. "And what would that be?"

He grinned. "Well, after tonight, I guess I can't call you 'Paleface.'"

Despite how swollen my face felt, no matter the pain that seemed to ricochet across my body like a bullet that didn't know where to land, I laughed. A full belly laugh that brought a smile to Cody's face.

"Thank you." I swallowed. "I don't think I ever thanked you. One night. Two rescues. You've met your hero quota."

His dark cheeks spiked with color, and I knew I had hit a soft spot. Detective Cody Pring liked being the hero in my story, and despite my guarded resistance to his charm, I knew it was a role well suited for him. But my life was too complicated to add a hero into the mix.

CHAPTER **TWENTY**

CODY

The train whistle blew in the distance. The deep bellow echoed in the early morning dawn and broke the silence in my truck.

"That's my wake-up call." Reese stared out the side window.

"Who needs an alarm clock when you've got Union Pacific on the job?" I said.

It was the first time she turned away from the window since we left the medical center. "You're right."

We were stopped at a red light on Central and East Lincolnway. Despite everything we'd both been through in the course of the last ten or twelve hours, I didn't want my time with this beautiful redhead to end. The rising sun caught the golden tones in her hair, and it looked like a halo circling her head. She was no angel, but she looked divine. I kept staring at her, and she didn't turn away.

"Is Reese a family name?" I asked.

She softly smiled. "It's short for Teresa."

"Oh."

She giggled. "Yeah, it's a Catholic thing. My full name is Mary Teresa, but every Catholic family has a Mary something. Mary Margaret. Mary Elizabeth. Mary Lynn. So, everyone named Mary usually goes by their middle name. I'm just happy my older brother couldn't pronounce Teresa, so he settled on Reese. Works for me."

"It suits you well," I said.

"And Cody? Isn't that a city in Wyoming?"

I glanced at the light that remained red. The light was sleeping like the rest of the city. "Cody is a town in Wyoming, founded by Colonel William 'Buffalo Bill' Cody himself."

"Nuh-uh."

I raised one hand. "Hundred percent. Buffalo Bill passed through the area and liked it so much he returned and started a town. My mom was in Cody when she met my dad."

When the light turned green, I crossed East Lincolnway and began the descent over the Greeley Highway overpass that crested across the city of Cheyenne, with the railroad streaming beneath us in a blur of black steel. The whistle echoed in the distance.

"Controlled mayhem," she said. "I've watched the track crew from my hotel window."

"Man, I bet that's a sight." I glanced her way, and her focus returned to the side window.

"It's hard to imagine, but a train has run through

Cheyenne since the late 1800s. In fact, if it wasn't for the transcontinental railroad, I doubt Cheyenne would be the city it is today, let alone the capital city."

My brief history lesson fell on deaf ears. Reese had no interest in Cheyenne or trains. But I had no interest in remaining mute.

"I don't know about you, but I think the train's whistle is romantic. You know what I mean?" I said.

She didn't respond, so I continued. "That whistle harkens back to days long ago when life seemed simpler. We weren't tied to electronics. Clocks stood tall or hung on the wall, not tied to our wrists with multifunctions that beep anytime a new email or text message surfaces. God forbid we disconnect from the world."

"I don't know if life was simpler. World War II ravaged people's lives and turned them inside out," she said soberly.

I nodded. "You're right. World War II did a number on my family—or at least my father's side of the family, when blacks served in combat and were often put on the front line." My truck reached the top of the overpass, giving a clear view of Cheyenne and the tall clock tower in the Depot that looked like it belonged in England. The grandfather-style clock tower was the city's only timepiece, keeping time for the downtown area since the late 1800s. The way it loomed over the city always reminded me of *Peter Pan*. I often looked for Tinker Bell buzzing around the clock's face, but she never appeared.

"Tell me more about World War II." Reese broke into my thoughts.

"Sure. My father's father, my grandfather, was in the Buffalo Division that served in combat in Italy."

"Buffalo Division?" She shook her head, and a long, crimson curl sprang forward. I so badly wanted to tuck it behind her ear, but after trying to brush away her hair earlier, I knew the last thing she wanted was some man's hands on her. Nightmare, ghost, or evil spirit, whatever Dixon and I witnessed in the stairwell was beyond explanation, and if I tried to do so out loud, they'd trade my badge and gun for a straitjacket and rubber room. I'd keep the conversation focused on what I could explain.

"Buffalo Soldiers, yeah, that comes from black military units carrying on the traditions of the original Buffalo Soldiers, who fought in the Spanish-American war in the late 1800s."

"I know that black men served in the military." Her tone was short, and her red eyes looked like sleep was needed in short order. "I just don't understand the 'Buffalo Soldiers' name. Is that because they were from Wyoming?"

"Got it. No, they weren't called Buffalo Soldiers because they were from Wyoming. Besides, our state flag has a bison, not buffalo on it, but many people make that mistake. It's as common as the misconception between shrimp and prawns. And now I'm suddenly craving some surf and turf." I hit my palm against the steering wheel and laughed, but by the aggravated expression on her face, she clearly didn't appreciate my humor. *My bad. Guess I'll save the lecture on the difference between buffalo and bison for another night.*

"Right, so Buffalo Soldiers. That originated when

the Native Americans began calling black cavalry troops Buffalo Soldiers because to the tribes, the soldiers' hair looked like the hair of buffalos—dense and curly." I kept one hand on the steering wheel and brushed my bald head with the other. "I guess I'd be a bald buffalo," I chuckled.

Again, my humor fell flat.

She shook her head. "That's not funny. That's an awful name." The look of disgust thankfully wasn't directed at me.

"Actually," I tentatively continued on a subject I hoped wouldn't upset her, "from what I've read, the black soldiers knew that the buffalo were sacred to the Native Americans for their strength and courage, so in a way, they saw that as a compliment."

This seemed to sit well with her because the scorn left her face. "As long as they were admired. Because anyone who served in any war should be treated well," she said.

"Absolutely. I support our troops for sure."

Her green eyes narrowed. "It's not *that* simple. In World War II, these men risked their lives, and it wasn't easy. It was awful. War was everywhere, and no one knew what would happen. I *felt it* when…." Her voice trailed off, and she turned to the side window and away from me.

I would bet that whatever or whoever that entity was in the stairwell had something to do with the bruises on Reese's arms. Burns? Maybe. But my gut told me she was shaken, and hard.

"So, I mentioned the transcontinental railroad," I said, and she nodded. "Well, some of Cheyenne's older residents were a result of the railroad. They came here to build the railroad and settled along Crow Creek." As I drove over a smaller overpass, I pointed to the creek that ran through the south side of town. "That's Crow Creek. It's low this time of year, but it's there."

She acknowledged it with a tilt of her head.

"Anyway, as the capital city grew, the growth seemed to mainly happen to the north and east. And, of course, the military base curtailed growth toward the west. The south side, where we're headed, was almost forgotten. And yet it's where Cheyenne began."

"Wait." She looked over her shoulder. "The base is behind us? And is that Fort F.E. Warren?"

"Yes to all your questions." I nodded. "It was an army base, and then after World War II, it became an air force base."

"Can I go there?"

"If you're accompanied by military personnel, but no, you can't just stroll onto base. And trust me"—I grinned—"when it's garage sale season and someone on base posts an ad in the newspaper, it creates a shit storm of confusion. Only military personnel are allowed on base, and visitors can be sponsored by base personnel without being accompanied, but it remains quite a process."

"Huh."

"Why all the interest in the base?"

"Oh, I just wondered about its history, and I'd like to see it. You know, take a tour."

History? The woman only really showed interest in

World War II and when I mentioned the base. The man in the military uniform flashed across my mind. *If he was the infamous Cheyenne cowboy Campbell Matthews, why was he in uniform?*

"So what else can you tell me?" She seemed to perk up.

"Well, this is the south side." I slowed when the light at Fox Farm Road turned yellow. "Most of the city's Hispanic population live on the south side, and for years they were treated pretty poorly. But a lot's changed due to a revitalization program that focused on the south side. A new high school and elementary were built. New housing sprung up, and the neighborhoods took pride in their community. It's no longer completely comprised with junk yards and trailer homes."

"And Wild Bill lives over here?"

"According to the address he texted you. He's over by the community college off College Avenue."

Greeley Highway was quiet. Commuters heading to Greeley, Colorado, on the historic two-lane highway were probably just waking up. Having Reese to myself, if even only for a few more minutes, was worth driving her to another man's house.

"Where do you live?" she asked.

"On the east side in the Avenues." My respected, historic neighborhood meant absolutely nothing to her.

"This area looks nice," she said, glancing at the neighborhoods we passed.

"The south side still has a lot of low-income families, but it's changed for the better. My grandmother on my mom's side remembers when realtors wouldn't show people of color—Hispanic as well as blacks—houses north of Pershing Boulevard," I said.

"Is your mom Hispanic?"

"Nah, my mom's as white and pale as you."

"Oh, but I'm not pale anymore, am I?" Reese briefly smiled and flipped the sun visor toward her. Thankfully, my truck wasn't equipped with a vanity mirror on the flip side. I sighed in relief. She was finally beginning to relax. The last thing she needed was to see her burnt face in the daylight. Not yet.

She pushed the visor back against the truck ceiling. "So not showing homes in a certain area of Cheyenne." She blew out a mouthful of air. "Does that kind of blatant discrimination still exist? I mean, I shouldn't even have to ask, but, well, the West is an entirely new experience for me."

"That ended decades ago. My granny just liked to remind my mom that there was a point in time when her only son wouldn't have been able to own a home on the Upper East Side and there were some restaurants that I wouldn't have been able to eat in, but I could have worked at." I rubbed my chin, which was begging for a razor. "A lot has changed. Some people still see the south side as a poor ghetto, but…."

"This ain't no ghetto," she said, finishing my thoughts. "I went to college in Los Angeles, and I've seen ghetto."

"Is that where you're from? LA?"

She shook her head and another curl escaped. "No, just went to school there. I lived and worked in the Bay area by

San Francisco."

"I've never been to California," I said.

Her face brightened. "Oh, it's amazing. You'd love it."

I softly smiled as I turned left onto College Avenue toward Wild Bill's house. "I bet I would, but Wyoming will always be home."

As if on cue, a strong Wyoming wind howled against the closed windows, and a burst of rain streamed against the windshield.

"I could do without the wind and the unpredictable showers," she said with a brief chuckle.

"That's Wyoming," I said, smiling. "It's the Wild West, baby. You can't change the untamed."

She raised an eyebrow, and her lips curved into that bewitching smile that left me speechless. The sudden spark in her hazel eyes lifted my spirits and buoyed my hopes that this wouldn't be the last time I spent a morning beside her.

CHAPTER **TWENTY-ONE**

REESE

Wild Bill's home was what I imagined corporate had lined up for me. It was an apartment above a garage with a large, main brick house in the distance. I limped toward the staircase and shook my head.

"Seriously? Another flight of stairs." I exhaled, but before I placed my foot on the first step, Cody swept me into his arms.

"When are you going to realize my job is to get you from point A to point B without a scratch?"

I wrapped my arms around his neck and felt like I could fall asleep. He was still in jeans but had on a different shirt than I saw earlier. And he smelled good—woodsy with a hint of spice. When we reached the top step, Wild Bill opened the door and I quickly raised my head off Cody's shoulder.

Cody carried me inside the one-room studio loft.

The front hallway led directly into a small kitchen, which separated his living room, which also served as his bedroom. A large bed was tucked in the corner of the room beside what looked like a closet.

"I changed the sheets so the bed is all yours. I'll sleep on the couch," Wild Bill said.

I glanced at Cody, who lingered in the hallway. He handed Wild Bill a business card. "All my contact info is on there. If you need anything."

"Thanks," Wild Bill said.

I stared at the bed positioned in the dark corner. "I'd rather sleep on the couch," I said.

"Sure. Whatever makes you more comfortable," Wild Bill said.

Cody nodded, still seeming to survey the situation. I knew he wouldn't leave until he thought I was okay.

"Here's my card too." He handed it to me, and I tucked it into the pocket of his jacket, beside my phone.

"Wild Bill, do you have a charger?" I handed him my iPhone.

"Absolutely." He took my phone into his kitchen, and I sat on the couch and propped my leg on a large, odd-shaped tree stump that served as an end table. Television and cable remotes were positioned on the glassy surface that looked like it had been coated with clear shellac. I would have left the wood untreated, but it wasn't my stump.

I glanced at Cody. "Thanks again. I'm okay."

"Copy that," he said.

I noticed that whenever he got nervous or maybe unsure

of himself, he resorted back to what he knew. And he knew how to be a cop. Or at least, that's where he seemed most comfortable.

"I'm on call this weekend, so if you need anything," he said again to Wild Bill, who shook his hand before closing the door behind him.

When Cody left, that deep ache of loneliness I felt when Campbell and Ella disappeared from my dream returned. It sank into the pit of my stomach.

"I'm just tired," I said, rationalizing my emotions, but Wild Bill responded.

"I bet." He ducked into his horseshoe-shaped kitchen and returned with a cup of dark tea with what looked like berries and leaves floating along the surface. "It's herbal tea."

I raised my eyebrows, and it stung my face. It felt like I had fallen asleep in the sun. My skin was tight, and even smiling hurt. I stared at the tea.

"How's your face?" Wild Bill asked.

A giggle escaped my lips. "Cody says he won't be able to call me 'Paleface' anymore."

Wild Bill laughed. "That works. I was thinking you look more like a member of my tribe than I do. Want to open a casino with me?"

I laughed, and it released some of the tension in my body. "A casino would work for me because I'm *never* going in that hotel again."

Wild Bill sat on the floor in front of the couch. It seemed like everyone was afraid of crowding me, like I'd snap—

or maybe it was my face. I'd glimpsed myself in the small hospital mirror, and it was red, but I didn't think it looked that bad. Maybe I was wrong.

"I'm not going back," I said. "So, consider yourself promoted, because everything people say about that hotel is true."

Wild Bill said nothing.

"Except it's not haunted, it's tormented."

"What happened?" he asked.

It was the first time I had been asked that question. Or maybe it was the first time I heard it. "I got trapped in the boiler room because the key Toby gave me is worthless. And don't even get me started on the elevator." I lifted the cup of tea to my lips and blew on the steam. I carefully took a sip, and hints of lemon, blackcurrant, and orange peel blended together and soothed my throat.

"Reese, what happened *after* you got stuck?"

I stared at the tea. "I dreamt about Campbell."

"He visited you?"

"No." The answer was quick on my lips. "He was in my dream. Or someone who told me he was Campbell Matthews. He was in an officer's uniform, and she was in a beautiful yellow dress."

"She?"

"Estelle. But he called her Ella. She was beautiful, and they were in love." That euphoric feeling I had when their story played out before me returned, and I smiled. "Oh, Wild Bill, they were so in love. He told her he had a crush on her." I tilted my head. "Isn't that so sweet?"

"There is nothing sweeter than first love."

"I agree. And they *loved* each other. I mean, they were crazy about each other," I said, wanting to stay in the reverie of their courtship.

"That sounds like a wonderful visit," he said.

I closed my eyes and tried to black out the rest of the dream. "No." I opened my eyes and looked at Wild Bill. "If the story had ended there under the penny moon, it would have been the most amazing dream of my life."

"But it didn't end there?"

I shook my head. "No. Suddenly, he appeared by himself, and he was…." I shuddered. "Blood was everywhere. He was in his officer's uniform, but…."

"Reese, that's how most people see him. No one's ever experienced him the way you did."

"You mean before he was bleeding?"

Wild Bill nodded. "When he last appeared to you, did he say anything?"

"Yeah, he told me that he married Ella a year later, but they had to postpone their honeymoon and that he didn't see her again until June at my hotel. He actually called it my hotel. That's why I know it was just a horrible nightmare. I refer to the Point as my hotel, but it's not my hotel. I'm just the GM. It was my subconscious talking, and the dream happened because of all the talk I've heard about Campbell from Zavi, Toby, and even you." I shook a finger at him like I was scolding him, which had no effect.

"Perhaps it was a dream," he said. "Though I'm curious. Did Campbell say anything else? When he appeared to you all bloody."

"Just that he wanted me to find out, or piece together, why his happiness turned tragic." A cold chill ran down my spine. "Nope. Not going to happen. Campbell can haunt someone else."

"Reese, life isn't always light and pretty. There are dark and scary times as well," Wild Bill said.

"I know that," I snapped.

"Okay, but it's like that in the afterlife too, except the light and pretty is what some folks call 'heaven' or the 'happy hunting grounds.' But for those lost spirits who were wronged in this life and never avenged, the dark and scary stays in this world until they receive justice and can truly rest in eternal peace. Campbell is just such a spirit, and he has attached himself to you because he believes you can grant him the justice and peace he never received." Wild Bill paused. "My ancestors would call you 'in touch with spirits,' but in this day and age, you're—"

"Pretty much fucked?" I said.

He chuckled. "No. But with the contact you had with Campbell, you could have your very own reality TV series with cable stations fighting amongst each other for your story, which would raise the price. In which case, you'd have some serious startup money for our casino."

I laughed. "That's not what you were going to say."

He smiled. "No, but it made you laugh."

"It did." I yawned, and Wild Bill got up, went to his bed, and brought a pillow and a striped blanket that he placed at my feet. The blanket had a simple pattern: green stripe, yellow stripe, red stripe, and indigo stripe against a white background that was bookended on the top and bottom ends of the blanket.

"I've only seen this kind of blanket in Wyoming." I gently touched the soft, worn wool.

"Hudson Bay blanket. They're big in these parts," he said.

And before I could ask why, he told me. Wyomingites were like that—they were proud of their heritage and what made the West uniquely its own territory.

"These blankets were traded with Indians in exchange for furs and pelts. The four colors were popular and easy to dye with wool. But for a Native, the colors represented something else." Wild Bill nodded toward the stripes at my feet. "Green means new life, yellow relates to harvest and sunshine, red often stands for battle or hunting, and indigo is water."

"Oh my gosh." I set down my tea. "This would be *perfect* in the hotel. Can you just see it? It would add historical charm while updating the gold-colored quilts that we have in the rooms." The thought flew out of my mouth before I had time to realize what I'd said. "Scratch that. I didn't mean it. I'm tired."

Wild Bill gently smiled, and his dimples softly appeared. "Reese, you've had a long night that's extended into morning." He chuckled. "If you need anything, I'm just over there." He cocked his head toward the dark corner of his room, and began to stand.

"Could you just sit with me a little while longer?" I asked.

"Of course." He resumed his post across from me. "Besides, I'm in no hurry to get to the hotel. I'm told the boss will be out today."

I shook my head. "Yeah, she's permanently out from what I've been told."

"All because of Campbell?" The look on Wild Bill's face could only be described as shocked. "You were such a doubter."

"Listen, seeing, or rather, dreaming is believing. And there's no stronger believer than a convert. The most hard-core skeptic would believe in ghosts in a heartbeat if they continually saw one in their dreams," I said, and raised a hand. "Don't get me wrong. I really *don't* believe in the actuality of ghosts, but I *do* believe that this Campbell guy existed and his life is somehow imprinted at the hotel. And since, as you pointed out, he's so keen on me, I'm not in any hurry to return to the hotel where he can torment me in my sleep. Once is enough. I'm out. Done. Through. Finished."

Wild Bill crossed his legs, and his long braid fell on his shoulder. His dark eyes no longer reminded me of bedroom eyes, especially since I was in his bedroom. Now I saw something deeper, something wiser.

"When I was little, my grandfather told me a Native American legend about wolves. According to the story, the grandson of an old Cherokee chief asked his grandfather, 'Why is life so unhappy?' The wise chief thought for a moment and then asked his grandson to listen to the wolves howling in the distance. The boy listened."

Wild Bill paused. Surrounded by Native American

artwork that hung on the walls behind him, and the tree stump that my leg rested upon, I listened, thinking maybe I'd hear a wolf in the distance.

Wild Bill continued. "The grandfather said, 'A fight is going on inside me. It is a terrible fight, and it is between two wolves. One is evil—he is anger, envy, sorrow, regret, greed, arrogance, self-pity, guilt, resentment, inferiority, lies, false pride, superiority, and ego.' He continued, 'The other is good—he is joy, peace, love, hope, serenity, humility, kindness, benevolence, empathy, generosity, truth, compassion, and faith. The same fight is going on inside you—and inside every other person, too.' The grandson thought about that for a moment and then asked his grandfather, 'Which wolf will win?' The old Cherokee simply replied, 'The one you feed.'"

Wild Bill again paused a beat. "I see two wolves fighting inside you, Reese. One wolf wants you to tuck tail and run away from the hotel and your responsibility, taking cover in self-pity and anger. But the other wolf, the one that felt compassion, empathy, and even love when you experienced Campbell—before and after whatever drove him to his death—is also present. That wolf wants you to stay at the hotel and use that compassion to bring Campbell to rest. The fight before you is very real, and only you can decide which wolf you'll feed."

Nope. Not going there. Great parable, but not taking the bait. I've made my decision. I'm packing my bags and heading back to spiritless, sunny California.

"You're right, I'm tired." I grabbed the pillow, tucked it

under my head, pulled the blanket around me, and closed my eyes. I didn't want to think of wolves, Campbell, the hotel, or any responsibility. The only person who hadn't pressed on me, or needed me to be in charge, was the one whose scent lingered on my hospital scrubs. I tucked my nose beneath my top and inhaled his woodsy, spicy scent, knowing it had to bring sweet dreams.

CHAPTER TWENTY-TWO

CODY

Two plates of eggs, thick bacon, and crispy hash browns arrived along with a pot of coffee, and for a few moments, the conversation traveled to lighter channels.

"What is it about breakfast that tastes so good? No matter what time it is, breakfast is my favorite meal."

I smiled in my sister's direction. Her blonde hair fell to her nape, offsetting her large brown eyes and her milky-white complexion. At five eleven, she had a model's physique—tall, willowy, and all legs. Yet the wholesomeness she exuded gave her an innocent appeal that I watched men gravitate toward. She attracted admiring glances from passersby in the restaurant. She was modest about her beauty, but she was a beauty.

In a pencil-slim tweed skirt, high boots, and an ivory blouse with a simple silver chain that lay between her soft curves, she was the very picture of elegance and class. She tucked her hair behind her ear and dug into her breakfast.

"If you don't want all your bacon, it's mine," she said around a mouthful. "I know you're weird about eating too much grease, which I just don't understand." She pointed her fork toward me. "Greasy food is the best. Hell, we were raised on grease."

"Peach, not all of us were blessed with your metabolism," I said.

She tilted her head and her blonde hair hung like a ray of sunshine. "Cody Bear, you haven't called me Peach in a very long time."

I swallowed hard and moved the hash browns around on my plate. Her hand reached across the table and squeezed mine.

"Tim told me about last night," she said. "Or I guess early morning."

I bit the inside of my lip.

"Thank God that woman wasn't raped." She let go of my hand and picked up her fork. "That's a nightmare you may never wake up from."

"Peach…." I didn't know what to say. The restaurant buzzed with morning commuters grabbing coffee for the road, and the arrival of older patrons, who sat in their regular booths for the $4.99 breakfast, free newspaper, and limitless coffee.

Sheridan placed her fork on the edge of her plate. "Cody Bear, I know what you're thinking, but don't go into that well. It sounds like this woman was amazingly brave—being stuck in a boiler room?" She shuddered. "No, thank you. That's where Freddy Krueger lives."

I nodded and looked at my eggs, which appeared to be undercooked. "Yeah, I took her to the hospital and stayed with her while they, uh, you know, checked her out."

"That's what Tim said."

"Yeah, she was pretty shaken up. I wanted to do more." I cut into my eggs, and when they began to run, I pushed them to the side of my plate.

"I'm sure you did everything you could for her."

"As much as she'd allow me. She's a bit stubborn."

"So you have something in common," Peach said with a smile.

"Cute." I salted my hash browns.

"Actually, Tim said the woman was cute and he thought you were crushing on her. Apparently, you've met her before?"

I rolled my eyes. "I literally ran into her when she was running. I was leaving the Steakhouse Saloon from the side door and we collided. It wasn't my best moment, and she was *not* about to let me forget it." I inhaled, and on the exhale, I thought about the fiery redhead and how she smelled. "All I did was carry her from the alley to Capitol Avenue, where it was lit."

"Cody, why didn't you drive her home?"

"Oh, gee, I wonder why I didn't think of that." I ripped off the end of a sugar packet and poured the contents in my coffee. "She wouldn't let me. But I offered."

"Was she afraid of you?" My sister lowered her voice. "Like was it a *black* thing?"

I laughed. "No, Peach, it wasn't a black thing. I don't

even think the woman realized I was black. She was so mad at me."

Peach tilted her head. "Ah, you like her."

"*Like her?*" I puffed out a mouthful of air. "I don't even know her." I paused. "I mean, I wouldn't mind *getting* to know her, but…." The night replayed in my mind. "After we found her in the boiler room and she was half-naked…."

My sister's tone matched her empathy. "That must have been hard for you."

I stared at my plate, but all I saw was the vacancy in Reese's eyes. I'd only seen that look one other time in my life.

"Cody, you do know it wasn't your fault any more than it was mine. We were too young to be left alone with him."

When I didn't say anything, she did.

"And, Cody Bear, it's not Momma's fault either. She had no reason not to trust her brother. It'd be like me not trusting you." Her brown eyes widened. "I can't even imagine that. Momma was horrified when she found out."

"Peach, she only found out because…." The image of my sister's room shot across my mind with the intensity of a PTSD flashback.

"There was blood all over my sheets. It's okay to talk about it." She paused, and I made eye contact with her.

"When you found this woman tonight, it probably brought up a lot of feelings for you."

My stomach tightened into a knot, and my shoulders felt like someone was pressing down hard on them and I couldn't shake the weight. Physical pain I could handle, but the dull ache that pulled at my chest felt like my heart was weeping. *Stupid. Whose heart weeps?*

"Cody, what happened tonight?" My sister knew I couldn't tell her names or details, but that's not what she was asking.

"Her clothes were in a pile…." Peach's clothes had been in a folded stack in her room, which was worse than if they had been scattered. Neat, orderly, arranged clothes revealed intent. The bastard had premeditated his act of violence against my sister.

"Oh, Cody Bear, I'm so sorry."

Her voice was a salve. Peach knew. Fuck, she lived through the horror, I just experienced it from outside her bedroom door.

"Seeing her in just her underwear and bra…." I swallowed hard, yet my voice still sounded small. "Peach, I didn't know what to do." It was the same way I'd found Peach.

"Counseling has *really* helped," she said gently. "Hell, I've been in counseling for years—I think in total I logged two decades' worth of time on the couch." Her laughter was meant to make me feel good, but it didn't.

"Cody, his actions don't define me. Any more than they would have for this woman if she had been raped. It took a long time, but by working with a therapist trained in trauma, the impact of what he did to me no longer owns me. If I've learned anything in counseling, it's that what happened to me was not my fault. That seems so obvious, but I also learned it's normal to try to make sense of what happened and second-guess my actions—like if I hadn't been playing dress up, then maybe...." She shook her head.

The knot in my gut twisted. "Peach, if I had just come into your room…. I knew something wasn't right."

"Cody, you can't do that to yourself. You can't second-guess what an eight-year-old would or should have done. You were eight. I was ten. Neither of us ever thought he would do that. Why would we? We were children. Neither of us knew what to do."

She took a sip of coffee. "And neither did Momma. It happened twenty-one years ago. Should she have called the cops? Probably. But it was her brother, and if she loved him half as much as I love you, it would be an impossible choice."

"No." I shook my head. "You were the child. He was the adult. There is no choice."

"And that's why you're a great cop. And," her voice softened, "you'll be an even better protective daddy. But blaming Momma *doesn't help me*."

Her brown eyes were touched with a hint of sadness, and it felt like my weepy heart plummeted to my gut.

"Peach, don't be sad. I shouldn't have brought this up."

When Peach smiled, it brightened the room. "Cody Bear, you didn't do anything wrong. It's okay. Between this woman in the boiler room and that dog you found, it's been a shit night."

I chuckled. "Yeah, it has."

"How's the dog?"

"The vet called dispatch, and so far, so good. The dog's

hanging on—he's a survivor." I exhaled, and the tension in my shoulders lessened a little.

"The dog sounds like you. Or our family." She laughed. "When I think back to our childhood, Momma did the best she could raising two kids by two different men all by herself without child support. We lived on the generosity of strangers' tips who took a liking to Momma in that pink waitress uniform."

The image of my short, full-figured momma in a bright pink uniform made me chuckle. "She looked like a puffed pastry."

My sister giggled. "For a white woman, Momma had a booty on her."

"Hundred percent. Remember how when people complemented Momma on not having wrinkles, she'd say, 'Fat don't crack'?" I burst out laughing. "My God, that was so wrong, but it was so funny."

"That's what I like to see." My sister grabbed the juiciest piece of bacon off my plate and popped it into her mouth.

"Hey!"

Her brown eyes danced along with a playful smile on her face.

"You're a pain in my ass," I said.

She shrugged. "That's what big sisters are for." She forked a hash brown chunk and waved it in the air. "Oh look, Cody Bear, it's crispy, greasy, and yummy." She moved her fork like an airplane before it landed in her mouth.

I shook my head. "It's unbelievable we're related."

"Ah, you love me."

"Hundred percent." I reached across and grabbed the last piece of bacon on her plate and dropped it in my mouth before her busy hands could take it back.

"Cody!" Her voice rose, and the older military vets in the corner booth glanced in our direction.

I nodded toward them; they in turn took one look at my sister and smiled. Peach was like a lyric in an Eagles song. The girl could open doors with a smile.

"So, let me guess, my partner's home asleep?" I tried a bite of the egg that wasn't runny. It was still too soft for my liking. "Momma always knew how to tell the cook to make my eggs." I glanced at Peach, who poured each of us another cup of coffee and offered me a sugar packet while she hoarded the creamer.

"Peach? You're stalling. Where's Dixon?"

She set down her fork. "Now, before you get upset, I want you to understand that this was all my idea."

I exhaled. "What did you do? Please don't tell me you have my partner selling that crappy spray on the street corner."

She waved away my comment. "Actually, Tim's interviewing with DCI."

"For real?"

She nodded. "He needs a desk job, and…."

"And you think the Department of Criminal Investigations is going to keep him safe? He's going to be handling heavier caseloads. You'll never see him."

"But he won't be entering homes with crazy old women pointing pistols at his head."

"It was *my* head, actually," I said. "And yeah, he won't have the same kind of contact with criminals, but he's not going to be immune to them."

"I know that, but…." She stared at her plate. My sister was holding back.

"But what?"

Her brown eyes looked up at me. Eyes that had guided me throughout my childhood. Eyes that were vacant for years after she was raped. Now, they were looking to me for support, and I didn't know for what, only that she'd have it.

"Tim and I are going to have a baby."

My body flushed with a surge of warmth, and my eyes watered. "Oh, Peach. You're pregnant? You don't even look pregnant."

She smiled, and her eyes brimmed with tears. "Don't tell anyone yet. I just passed the first trimester, but we've lost a baby before."

I nodded, leaned across the table, and gently kissed her forehead. "This is different."

She nodded. "I know, right? It feels different. And I don't want to stress that Tim won't come home to me."

"I'd *never* let that happen," I said, wiping my eyes.

Her head titled again. "Cody Bear, you can't promise me that. Any more than Tim could promise to keep you safe."

"So DCI, huh?" I brushed the rim of my coffee cup with my thumb. The restaurant thinned of people as breakfast rolled toward lunch.

"They scheduled a weekend interview so he wouldn't have to take time off from work—other than being on call," she said.

"Does Chief know?" My sister's face answered for her. "Chief knows," I stated. "Apparently, the only person who *didn't* know was his partner."

"Cody, that's not fair. I told him not to tell you."

"Why?" I leaned toward her. "Why wouldn't you want me to know?"

She looked at me, and there wasn't anything I wouldn't do for her. "Because I knew how much it'd get into your head."

My sister relapsed into the role that had been her first in my life—protector. I should have been hers, but she was always mine.

"Cody, I need you to be sharp when you're in the field—especially when an old woman is pointing a gun at my husband's head."

"My head!" I flung my hands in the air a little more dramatically than I intended. "The Colt was pointed at *my* head, not Dixon's."

When my sister giggled, it was the sound of my childhood.

"Oh, cute, you were teasing me. Nice. Real nice." Yet I couldn't help but grin. My sister's happiness shone from her eyes, and it was beautiful.

She suddenly leaned out of the booth and waved. "It's Tim!"

I playfully rolled my eyes. "Here comes trouble." I glanced behind me as my partner sauntered into the restaurant and scooted into the booth beside my sister.

"So, how'd you do?" I asked, and Dixon quickly elbowed his wife.

"I thought you didn't want him to know?"

Peach giggled. "I can't keep secrets from Cody Bear."

I closed my eyes. *Here it comes.*

"Cody Bear, huh? Wow. That's a new one." Dixon laughed. "You never told me your middle name was Bear."

I opened my eyes and looked at him. "Well, then we're even. You didn't tell me about DCI, and"—I raised my hand—"don't put this on my sister. We've been partners longer than you've been married. Hell, I set you two up. You can tell me anything. Like if you're applying for a job with DCI or that your wife and my sister is pregnant."

Dixon's blue eyes widened. "Sheridan, is there anything you didn't tell him?"

"No, he doesn't know *everything*—like I never told him that we conceived the baby at his house." She burst out laughing, and I shook my head.

"Please tell me you're joking." But neither of them spoke. "For real?" I stared at them. "When?" They remained mute, and my mind cataloged when I'd even had my sister watch my house. I slapped the table, and my coffee cup shook.

"It was when I asked you to water my plants because I went to that concert at Red Rocks, right? And it was really hot that weekend. Shit, that was back in August."

They both nodded, and my sister beamed. "August 7, to be exact."

I shrugged. "I got nothing." I pushed my plate away. "I don't want to know where in my house you conceived my niece or nephew." I held up my hands. "Peach, that is *not* a dare or invitation to tell me. I do not want to know. In fact, I'd rather not know you even used my house. You're grown people with a place of your own. What the hell?"

Dixon laughed. "You're telling me you've never been caught up in the moment?"

I rubbed my beard that still hadn't seen a razor in two days. "Oh, I get caught up in the moment, and the next time I do, it's going to be at your house."

My sister radiated warmth and happiness, which was the best way to come down after a harrowing night and morning.

I drank the rest of my coffee. "What is it about diner coffee that makes the day look better?"

"Nothing. There's nothing about diner coffee. It's flat," Dixon said.

Peach wagged her finger back and forth. "No, sir. I'm with my brother on this one. Diner coffee is *the* only coffee worth paying for."

Dixon chuckled. "Sure." He cocked his head toward the coffeepot between us. "You better fill up then, we have a long night ahead of us."

"Are you still on that whole Halloween thing?" The skepticism dripped from my voice, but I did pour the last of the pot into my cup.

"You haven't checked your messages." When my partner spoke in absolutes, I knew it couldn't be good.

"What?" I didn't bother to retrieve my work cell.

"The governor's attending the costume party at the

Point tonight."

"And?" I waited before taking a drink.

"And we've been assigned to cover it."

I shrugged. "Okay. Walk in the park. The governor has his own security detail—not seeing a downside to this."

Dixon and my sister exchanged a glance.

"What?"

"Chief wants us to blend in and not be a notable presence in the room."

"Sure. That makes sense," I said. "We can hang on the periphery."

Peach laughed. "No, that's not quite your assignment."

I really didn't like how much my sister knew about my assignment before I did, but I had no one to blame. After I left Reese at Wild Bill's, I put my phone on the charger, caught two hours of sleep, and called Peach to meet for breakfast. I never checked my messages, and my cell hadn't dinged like I had missed something.

"Okay, Peach, what's our assignment?" I could play along.

She grinned and clapped. "Cody Bear, you and Tim get to dress up in costume!"

I instantly looked at my partner. "You're putting me on."

He flatly shook his head. "Negative."

"Chief wants us in costume?"

"Affirmative."

"What the hell?" I said.

"Oh, Cody Bear, it'll be so much fun. I'll help you and Tim find something fabulous to wear so you'll blend in."

I shrugged. "Well, unless you turn me invisible or Caucasian, I'll be noticed. And Peach, since both are permanent, it's just too big a price to pay for a party."

She giggled, and then her brown eyes softened. "Okay, okay, since blending in won't work, maybe we opt for standing out."

This intrigued me.

"Trust me?" she said.

"Always." I smiled.

The server appeared at our booth. "Will you be staying for lunch?" She smiled, and in her I saw Momma.

"No, thank you." I handed her our plates stacked together with the silverware on top, which would cut down her bussing time.

"Thank you." She looked surprised and cradled the plates in her arm like a baby that she shifted to her hip to reach into her apron pocket for the ticket. "I'll be your cashier."

I grabbed my wallet from my back pocket, withdrew a fifty, and handed it to her. "Let me get your change." As she walked away, I glanced at Peach, who grabbed her purse and pushed Dixon out of the booth.

"Doesn't Cody want his change? It's like forty bucks."

My sister and I looked at each other, then to him.

"Oh, that's right," he said. "No change. That's her tip."

I patted him heartily on the back. "Peach, didn't I tell you he was trainable?"

My sister's joyful laughter was all I heard as we left the restaurant.

CHAPTER **TWENTY-THREE**

REESE

There was a clamor of whispering voices.

"Should we wake her up?"

"I don't think so."

"But the hotel's hosting the Halloween party tonight."

"Who cares? We can do it."

"You and me, you mean?"

"No, me and Heidi Klum."

"Is she coming to the hotel?"

The next sound I heard was a loud smack.

"What'd you do that for?"

I opened my eyes, and Toby was rubbing the back of his head.

"Listen, you two doofuses, quit your yapping, I'm up," I said.

"Wouldn't the plural be doofi?" Wild Bill grinned.

"I swear, if both your intelligence was doubled, the two

of you combined would almost be a half-wit." But they were my half-wits, and when Toby rushed to the side of the couch, the concern in his brown eyes left me speechless.

He knelt before me. "How you feeling, Doc?" He looked on the verge of tears. "I'm so sorry you got stuck in the boiler room. When Otis returned and you weren't there, I just figured you had gone to your suite to drink. I wouldn't have gone home if I knew you were stuck."

"Tobness, it's okay. I'm fine."

"But your face?"

Wild Bill swiftly smacked the back of Toby's head again.

"Ouch! What the hell?" Toby turned on the heel of his boot. "Knock that shit off."

"What about my face?" My skin felt tight, but it didn't hurt.

Neither of them answered. Wild Bill crossed the room and pulled the cord to lift the blinds from one of the high windows in his loft. The room flooded with sunlight.

"What time is it?"

"Two," Toby said. "In the afternoon."

I laughed. "Thanks."

"You're about an hour shy of eight hours of sleep," Wild Bill said. "I'm sure you could sleep all day, but there's an email from corporate about the costume party."

I sat up, and it felt like my body had been hit by a Mack truck and then dragged along Greeley Highway. Wild Bill handed me a bottle of water. I twisted off the cap, and when the water touched my lips, it burned. I pulled away from the bottle, and Wild Bill gave me a round container of lip balm.

"Reese, you've got to drink. I read the hospital discharge papers, and you were pretty dehydrated."

I dipped my finger into the pot of aloe-vera-smelling balm and carefully dabbed my lips.

"Shit, that stings."

Toby grimaced. "I bet. Your lips look like Ronald McDonald's." As soon as the comment left his mouth, he ducked.

Wild Bill stood over him. "And you wonder why you're not in guest services."

I opted not to smile, not because I wasn't amused, but because it hurt. "Okay, tell me about this email."

Wild Bill reached behind him to the kitchen counter, unplugged my iPhone from the charger, and handed it to me. "I was cc'd on it, but it was addressed to you."

Swiping my phone awake woke more than a hundred emails waiting for me.

"What the hell?" I blinked, but the red circle floating above the blue mail icon still had 132 in it. "Did you guys burn down the hotel?"

They both shook their heads.

"Doc, it's probably everyone RSVPing for tonight's costume party."

"This late?" I looked at Wild Bill. "Didn't the invitations go out before I arrived on property—like in early October?"

"Yes. I took them to the post office myself, but...." Wild Bill's voice trailed off.

"*But?* I don't think I can handle any buts right now."

"But people in Wyoming are late to RSVP or they don't

at all," Wild Bill said.

"So?" I shrugged. "Chef is preparing a buffet to feed a small village."

Toby grimaced again.

"Oh my God—what?"

"You should probably read your email," Wild Bill said.

I slowly exhaled and scrolled to the email from Angus Thurman.

Reese,

When I didn't receive your current profit and loss statement, I looked at the calendar and realized you must be preparing for the annual costume party. Of course, this is a tradition the Point Resort has continued since we assumed ownership of the historic property.

After speaking with our media director, we've contracted a local photographer, Ryan Donihue, to photograph tonight's event. We've spoken to Ryan, who will post photos to our corporate website throughout the night. I think it will help attract visitors and other interested parties toward the hotel—especially when they experience all our wonderful amenities.

To that end, we'd like to have the costume party held on the rooftop.

My mouth fell open. "The rooftop? He wants the party

moved to the rooftop?"

Toby nodded, and Wild Bill spoke. "Keep reading—there's more."

"More? What more could he want? A fireworks show?"

"No, but only because that would cost money. However," Wild Bill said, "if you could arrange an aurora borealis, you'd be a corporate hero."

"Sure, I'll get right on that." I resumed reading the rest of the email.

> *From the most recent engineering report I read, the tennis court has been enclosed for the winter, which still hasn't hit your area yet! Such good timing for a wonderful rooftop costume party!*
>
> *I reached out to Governor Hawthorne directly, and he was enthusiastic to accept our annual invitation to join tonight's costume party. Please coordinate with his security personnel to ensure they have everything they need to protect Wyoming's most trusted official.*
>
> *Additionally, please comp suites for the governor and his staff. After reviewing the recent occupancy rate, which was rather low, our media director created a marketing blitz on social media and placed ads with the local radio station and newspaper. We'll be offering discounted hotel rates throughout the weekend and into midweek. With the governor on property, the fuller the better.*
>
> *I realize you've been occupying a suite at*

the hotel. I contacted our corporate realtor, who found a rental that's available immediately. You no longer have to wait to move in! A separate email with the address will be sent from our realtor. The security deposit and rent has already been wired to the property owner. All you have to do is move your things! We want to ensure every suite is available this weekend.

Thanks!

Angus Thurman

I stared at my cell phone. "When did he email this?"

"Late last night, probably when you were running," Toby said.

"I checked my email before I ran, and this wasn't there. I had another email from him. But this wasn't there." I shook my phone like a Magic 8-Ball, but it did nothing to erase my fate.

"Sometimes our Internet connection is slow or doesn't function," Toby said.

I held up my hand. "Don't even get me started on what does and does not function in that hotel."

Toby cringed. "Yeah, I don't know how you or those cops got stuck in the boiler room. Wild Bill and I personally checked all the locks, and the master key works in the stairwell just fine. And the door leading from the basement into the boiler room stairwell wasn't locked."

I must have had a disheartened look on my face, or maybe it was just my face, because Wild Bill elbowed Toby.

"Those old doors stick all the time, and until you've really had time using the master key, it can be tricky."

"Oh, sure, yeah, that happens," Toby said.

I tossed my phone on the cushion beside me and leaned back against the couch. "I was supposed to quit today."

"What?" Toby's eyes were as large as quarters. "Why would you want to quit, Doc? You just got here."

I glanced at Wild Bill and realized he hadn't told his working half about my dream. I gently smiled.

"Oh." I exhaled. "I was just tired and had a rough night. I'm not going anywhere." I shot Wild Bill a look. "Not yet, not with the governor coming. But doesn't the party start at eight?"

They both nodded.

I glanced behind Wild Bill to a photo on the mantle beside his television that I hadn't seen last night.

"Is that Millie?" I leaned forward and squinted. "That's Millie from the gift shop."

Wild Bill's face brightened, and his dimples seemed permanently embedded in his cheeks. "Yeah, that was at last year's summer staff barbecue."

"Oh, you're sweet on Millie," I said, and he didn't disagree.

"He may be sweet on Millie, but is Millie sweet on him?" Toby asked.

Wild Bill looked like he was ready to whack Toby again.

"Just saying," Toby said.

"Well, don't," I said, and redirected the conversation. "So, we've got six hours to move the party to the rooftop tennis court, move my entire life into some rental home, and reserve our best suites for the governor and his staff. I haven't showered, I'm in hospital scrubs, and, oh, here's a fun fact, I don't have a costume because I wasn't planning on the governor or a photographer being there tonight."

"I got to the hotel by ten, and Toby and I've been working on most of what needs to be done."

Wild Bill stood in front of me, ready to give me a full report, when I suddenly remembered.

"Oh, shit. What about Mr. P-nus and his tennis game?"

Wild Bill laughed and Toby scratched his head. "Who's Mr. Penis?"

"When I comp'd Mr. Nus's room for one night, it seemed to take the sting out of missing his scheduled tennis match," Wild Bill said.

"Oh, Robert Nus? Yeah, he's a regular," Toby said.

"Okay, what else?" I looked at Wild Bill.

"Chef wasn't pleased about the location switch, because Chef likes to complain when this *really* doesn't affect him at all. The banquet director wasn't too happy, but when we told him the governor and other VIPs would be there, he got on board," Wild Bill said. "We'll run food and servers through the elevator. And before you tell me that staff isn't supposed to use the elevator, we allow the housekeepers and room service to deliver to the upper floors so, unless we want cold food and sweaty servers, we're going to have to do the same thing with the banquet servers. We've got one elevator, and Otis is going to be working overtime tonight."

"Otis," I mumbled. My antagonism left a bitter taste in

my mouth. I wagged a finger at Toby. "You better make sure Otis behaves."

He held up his hand. "Already did. His British accent is turned up, and his control panel has been buffed and polished."

I rolled my eyes. "I still don't have a lot of faith in Otis, but since we don't have a service elevator, it's Otis or nothing."

Toby grinned. "Otis won't let you down."

Wild Bill interlaced his fingers together and shook his fist toward me. "Reese, before you react, hear me out."

"About?" I didn't like the uncertainty in my hotel manager's voice.

"I know how tight the budget is, but I thought since the governor and other VIPs would be attending the party, and many for the first time, that we should have a live band play and not just DJ house music. So, I phoned in a favor and have a band lined up."

"Smart move," I said.

The relief on Wild Bill's face was instant, and his hands relaxed.

"So that leaves booking suites, moving my life, and getting a costume," I said.

"All your personal belongings have been packed by housekeeping and are in the hotel shuttle downstairs, along with your car. That's why we're both here," Toby said with a smile. "I drove your car and Wild Bill drove the shuttle. We're here to help you move in!"

His enthusiasm was annoyingly sweet. "You *are* the

Tobmaster," I said.

Toby's face lit with excitement, and he clapped his hands. "After we move you in, we'll take you to the thrift store for a costume. Oh." His mouth widened along with his eyes. "We could get you a cigar and a pair of goggles for your forehead, and with your red face, you could be Hellboy. It's perfect."

I stared at Toby, and he wasn't laughing. *Oh my God, he's serious.*

"Or she could wear a Nazi uniform and be the Red Skull," Wild Bill said.

"And you both really wonder why you're still single?" I said.

They looked at each other and laughed. "Yeah, you're not tall enough to be Hellboy," Toby said. "And, Doc, I'm not single. I'm married."

"I'm single." Wild Bill shrugged. "And the more I think about it, Nazis aren't really politically correct."

Unreal. "Thanks, guys, but I'll figure something out." I carefully stood, and my left leg stood with me. I smiled. "Well, that's a good start. Now, let's go see where corporate relocated me."

CHAPTER **TWENTY-FOUR**

CODY

The olive-drab steel helmet was marred by a dent, and the uniform had faded. But when my sister pulled them out of her hope chest, my chest swelled with pride.

"Suggesting that Cody Bear blend in at this costume party was wrong. And I don't care if it was Chief's idea." Peach dusted off my grandfather's helmet. "Why should my handsome brother blend in, when he can stand out."

She placed the helmet on my head, and it fit.

"Buffalo Soldier in the heart of America," Dixon said, stealing a line from Bob Marley.

I grinned. "The helmet fits, but my granddad was a pretty thin private." I pulled the pressed pants off the hanger and checked the waist size.

"Damn. *Thirty*?" I chuckled and handed them to my sister. "Peach, this is a great idea, but how the hell do you expect my thirty-four-inch waist to fit into a slim thirty?"

"Listen, Private," my sister said. "If your grandfather could serve in Italy in the fall of 1944 with one of the army's entirely black units, we can figure out how to get your bubble butt into these pants."

I smiled. Peach was the family historian. When my dad did live with us, she kept a journal of his stories. On the rare occasions when Granddaddy Pring visited, she pulled out her journal and asked him questions. I only knew my dad's family history because of Peach.

"What about the jacket?" She handed it to me. "As long as your arms can fit, I can make the rest work."

I pulled off my gray V-neck sweater and was about to remove my white T-shirt when my sister wagged her finger.

"Keep it on."

I drew a deep breath, as if that'd even make a difference, and slipped one arm and then the other into the jacket. I slowly stretched my arms across my chest, and when the jacket didn't rip, I exhaled. "I don't remember Granddaddy being that broad."

"He kind of had that swimmers build—broad shoulders, narrow waist."

I surveyed the row of buttons and grimaced. "Uh, I don't think I can button it."

"That's okay." Peach dug through her cedar chest and pulled out a pair of dog tags that she roped around my neck.

I looked at myself in the reflection of the large-screen TV mounted on the wall in their bedroom. With the helmet on, jacket open, the white T-shirt, and dog tags hanging in the center of my chest, I looked like a soldier.

Damn, that's fly. I can't wait for Reese to see me in this. Will she even be there tonight?

"All I need are army-green pants, boots, and a holster."

Dixon's fingers streamed across his iPhone. "Hold up, dreadlock Rasta, to be authentic, the boots you want…." His blue eyes focused on the screen. "Okay, here it is. You want a pair of ankle-high, russet-brown combat boots with a two-buckle leather ankle strap. And the pants were actually wool trousers. Olive drab, not army green."

"I can see why you and my sister get along so well."

She flipped the helmet off my head and handed it to her husband. "If you touch the inside of the helmet, you can feel the divots left from shrapnel."

"Pretty impressive," Dixon said.

"What's even more impressive is that Cody's granddaddy was part of the 92nd Infantry Division, one of the *only* African-American units to see combat in Europe. Cody's granddaddy battled German troops in Italy." Peach sat on the edge of her bed.

My father wasn't a topic I much discussed, but my granddaddy was someone I wished I had known better. I admired his courage.

"He only died a few years ago, right?" Dixon looked like an idiot in my granddaddy's hat that was two times too big for him.

Before I could answer, Peach did. "Abner Pring was born in 1924, and when he was drafted in 1944, he was only nineteen. He died on June 30. He was eighty-five years young."

"Abner." Dixon nodded. "That's right. Wasn't that a family name?" He grinned.

"Momma wouldn't name her only son Abner, so she broke the family tradition," Peach said.

I rolled my eyes. "So instead, she named me after the town where I was conceived."

Peach laughed. "Thank God her and my daddy conceived me in Sheridan and not Baggs, Casper, or Jackson."

My sister and I often joked, naming all the small Wyoming towns we could have been named after.

"Yeah, I could've been Graybull, Lyman, or Manville."

Dixon laughed. "Don't get me wrong, I love your momma, but we are *not* carrying on that naming tradition."

"I don't know, Dixon, since my niece or nephew was conceived in my house, he or she could be named after the house of Cody or the city of Cheyenne. Seems like a win-win to me."

Dixon arched an eyebrow toward my sister. "Actually, Cheyenne is a cute name for a girl."

She smiled and gently rubbed her belly "Oh my gosh! I *totally* thought that, too!" When my sister got excited about something, her big brown eyes sparkled.

"Yeah, yeah, yeah. Cody or Cheyenne. Cute names. But that doesn't solve my costume problem."

"Or mine. What am I going to wear?" Dixon and I looked at my sister, who stretched across the bed in their master bedroom and grabbed her sewing box on the lower ledge of her nightstand.

"What time do you need your costumes?" She rolled

back into a sitting position and propped pillows behind her. After breakfast, her belly puffed out. Or maybe I just now noticed.

I glanced at Dixon. "What time does Chief want us there?"

"The party starts at eight, so we should be there by seven? Seven thirty, latest."

My sister checked the Fitbit on her wrist and massaged her forehead. "Okay, it's going to be tight, but I can do it."

"Sheridan, you still haven't told me what I'm going to wear."

She grinned. "Don't worry, baby. I'll make sure you stand out and match your partner's buffalo theme."

Dixon elbowed me. "Hear that? I'll probably be a Buffalo Bills football player, or your namesake, Buffalo Bill Cody. Either is fine because they're both masculine and cool."

I rolled my eyes. "My sister's probably got Cinderella's fairy godmother on retainer, and if I don't have you back by midnight, chances are I'll be coming home wearing a pair of pumpkin pants."

CHAPTER **TWENTY-FIVE**

REESE

"So, where's my new abode?" My attitude had improved dramatically with the help of the breakfast burrito waiting for me in the hotel shuttle. Wild Bill had volunteered to drive my car and leave it for me at my rental so he could return to the hotel to tie up loose ends for tonight's party while Toby and I met my new landlord. I had a full stomach, which not even the sight of my highly paid engineer playing chauffeur could upset.

"Reese, you're going to love it. I can't believe how lucky you got."

"And what's so lucky about this rental?"

"Do you want the whole story or just the 411?" Toby glanced at me while he drove from Wild Bill's south side home toward downtown Cheyenne.

"Give me the full scoop," I said.

"Really?"

"Yeah, Tobster, lay it all on me."

"Okay, so your rental is on Evans and 22nd Street in downtown Cheyenne, which is actually pretty close to the hotel. Wild Bill already texted that it only took him seven minutes to walk to the hotel. So that's a plus."

"I like it," I said.

"Okay, so on Evans, there are four homes identical in architecture and design. These red-brick, single-family homes were built in 1900 for four sisters." When I didn't comment, he glanced at me and I gave him a reassuring thumbs-up.

"Four sisters, four homes," I said.

He smiled. "These homes are located in the Rainsford Historic District. You'll notice historical markers posted in the area."

"Rainsford? Person or... ghost?" I giggled, and Toby grinned.

"I'm glad being locked in the boiler room didn't dampen your spirits," he said.

"Nope, just my hair and face. That steam did a number on me." I really did look like Hellboy.

"It's the oddest thing, neither Wild Bill nor I could find a pressure leak."

I shrugged. "Eh, maybe I sleepwalked into the demon boiler. Who knows? It was a trippy night. I'm beyond grateful I don't have to sleep in the hotel anymore. I will give you and Wild Bill this—there's a lot of history there."

"Told you." He grinned.

I didn't want to talk about Campbell. I was relaxed and

rested; there was no reason to stir up a bad spirit. Besides, why harp on what amounted to nothing more than a bad dream?

"So Rainsford?" I redirected the conversation.

"Right. George Rainsford was a New York architect who came west in the late 1870s to try his hand at horse ranching. He ended up doing well and gained a strong reputation for the quality of his stock."

"So, was he an architect or horse breeder? I'm confused."

"He came to Cheyenne to breed horses, but as a hobby and favor to his cattle-ranching friends, he continued to practice architecture."

"Very cool. I assume he built these four homes for four sisters?"

"I think he *may* have because his design style leaned toward traditional styles with varied roof shapes. But a lot of builders borrowed his designs. The four sisters' homes have a Victorian influence."

"Victorian, huh? That sounds nice."

"Reese, it's really nice, and you're in a *great* neighborhood, albeit it's old. But most historic things are." He chuckled.

"I can't wait." We crested the railroad overpass. I glanced at the trains, and my thoughts turned to Cody. My talkative, thoughtful, protective cop. My smile turned to a frown when I realized how curt I'd been. I did thank him, but it probably seemed empty in comparison to my abrupt tone. I exhaled. *I'll make it right later. I can't focus on him now—not with Governor Hawthorne due at the hotel in less than six hours.*

"So, the homes along Evans once belonged to the richest cattle barons in Cheyenne. Old-timers still call the area 'Cattle Baron Row.'"

"I think I'll call it home."

Toby turned on 21st Street and pointed toward a home that could only be described as a stately manor. "That's the former governor's mansion. You've got to walk the neighborhood to see all the different homes and history."

"Will do. This looks ah-mazing, but I'm still not sure why four sisters needed four different homes? Were they spinsters?"

Toby's laughter wheezed out of him.

"Not spinsters. They just had a rich daddy who built a home when each of his daughters married."

"Gives new meaning to the word 'dowry,'" I said.

The hotel shuttle slowed, and Toby pulled along the curb in front of a two-story brick home that was bookended by twin homes on either side.

"Uh, that's odd." He glanced at the address. "I thought you were in one of the four sisters' homes."

He checked the address against the four cookie-cutter homes that were in pristine condition. There was a vacant sliver of land and then another home, which looked like it was made with the remnants leftover from building the four sisters' homes. It wasn't ugly, but it wasn't deliberately adorable. The home looked like an afterthought.

"Oh." Toby's voice dropped, and he backed the shuttle to the front of the fifth home, where my car was parked.

"This is your rental." He leaned toward me and squinted at the number on the house. "Yup. This is the one. Okay, so the property has about 1,575 finished square feet."

Leave it to my engineer to know the specifics.

"But for being old, it actually looks like it's in great, great shape. And you know what, it's kind of cute," he said.

It was hard, though, not to compare. The four sisters' homes were framed with scallops painted cream, which contrasted beautifully against the rich red brick. A small porch with four ivory posts gave the historic homes country charm. Fireplaces piped out of the high roof pitch were just waiting for Santa. While the four sisters' homes were an identical quartet, they worked and collectively brightened the street.

I glanced at my rental. Instead of creamy scallops, the house was solid brick. A steepled roof design made it appear pointed and hard. A single upstairs window looked lonely and forgotten compared to the sisters' two upstairs windows, where it looked like courting began and ended beneath the inviting frames.

The only consistency this house had with the four sisters' was the four-poster porch with a slanted roof. But when I did a double take, the house corporate rented for me had a mismatched front door that was a hodgepodge of brown and tan. It was hideous. And there wasn't a wrought-iron fence enclosing the front yard like the sisters' homes.

I knew it was only a rental, but my chest deflated. *Bummer*.

A woman stepped onto the porch. She stood in the

shadows, so it was hard to see her. Even though the windows in the shuttle were closed, I lowered my voice. "Is that my landlord?"

"I think so. Let's go meet her."

My hair was pulled into a ponytail, but I quickly tucked any loose curls behind my ear. My face was redder than a beet, my navy hospital scrubs were three sizes too big, and even in a knee brace, I gimped as I walked toward her.

"Hi. I'm Reese and I kind of look like the walking wounded," I said as I approached. "I'm like that picture that's in any American history book I've ever opened. You know, the one where there's three men marching on the battlefield and two of them are playing the drums and one is playing the flute while an American flag waves in the background."

When the woman said nothing, but instead eyed me from head to toe, I was pretty sure I wasn't getting the keys to her house.

"Is this your home?" I asked.

"Once. A very long time ago." She walked out of the shadows, and her hair shone like silver. "It's called *The Spirit of '76.*"

"Oh, that's a great name for a home," I said.

Her laughter was surprisingly light compared to her dark eyes. "Sweet child, that's not the name of my home, it's the name of the painting you referenced."

"Oh," I said, and looked at Toby who had a forced grin.

"*The Spirit of '76* is an oil painting by Archibald Willard. It's quite famous."

"Thank you, I never knew the name. I just know that

the guy playing the flute looks pretty worse for wear. And I remember he had a bandage around his head because I always thought, despite a head wound, he kept playing the flute." I stuck my leg out. "All I'm missing is the head bandage and flute, because with this bum knee and burnt face, I think I could pass as his double."

She stood on the porch blocking the entrance to the house.

"It's a fife," she said.

"Excuse me?" I looked from her to Toby, who was quieter than I'd ever experienced him.

"The instrument is a fife, not flute. It's part of the flute family, but a fife has a higher pitch and it's smaller. A fifer plays the fife, and they accompany drums in a military or marching band," she said.

"I did not know that," I said, wondering what Pandora's box I opened with a simple picture.

She took a step off the porch and positioned herself on the top step. "Two of my sisters and I dressed like *The Spirit of '76* for Halloween one year. I was the youngest, so I was the little drummer boy, and my oldest sister wore a white wig to look like the older drummer. My middle sister always had a darker complexion because she loved the sun, so she dressed like the fifer."

"I bet that was adorable," I said.

What looked like her best attempt at a smile appeared across her wrinkled face. "Our mother sewed uniforms to look exactly like that painting, and I remember my father took us to the country club where we were quite the hit.

We won first place in the costume contest."

"Oh, that's awesome," I said, and I meant it. I could imagine a much younger version of her dressed as a drummer boy. I bet her gray hair was once blonde. Then it hit me.

"Uh, you wouldn't still happen to have those costumes, would you?"

She turned toward the house and looked at the sole window on the second floor. "If memory serves me correctly, they're still in a box in the upstairs closet."

"Oh my gosh!" I tried to jump for joy, but my leg failed the attempt. "Do you think I could borrow one of the costumes? I mean, if you think they'd fit and if that's not too creepy."

"Is it for Halloween?" she asked.

I grinned in answer and held out my hand to formally introduce myself, but my hand wasn't met by hers. I lowered it quickly and felt my body flush with embarrassment. "Uh, yeah, hi, well as I said earlier, I'm Reese. Uh, actually Reese Pemberton and I'm the new general manager at the Historic Wyoming Point Resort here in Cheyenne. I believe I'm your new renter. Our corporate office"—I glanced at Toby—"sent us an email this morning or last night that our annual costume party will be attended by Governor Hawthorne, and well, it's kind of important that I have a costume. But with this knee, I wasn't sure what I would do."

"The general manager?" She raised a dark eyebrow.

"Yes, ma'am."

"Maybe I should have asked for higher rent."

I laughed, but she didn't.

"The corporate office coordinates the rental properties," Toby said. They were the first words he'd spoken since we arrived. "Reese may be the general manager, but corporate makes the final call on all finances."

I was about to call bullshit on his last statement, but something inside me silenced that impulse.

The woman focused intently on Toby. "Who are you?"

"I'm Toby Anderson, the chief engineer at the Point." He took a step toward her and extended his hand. "I've long admired the homes along Evans Avenue."

She quickly shook his hand and then wiped her hand on her dress without apology, like there was something dirty about my chief engineer that she had to rid herself of.

I was about to say something when she spoke.

"There are only four houses people admire on this side of Evans Avenue." Her chin jutted toward the four sisters' houses less than twenty yards from her porch. "People admire them for the same reason they admired the sisters— they present a nice appearance. But looks," she said, and eyed me, "aren't everything now, are they?"

Seriously? Did this old lady just slam me?

"You'll be needing these." She reached into the pocket of her dress and handed me a set a house keys.

Something smelled rank when I stepped onto the top stair beside her, and I prayed to God it wasn't my new home.

"*The Spirit of '76.*" Her eyes weren't dark, but rather gray like her hair. "I've always liked that painting. If any of the costumes fit, you are welcome to borrow them," she said.

"As I told the realtor who contacted me, I've never rented this house before, so it has a few of my belongings in it. I'd prefer that they remained as you find them."

"Of course." *Maybe that's why she's so protective. I'm her first renter.*

"Besides, there wouldn't be anything of interest to a young woman like yourself. It's just clothing and collectables from yesteryear. I had my grandson put most of the boxes in the basement cellar before he had to go away, but I think there may be a box on the top shelf in the bedroom closet. You'll find your costume there."

"Thank you."

She appeared ready to walk away without giving us a tour, or further interview and instructions, but then she gently placed her hand on my shoulder. She had a cool touch, but her voice was surprisingly warm.

"Don't let your knee or anything superficial keep you from living your life. If you think you'd make a great Revolutionary War soldier, then by all means, dress the part. But"—she made direct eye contact with me—"with your hair and healthy bosom, you'd make a great cigarette girl, and I know *that* costume's in there as well."

I knew it was a compliment, but I wanted to die. *Bosom? Oh my God. How could she tell I'm a size C in these scrubs? And who says bosom anymore?*

Thankfully, she glanced at Toby. "I'm sure it wouldn't be hard for you to put together a cigarette tray with a black silky strap that loops around her neck. You know what I'm talking about, don't you?"

"Yes, ma'am, I do. It's like a portable concession but for cigarettes and cigars, right?"

"That's right."

Her attention turned to me again. "Fill the box with candy and fun things to hand out. The box will cover your knee, but the dress…" She grinned. "The dress will distract even a gay man"—she nodded toward Toby, as if he were the gay man in question—"from your leg."

I was ready to rebuke her homophobia when Toby cut me off. "Thank you for all your help."

He didn't mince words or try to conceal the hardened expression he directed toward this woman he was more than happy to see leave.

"What's your name?" I said before she did.

"Mrs. Reed. Mrs. Ames Reed."

CHAPTER TWENTY-SIX

CODY

"Sheridan, this is *not at all* what we agreed upon." Dixon stood grumpily with his hands out like he was waiting for someone to tell him where to put them.

It was hard to take him seriously while he was sandwiched between two perfectly circular foil-covered cardboard pieces. Combined with his gray jeans and silver long-sleeved shirt, he shone like a new penny. Only with a Native American drawn in black ink on one side and an American bison on the other, the costume brought the Buffalo nickel to life. There were so many jokes racing through my mind, but for the sake of my sister, I swallowed my laughter and jabs.

"Dixon, buddy, you look fly," I said.

When he tilted his head, his costume rotated.

"Uh, buddy, you may not want to do that when we're at the party tonight."

"Oh, really, why's that?" He tilted again, and I bit the inside of my cheek.

"You look like you're going to roll away," I said, and then couldn't stop my own roll. "Now I know why the expression is 'turn on a dime' and not 'turn on a nickel,' because you have about as much poise and grace as a drunken elephant on a tightrope. And if you fall down as you're spinning, I'm calling tails."

"Nuh-uh, this is crap. Sheridan, you promised I'd stand out."

"Buddy, you do stand out," I said.

"Sweetheart, I said that you'd stand out *and* match your partner's buffalo theme, and you do." My sister could tame a wild boar.

"I'm a nickel!"

"You're a straight-up dime to me, baby." My sister cooed something in his ear before she kissed his cheek.

"Promise?" he said, and my sister smiled mischievously. I didn't even want to know what she offered my partner to have him wear the costume.

I shuddered at the thought. "Okay, okay, enough of that shit. We've got a costume party to go to."

I took one last look at myself in the olive-drab wool pants my sister managed to score at the army surplus store.

"They're a little snug," she said, tugging at the pant leg to straighten the seam. "But that's because you've got such a big ass."

"Thanks. I was actually feeling pretty good about myself."

"Ha. Serves you right, bubble butt." Dixon stood tall in his nickel costume, and I waved him away.

"What is that, your five cents?" I said with a grin. "I could go on like this all night."

"That's what she said," my sister chimed in, and we both laughed.

She quickly brushed a cloth over the buckles on my boots, which she'd also found at the surplus store.

"Peach, you really outdid yourself." I held out my hand while she stood and placed my granddaddy's helmet on my head. She tilted the helmet so it lay at an angle.

"The uniform may be olive drab, but little brother, those eyes of yours aren't." My sister was the first person to make me see past the oddity of a little black boy with green eyes to the beauty of it.

She placed an open pack of Lucky Strike cigarettes in the front pocket of my jacket and a chrome lighter in my other pocket.

"This is not an invitation for you to pick up a bad habit," she said. "I just saw these at the army store, and I had to have them to complete the look."

I took one last glimpse of myself in the full-length mirror, and I was one badass Buffalo Soldier.

"I can't go to this party as a nickel." Dixon's fair skin reddened.

"You better calm down, partner, because you're so red in the face folks are going to think you're trying to be both sides of the nickel, buffalo and Indian, and that would be rather insensitive and intolerant of you." I pushed up the sleeves of my granddaddy's army jacket, which made my dog tags rattle together. "Dixon, the last thing I need is to be called a racist by association and have a complaint filed against me. And just imagine that, a black man required to go to a racial tolerance seminar, all because his partner can't laugh at himself." I took a solid step toward him, reached between his nickel plating, and gripped his shoulder. "After all the hard work your wife put into making that one-of-a-kind costume, you need to get your head on straight, profusely thank my sister, and then let's head out to the party before I put my soldier's boot up your silver ass."

That's right, Buffalo Soldier in the heart of America ready to break some hearts.

CHAPTER TWENTY-SEVEN

REESE

"Oh. This is shorter than I imagined." I grabbed my cell phone, took a selfie in the full-length mirror that hung on the back of the upstairs bedroom door, and texted *Do I look like a hooker?* to the one person I knew would be honest.

KitKat: Red & black lace—all u need r ruby red lips & u've got the saloon-girl thing down.

Me: Not exactly the look I was going for.

I added a picture of the shiny black-lacquered room service tray of which Toby had looped a silky, black ribbon through the handles.

KitKat: Cigarette or candy girl. Cute

Me: Honest?

No sooner had the message flown away than my cell rang.

"Hey, KitKat," I said, answering the phone.

"How's my favorite sister?"

"I'm your only sister." I laughed.

"Reese's Pieces, what's with the knee brace?"

"The short version is I ran into a door or the door ran into me—I'm still not sure. Suffice to say, I ended up with a sprained ligament. Nothing I can't handle. Now, the cop who carried me to safety, not sure about him, but otherwise I'm good."

"Whoa, whoa, whoa. Cop? What cop? And he carried you?"

"Yeah, it's really not that big a deal. His name's Cody Pring—sounds like a potato chip. Anyway, he carried me after I hurt my knee outside the bar and then again up these stairs at the hotel when I got locked in the boiler room."

"Reese, what the hell? Maybe you should change costumes and go as Calamity Jane instead."

I laughed. "There're a lot of costumes stuffed in this plastic bin, but I didn't see any frontier costumes. Though didn't Calamity Jane and Wild Bill Hickok hang out?"

Now my sister laughed. "If knowing and respecting each other constitutes as hanging out, then yes, they hung."

"My hotel manager, my number two in charge, is William Goldstein, but he goes by the name Wild Bill."

"Really?"

"I knew that'd pique your love of history. And here's another little fun fact, Wild Bill is a Native American."

"With Jewish ties?"

"Yup. When he took me on a tour of the hotel, I asked him about his last name and he told me his parents were the ultimate marriage of the tribes."

"When someone says they are a 'member of the tribe' it means they're Jewish," my older sister said.

"Wow. Thanks for clarifying that for me, KitKat. I wouldn't have been able to piece that together."

"Well, your PhD is in the put-me-to-sleep physics field and not keep-me-awake-with-vivid-scary-stories forensics."

"You're a brat. And you didn't know that tribe reference from forensics, but your boring interest in history. Talk about instant yawn fest." Her laughter was a touchstone to our childhood. "I miss you, KitKat."

"I miss you too, Reese's Pieces."

"I'm supposed to be a cigarette girl," I said, glancing in the mirror. "I don't know if you could see my shoes, but I'm wearing my red peep-toe pumps."

"Those are pretty high, aren't they?"

I shrugged. "The governor's going to be at the hotel. I can't be in boring flats. Besides"—I turned sideways and liked how the higher heel added about three inches to my leg—"I plan on standing in the corner all night with my bum leg bent like I'm flirting." I ran my hand along the black fishnet stockings that clipped to a red satin garter belt. "I'm wearing that bra and garter set we bought at that lingerie store that was going out of business."

"Reese, it's not a bra. It's two open cups your breasts sit on like a shelf."

I nodded and glided my hand down the front of the red satin corset that hugged my body and brought attention to what Mrs. Reed referred to as my healthy bosom.

"Well, that bra's the only strapless one I could find in all my crap, and it works pretty damn nicely. Besides, nothing will draw attention away from my knee like a healthy rack and black fishnet stockings."

"Or draw more attention to it," my sister said.

"No, sadly, what draws the most attention is my red face."

"Yeah, I wasn't going to say anything, but what the hell? Did you fall asleep in the sun? Does Wyoming even have sun in October?"

I needed to laugh. "I didn't fall asleep in the sun, which we do have. Hell, the sun's been out so much, we haven't even had snow yet. Although I don't think the two cancel each other out, but I'm a So Cal girl, what the hell do I know about snow?" I chuckled. "Anyway, about my face—I dozed off in the boiler room, and I think all the steam zapped me. I also have these weird bruises on my arms. I must have banged into something." I glanced at my forearms. I'd covered them with makeup and dusting powder, which helped but didn't completely erase the discoloration.

"Did you see someone about your face? It looks pretty red."

"Yeah, I went to the hospital last night for my face, and Cody the cop thought I had been raped."

"What?" Her voice noticeably rose.

"Katherine, I'm okay. I wasn't raped. But when Cody found me in my underwear—and not the good stuff—and jog bra and heard me yelling, he—"

"Did the right thing."

"Exactly. Thankfully, the sexual assault nurse wasn't as

alarmed when she saw me. She checked me out and knew nothing had happened, so I didn't have to go through a full exam."

"Oh, Reese, I'm sorry."

I swallowed. "It was a really shitty night, and I had this horrible nightmare, that's why I screamed. But I wasn't hurt by anyone—just my subconscious."

"You've always had an overactive imagination."

"I know, and that's all it was. But I was pretty shaken. I wanted to quit, I even told Wild Bill I was through, but"—I took a look at myself in the mirror—"I was overtired, hungry, and wasn't thinking clearly."

"And you are with this costume?" Her voice was playful, but I knew my older sister was looking out for me.

"Ah, KitKat, don't be a hater. I want to have fun. Hell, I *need* to have fun. So tonight, I'm going for that timeless, yet romantically seductive look. Did you see my hair? After I washed it, I pinned big strands with bobby pins and then blasted it with the hair dryer. When I removed the bobby pins, my hair unwound into large waves."

"I *love* how you created a deep part and let your hair naturally fall into place. Daddy always said your hair was your crowning glory. And just so you know, in case anyone asks, what you did to your hair is called pin curls," she said. "It's actually a thing."

"Whatever. I googled hairstyles of the forties and figured I could do this. Then I spritzed the hell out of it with hair spray. I told you, I'm going for a classy, yet showy look."

"Well, actually," her voice shifted, "historically, cigarette girls were hired to flirt with customers and serve as eye candy."

I glanced at the layers of black lace tulle that puffed out my red skirt and smiled. "Eye candy, huh?"

"Yes, Reese, and from the pic you texted, no one's going to be interested in whatever you're offering on that tray."

"I'm good with that."

My sister laughed. "You're such a goof. How's life in Wyoming treating you anyway?"

"It's been a bit bumpy, but I got the keys today to the rental home corporate lined up." I glanced at the rose-accented cream wallpaper that covered the walls in the master bedroom. "It's really cute. Not much curb appeal— simple red brick siding, but the inside is actually sweet. Hardwood floors, pink-tiled bathroom with chrome fixtures, and different floral wallpaper on nearly every wall in the house. The owner's never rented the house, and it pretty much looks untouched by time. The box of costumes was in great shape. The lighting kind of sucks. There's floor lamps in every room, and it's only two bedrooms. I guess they didn't believe in big families. Or all the kids stayed in one room. I don't know."

"How's the kitchen?"

This made me burst out laughing. "A lot of cupboards? I barely set foot in it. You know the only thing a kitchen's good for is to toss the mail and keep a dead plant."

"You are eating, right?"

"Had a breakfast burrito today."

"Good girl."

I grinned. "Thank you." I paused, and for a moment, Campbell flashed across my mind. I shook my head, erasing the nightmare. "I so want to talk with you, there's still so much to catch up on, but I've got to get to the hotel. My staff's been amazing and set everything up for me. My engineer even went to every liquor store in Cheyenne and bought every bubblegum cigar and box of candy cigarettes he could find. But at some point, I've literally got to strap on the cigarette tray and serve as eye candy at the party. It's about all I can do with this knee." I nervously laughed and looked at myself in the mirror. "Oh, KitKat, what was I thinking?"

"You were thinking that you were harkening back the not-quite-so-good old days when women's rights and the Surgeon General's warning didn't exist."

I giggled.

"Reese, you deserve to have a night to be your goofy self. So go have fun, little sister. Happy Halloween! Go make some new memories."

CHAPTER TWENTY-EIGHT

CODY

The tennis court was clear of debris, water, and other remnants, like leaves, that normally gathered in the corners. The net was gone and the wind screens that were attached to the rooftop fence system had also been removed, replaced by a heavy tarp that billowed in the wind.

White lights were strung across the dark tarp to look like twinkling stars across a Wyoming sky. A wooden dance floor covered the surface of the hard court. Four heat lamps with pumpkins, gourds, and logs lying at their base were stationed in the corners of the court, keeping the autumn chill at bay.

A buffet station was positioned beside a portable bar. The banquet servers and bartender were dressed in black tuxedos, white shirts, and orange bow ties. They looked professional and festive.

A western band was practicing their set list on the

elevated stage centered in front of the dance floor. The doors to the rooftop party opened in thirty minutes, and already the sweet sound of country music could be heard across Cheyenne. Or so my engineer had bragged when I arrived. Round eight and ten top tables were positioned around the dance floor. Boughs of harvest leaves and additional lights were draped across the roof of the enclosed courts.

The crystal centerpieces glinted in the warm candlelight. The tennis court had been transformed into an enchanted, autumnal celebration. I expected fairies to magically appear and woodland creatures to pop out from behind the logs positioned beside the heat lamps. Instead, *he* appeared.

In a military jacket, dingy white T-shirt, and pants that hugged his thighs, with dog tags that swayed against his broad chest when he approached, he had this sleek, slightly beat-up look that was absolutely sexy. When he removed his helmet and tucked it beneath his arm, I was sure my good knee would give out.

"A real cheesy pickup line would be to ask your sign, but judging by your costume, I'm guessing that would be Cancer." A satisfied smile crossed his face.

"You really are an idiot," I said without breaking a smile. "If you *just* hadn't opened your mouth." I'd turned to walk away when he reached for me. His touch sent my heart racing. Maybe it was the costume, but I played it cool. *How far will you go to have me?*

"Listen, doll, what's a soldier got to do for a pack of smokes?"

***

CODY

She smiled at me over her shoulder and waves of red hair cascaded down her back. Something inside of me knew I'd never be able to keep this woman at arm's length. *What is it about this redhead? Seriously? Does it really matter?* In fishnet stockings and nothing more than a corset and short skirt, she burned with desire. Or maybe I did. I couldn't think straight around her.

Her hazel eyes flashed to the single chevron on my shoulder.

"Private, who's your CO?"

Private? Commanding Officer? Impressive. But from the spark in her eyes, she wanted to do more than impress me with her military knowledge. She wanted to play. And I was more than game.

"Wyman. General Wyman." My hand was still on her wrist. She glanced at my hand and then into my eyes, and I swore time stood still. I wasn't on assignment. The governor wasn't two floors down preparing for the costume ball, my partner wasn't standing beneath the heat lamp looking like his silver costume could double as a thermal conductor, and I wasn't a detective. I was a single guy talking to what I hoped was a single gal.

"And you are?" That one reddish eyebrow rose, and my pants got even tighter.

"Private Pring on a training holiday."

Even though her face was the color of lobster, the rest of her skin was alabaster—like it had never been touched. "And you chose the Point for your free day off?"

"Heard about the party and the women. I was told they could make a soldier forget."

"Soldier, all I've got are cigarettes and cigars. If that'll help you forget, then drop your dime in my box."

"Is that what they're calling it now?"

Her lips curved into a smile, her red face flushed, and she pivoted on the nastiest red shoes I'd ever seen as she tried to free herself from me. But I wasn't about to let go. "Doll, where you going?"

The bassist struck a strutting groove, accompanied by a slinky guitar riff, and I knew the song. When the lead singer began Chase Bryant's "Little Bit of You," I wanted more than just a little bit of her. The girl was fine. I gently tugged her wrist, pulling her toward me. I carefully removed her cigarette tray, placed it on a table beside my helmet, and led her to the dance floor.

"Bring it close." I wrapped my hand around her waist and swayed to the music.

She feigned disinterest, looking everywhere but at me. When I began to sing in her ear, her body relaxed into me, her eyes sparkled, and when her hand gently stroked the side of my face, I forgot the next lyric.

"I like the stubble," she said.

"I'll never shave again."

Her laughter was as beautiful as she was. The beat to the music picked up tempo, and I instinctively swung her out.

Fuck. Her knee.

But even with a brace hugging her knee, Reese played along. Her skirt kicked up and her long legs sashayed seductively back to me. Her bare shoulders that rolled, keeping rhythm with the music, were almost as enticing as her legs. Alone on the dance floor, with her in my arms, she came alive to the song's foot-tapping, romantic beat. With the lights twinkling and the sweet scent of lavender, rose, and jasmine that clung to her shoulders, I didn't want the song to ever end. But it did, and then the lead singer spoke directly to Reese.

"Wild Bill told me you've had a rough welcome to Wyoming. So, before the doors open, we wanted to bring the party to you," he said.

Reese tilted her head, and her hair swayed across her shoulder. "Thank you."

He glanced at someone behind us. I turned, and Wild Bill stood beside Millie.

"Oh, they're here together." Reese waved at them.

"All right, we've got one more song for you, and we're kicking it off old-school," the singer said.

The band struck a different chord and the slow, steady beat of a blues guitar accompanied by the smooth-edged vocals of the Vaughan Brothers' "Tick Tock" filled the rooftop.

A slower, seductive beat. I pressed Reese into me and slowly ground against her. I didn't care who on the rooftop saw or what they thought. After the harrowing night I'd had with a crazy old, gun-toting rich bitch, tortured dog, and then finding a terrified Reese, this was our time.

I sang in her ear, and she rocked against me and sang along.

"You're here because of the governor," she said when the music began to fade.

"I am."

"Long night?"

"I sure hope so," I said, and the smile on her face made me want to grab her hand and run off with her. Instead, I gently, politely pecked her cheek with a chaste kiss. "Thank you for the dances."

Her hand softy cupped my cheek as her face moved toward mine. Her lips were warm, inviting, and when her tongue tenderly made its way into my mouth, I pressed into her. Our lips met in a very hot, very passionate kiss. She tasted sweet, but her kiss wasn't. It was a kiss that got my hormones racing with one thought—when could I get her alone.

CHAPTER **TWENTY-NINE**

REESE

Zavi appeared beside me, dressed as Zorro, and handed me a cold craft beer. "Who's the guy?"

I took a sip and rolled my shoulder playfully. "What guy?"

"Sure." Zavi's mask made his brown eyes look darker. "There's two black guys at this party—me and army man—and from the looks of it, you're ready to enlist."

I laughed. "That's Detective Cody Pring. Or Private Pring, depends on where we are."

Zavi tapped the tip of his sword on the dance floor. "So why are you standing here while he's over there?"

I shrugged and took another sip. The autumn ale was smooth and rich, and the hint of pumpkin was delicious. "I don't know? We both have jobs to do. And the governor's here."

"The governor is fine. Look at him. He's surrounded by

people, and thanks to all the banquet servers on duty, his glass hasn't gone empty once," Zavi said.

"Yes, but neither of us can just leave with Wyoming's top official on property," I said.

"Who said anything about leaving?"

I stared at him. "What are you talking about?"

"I know Wild Bill gave you a *full* tour of the property, so I'm sure he showed you the room behind the library."

"Oh, yeah." I nodded. "It leads, or rather, led to the old tunnel system. That was so weird. I thought the rumors that the hotel had a bordello were just that: rumors. But apparently the tunnel system extends to the capitol building, where senators and congressmen would access the hotel without anyone knowing."

"True story."

"Talk about the wild west. When Wild Bill hit the bookcase with his palm, I didn't know what he was doing. But then the bookcase slid across to this hallway. Crazy." I took a longer sip.

"What's crazy is not taking advantage of the love lounge."

"The what?" I almost choked on my IPA.

"Listen, it's the not-so-secret chamber, and sometimes the staff likes to hang out. That's why it has artwork on the walls, condoms in the end table.... We've all left our mark."

"Is that so?"

He grinned. "Yes, ma'am. And since housekeeping regularly services the private suite, it's always well-maintained. But you know that. You saw it."

"The things I learn after a few beers."

"Secret tunnels and hidden rooms aren't always scary. Sometimes, they're just fun." Zavi tapped his sword on the covered court. "And, boss, you need to have some fun. Wild Bill and Toby didn't call everyone on staff to make this party a hit for the governor. They did it for you." He turned to face me and his black cape swirled behind him. "I heard about you getting stuck in the boiler room. That sucks. All we want is for you to have a good time here. No one wants you to leave."

I touched his shoulder. "Zavi, I'm not going anywhere. And it's not your job to ensure I have a good time." I thought about corporate's plans to sell the property in the spring. "I'm not a quitter." *Corporate may be, but I'm not.* "I'm here to see this through."

Zavi reached over my head and lifted the cigarette tray off my shoulders. He was not nearly as smooth as Cody, but the gesture was nonetheless thoughtful and a bit confusing.

"Whatcha doing?" I asked, when he set my tray on a chair.

Zavi flashed a smile and swept his cape dramatically. "Dance! You must dance!"

I thought about my sister and creating new memories. "Okay, I will."

I walked toward Cody, who stood beside a man dressed in silver. When I got closer, I realized it was his partner.

"It's Dixon, right?" I said when I reached them.

"That's correct, Ms. Pemberton."

I laughed. "It's Reese. And I wanted to thank you for

your help last night."

"Cody did all the work," he said, deflecting to his partner, who grinned.

"I always do all the work," Cody said.

Dixon rolled his eyes. "Sure, whatever."

"I like your costume." I glanced at the backside. "A Buffalo nickel. That's clever."

Dixon smiled proudly. "My wife made it for me."

"What a great idea. You'll have to enter the costume contest," I said.

He adamantly shook his head. "No, probably not a good idea since we're on the job, but thanks."

I turned my focus to Cody. "Private, would you like to dance?"

He grinned, passed his helmet to his partner, and took my hand. When we were on the dance floor, I slipped naturally into his arms. In my higher heels, I was taller, but not tall enough to be eye to eye with him or have his ear, so I did the next best thing. I draped my arm around his neck and gently pulled him toward me.

"Get me out of here," I whispered in his ear.

He pulled back and looked at me. "For real?"

I slowly nodded. He took my hand and led me toward the elevator.

CHAPTER **THIRTY**

CODY

"Since I can't leave the property, and I can't drink while I'm on duty"—I led Reese toward the downstairs bar—"let me buy you a drink."

Her hair slowly swept across her shoulders as she shook her head. "No."

"Oh-kay." I glanced around the hotel lobby. "Well, we could sit in the… I think it's a parlor, right?"

Her finger swung back and forth seductively.

"No, it's not a parlor, or no to sitting there?"

She took my hand and led me to the only public stairs in the hotel, which led to the second floor. I knew this because Dixon and I had canvassed the hotel and blueprints of it before the governor arrived. What I didn't know was that the bookcase in the second-floor library was apparently built on tracks in the floor and slid open with the right touch. And there was no doubt in my mind that Reese had the right touch.

"And what do we have here?" I reached into the back waistband of my pants for my Glock.

Her eyes focused on my gun—and not the one that throbbed in my pants.

"This wasn't in the blueprints we were given," I said.

"I don't think it's on the blueprints. I forgot about it until Zavi reminded me. It leads to a room, complete with a fireplace. I don't think it's operable anymore, and I wouldn't want to test it, but the room was built for dignitaries like the governor who wanted to use the *other* amenities the hotel offered in the early 1900s."

"Other amenities?" I glanced at her.

"Uh, the oldest profession?"

"So they had a bakery, you say? And let me guess, the only item on the menu was a collection of tarts."

Reese's head tilted back and she laughed. "Exactly."

I grabbed the flashlight clipped to the side of my belt and shone the light into the narrow passageway. "I've got to admit I don't think you're ever too old or too jaded to think secret passageways are the coolest thing ever."

Her eyes lit with excitement. "So you're not scared?"

"Scared." I grunted. "I'm not scared. Who said anything about being scared?"

She chuckled and grabbed my forearm, which I instantly flexed. "Good to know." Her eyebrow rose. "This can be our own escape from the world—for just a little bit. I'm told it has *everything* you'd need for a little R&R."

"Everything?"

A devil-may-care grin crossed her face. "Everything."

Even if I was a little freaked out by the dank, dark hallway and chamber hidden behind the wall, I sure as shit wasn't going to show it. I grabbed my work phone and texted Dixon.

Me: Taking thirty

I really wanted more time with this redhead who elevated my flirting—and just about everything else.

The passageway led to a room that wasn't makeshift. It was actually framed with a locking door and tongue-and-groove pinewood that lined the walls and ceiling. A freestanding electric fireplace was in the corner, which made me chuckle.

"Uh, Reese, that's an electric fireplace."

"I know, we probably shouldn't burn anything in it," she said, and I grinned.

"Oh, you are from California. An electric fireplace doesn't use logs, it uses electricity."

She still seemed confused.

"You plug it in, turn on a switch, and get fake flames that kick out heat."

"Oh." Her mouth fell open. "I didn't know that."

"Stick with me, doll." I reverted back to my army role.

She responded by sitting in the corner on the ample leather couch, crossing her legs and letting her long gams flash in my direction.

"How's your knee?" I didn't want to waste time talking about her knee or anything, but I was raised to be a gentleman. So even when my desire wanted to ignore my upbringing, I didn't allow it.

"I don't know. Why don't you check it for me?"

When I locked gazes with her, her hazel eyes looked a little sleepy. I knew she wasn't ready for a nap, but she was ready for bed. She had a restful, dreamy look about her that craved naked escapism, and I wasn't about to disappoint.

I carefully tore apart the two Velcro straps that held her knee brace in place. The brace fell to the floor and her fishnet-covered knee bent toward me. It wasn't as badly swollen as before. Still, I gently massaged it as my hand slowly made its way along the inside of her thigh.

I stopped short and raised my brows. "Are you wearing a garter?"

She gazed downward at me through her long, dark lashes. Her come-hither look sent a signal straight to my cock, which pulsed hard.

She slowly inched off her skirt, and beneath the lace was more lace. *Sexy.* Red silky straps held her fishnet stockings attached to a high-waist, lacy, scallop-edged garter. A tiny pair of panties barely covered her patch. I couldn't tell if she had hardwood, full carpet, or a landing strip. I was hoping for hardwood. Something about a naked pussy drove me nuts. My hand reached behind her and dug into her fleshy ass.

"A thong and garter. You're the best-kept secret at this hotel."

The corners of her mouth turned upward into a beautiful smile. "Thank you, Private. And perhaps you could help?" She turned, revealing the back of her corset. A row of tiny buttons traced her spine. I slowly began unbuttoning her. When the final button was unfastened, she turned back to me and slowly pulled away the corset.

Her breasts were instantly exposed. Plump breasts with erect cherry-red nipples were cradled on the cups of her bra. She slowly stood, and in a garter and thong, with full, supple breasts poking out, everything about her teased and tantalized. She looked like a showgirl. She pushed off my jacket and slid her hands beneath my T-shirt, feeling my chest. Her hand warmed me. I pulled off my T-shirt, and she pressed her tits against me.

I held her plump ass and slowly slid my finger along the thong that rode between her cheeks. Her body responded, and she wrapped her leg around mine and pressed into me. My cock rose to meet her. I unhooked my gun belt and laid it on the table beside the couch. She fumbled with the button on my wool pants. I held her wrist, unhooked my pants with one hand, and let them fall as far as they would. My cock stopped most of the progress. I released her and bent down to unbuckle my boots and toss them aside. My pants fell to the floor, and I kicked them off. But before I could straighten, her red heel rose and planted itself on my thigh. She gently pressed into me, and my desire heightened. As I knelt with my arms stretched toward her, I felt like Atlas, and she was my world.

I didn't know what it was about this redhead, but being with her didn't feel like I was running away. It actually felt like I was running toward something. But I had to be sure.

"I don't want just a random hookup." The words blurted

from my mouth.

She gazed down at me and grinned. "Private Pring, is that all you think this is?"

With her heel pressed into my thigh, I wanted nothing more than to get things going and going good, but something inside me wasn't convinced. "I don't know what this is."

Her eyes softened. "Cody, I usually don't *do* this." She paused. "But I also usually don't get slammed into by a bar door while I'm jogging, and then get stuck in a boiler room in the same night—and rescued by the same man."

I felt my face burn with a mixture of embarrassment and pride.

"So, this is new for me too," she said. "But I thought it was time to break free, have some fun, and you were my first choice." She giggled. "Truth be told, you were my only choice, so I'm *really* glad you didn't refuse me my whimsy."

"Refuse you? Reese, I could live to be a hundred and I wouldn't be able to refuse you anything."

I couldn't tell if she was shocked in a good or bad way. I opted to shut up, change gears, and nibble on the inside of her thigh while my tongue trailed toward her clit. Heat radiated off her panties when I pushed the silky material aside and tongued her. A small strip of hair made me glad she hadn't shaved it off. Her hands grabbed the sides of my head and pressed my mouth further into her. The way her lips swelled and the juice flowed so readily was primal. It was a signal to my cock that she wasn't just ready for me, she wanted me.

But I wasn't ready. Not until I heard the sweet echo of

her orgasm. My tongue did a tango against her clit, moving it back and forth, backing off, and before I gently charged toward it, I reached up and tautly held her nipple. She gasped and then pressed her clit toward my lips. I watched her reaction as I suckled on it. Her mouth opened like she was about to roar. And when I ran my tongue along her swollen lips and dipped inside her sweet wetness, the sound she emitted was raw, primitive, and sexier than anything I'd ever heard.

"Yes. Right. There."

My hand remained clamped on her nipple, and my tongue continued to play hide-and-seek with her clit. I'd rush it, then back off, then rush it again. It was a pace that sent her to a fevered pitch of euphoria.

"Oh my God," she cried.

She threw her head back and sweat beaded between her breasts, but I didn't stop. I wouldn't, not until she had another orgasm. There was nothing composed about me or what I was doing. I operated from lust, passion, and point of climax. I wanted her to have an eyes-open, screaming orgasm she'd never forget.

I had less than thirty minutes, and I wanted to taste and feel every part of her. I released her nipple, looped my arm under knee, and turned her around.

"Kneel. I mean, if you can."

"Oh, I can," she said. And from the look in her eyes, I knew, bum knee or not, she was more than game for adventure.

I brought her arms up and placed them against the wall

while she knelt on the couch. I spread her legs apart and frisked every curve, dip, and crevice of her body with my hands. I pressed my shoulder into her back as my hand felt along the seam of her fishnet stockings that stopped short of her ass. I grabbed my Leatherman tool from my belt, flipped it open, and placed the blade against the side of her panty and cut. I did the same with the other side, and her panties dropped between us on the couch. Her red lace garter belt hugged her waist, and nothing stood in my way of what I desired most.

I knelt on the floor in front of the couch and slowly licked her cheeks. Her body tensed. I repeated, increasing my rhythm until she surrendered to the sensation of my tongue on her sensitive skin. I parted her ass and buried my mouth inside her while my finger reached beneath her and fingered her. She dripped with wetness that I slathered on the shaft of my cock.

"Condoms. Where are they?" I kept my tone sharp and direct, and she responded by pointing toward the side table. I opened the drawer, and a large box of Magnum condoms was tucked inside. I grabbed a packet, ripped it open with my teeth, and placed it on my cock.

I stood behind her and placed the tip of my cock between her legs. When she didn't stop me and instead pushed against me, I moved toward her wetness.

Her hands remained pressed against the wall, and I remained pressed against the edge of entry.

"Am I hurting you?"

She looked over her shoulder, and her eyes were dark

with desire. "Fuck me."

Despite her command and her groans that filled the room, I slowly moved my cock toward her pussy. There was a moment when I either had to push forward or back off.

She turned again, and this time her eyes flashed and her tone was sharp. "Private, are you man enough to fuck me, or do I need to get someone else to do the job for you?"

"No, ma'am." My response was instinctive to her authority. I wasn't in charge. *Who am I kidding?* I may have the cock, but she directed every move I made. And the more she dominated the situation, the more I thought I wanted her to.

"Okay then, Private, take your big cock and fuck me—hard. And if by some miracle you don't prematurely lose your load, then you can fuck me again. Understood?"

My cock throbbed, and it was a miracle I hadn't lost my load. Still, I took my time entering her, and as soon as I did, I had to slow my roll or I'd lose it altogether. But she didn't know slow. She rocked back and forth against my cock.

I had to take charge or face humiliation. I grabbed her hips, thrust into her, and took control. She cooed and practically purred.

"That's right."

I moved in and out of her with a burning desire only she could quench. Her cries filled the room. I pulled out and flipped her around so her breasts faced me.

"I want your tits. Your big nipples." I tugged on one with my teeth, pulling it to the pressure point and then backing off. Taking her to the tipping point was tested when she mounted me. She hopped on my cock, held onto my shoulders, wrapped her legs around me, and rode me like a rented mule. With her nipple between my teeth and her other breast bouncing, she made me feel like a man. And when I was with Reese, I wanted to be that guy. That guy who did the right thing and was man enough to let down his guard so a beautiful woman like this felt safe and secure to open herself to me. My cock slid in and out of her wetness. I released her nipple and looked at her.

"I'm not sure how much longer I can last," I said.

The corners of her mouth drooped slightly downward—not a full-on pout, but enough to mimic a frown and inspire me to get a grip. The woman was insatiable. Or maybe she hadn't ever been properly fucked. Either way, I had to cowboy up and fuck her proper.

But when her breasts continued to bounce, teasing me, taunting me, and her pussy maintained a tight choke hold around my cock, I wasn't sure I'd last. Everything about her was a perfect fit. I wanted to last forever, but I'd settle for lasting another five minutes.

"I'm sorry you can't last," she said. "I thought I picked a man—not a boy."

She's good. Her jibe spurred me and hardened my cock until I thought my foreskin would tear. Her nails dug into my shoulders, and her stockinged legs wrapped around my waist. I nipped her nipple with my teeth, and she screamed with delight.

"Hell yes, Private. More. Now!"

I pinched her other nipple and gave a little nip to her tit.

I quickly discovered Reese liked a little bit of pain with her pleasure. And as long as I didn't draw blood, I was down. In turn, her heels dug into my ass, and together the pleasure and pain were in sync. Big time.

Her mouth found mine, and the tip of her tongue played with me, and I imagined it on the head of my cock. This beautiful redhead was driving me crazy with pleasure.

She ground hard on me. Her sexuality was as open as her passion that knew no bounds.

"Cody."

It was the first time she called my name.

"I want you," she cooed.

Her voice was a soft directive to my heart. Her desire for pleasure and for me to be in charge brought out my best. I leaned into her, burrowing my cock into her slippery, swollen pussy. She arched, and I held the small of her back. She screamed, and warmth oozed over my cock. *That's three.* I no longer had to wait.

"I'll teach you to sass me." I pulled out and turned her around. "Grab the back of the couch, spread your legs, and shut. The. Fuck. Up."

My cock had a full load ready to discharge. I slowly slipped into her pussy, and the tightness from entering her from behind was beyond my ability to maintain control. But I grabbed her hips and got three long, deep, penetrating strokes into her hot, tight little pussy before I erupted deep inside her.

No sooner had I collapsed on top of her than my cell phone buzzed on the end table.

"I think my thirty went into sixty," I said into her velvety hair.

Her lips found mine and tenderly kissed me. "No regrets."

"With you?" I said. "Never."

CHAPTER **THIRTY-ONE**

REESE

"You go ahead, I'll clean up."

Cody shook his head. "Yeah, I don't like the idea of leaving you behind."

"Listen, soldier, I'm fine. Besides, I want to bask in the afterglow a little while longer." I smiled. "And stash the evidence of our playtime."

A sheepish grin filled his masculine face. "Uh, sorry about your panties."

"I'm not."

Cody waited. His sense of duty was honorable, but more than that, it endeared him to me in a way I couldn't explain. When I was with him, I knew he had my best interests at heart. Hell, the man was all heart.

"Hey," I said, and eyes I could get lost into locked on to mine. "Are we good? I mean, I wanted this and I think you did too?"

"Definitely." He stood with his jacket slung over his shoulder, and if it were at all possible, he looked even sexier. "Just so we're clear—I'm not into a one and done with you."

I grinned. "Really?'

"Reese, you're not a one-and-done kind of girl. Not for me."

I didn't know what to say. It felt like my whole body lit up into a smile.

"So listen," he said, "if you're not back to the rooftop by the time the party ends, I'm coming back to find you."

"That's my plan," I said with a wink.

He laughed.

"Can you find your way back? To the library?" I asked.

"Yes. The better question is, can you?"

"Absolutely, and if by some dumb luck I get stuck, I'm not in the boiler room. Zavi was right, this is a little love lounge."

"Love lounge?" The green in his eyes sparkled in the soft light.

I shrugged. "Not my idea, but it is catchy. I was also told that housekeeping services the suite just like a regular guest room, so at least it's clean."

"Wasn't worried about it." Cody leaned over and kissed me. "See you later?"

I smiled. "I'd like that."

He looked at me and any embarrassment that may have wanted to linger, vanished. Cody wasn't judging me, so why should I?

"Uh, so, maybe we could get breakfast?" This could go one of two ways—either he's in or it was a one-time thing.

"Definitely breakfast," he said, and cupped my face. His lips lingered on mine as we kissed, which showed me Cody wasn't a one-time thing. As he walked away, I couldn't have felt happier.

After he left, I quickly put the minisuite and myself back together. Beneath the end table was a wicker basket filled with everything we offered at the front desk for guests who arrived unexpectedly due to a snowstorm and required overnight essentials. There was a package of makeup remover sheets, body spray, deodorant, toothbrush, toothpaste, comb, and feminine hygiene products. It had everything I needed after an off-the-charts sexcapade.

I stashed my ripped panties in the back of my skirt that my corset covered. I lay on the couch and elevated my knee with a pillow. *Just five minutes.* I still wasn't caught up on sleep. And there was something about this private suite that relaxed me. Or maybe it was the three orgasms Cody gave me. The man was a dreamy, steamy sex machine. I closed my eyes, and the buzz of a trumpet and the brilliant flare of a brass trombone echoed through the walls. *Must be the band.* The singer's voice sounded different, though.

The melody was jazzy, but that couldn't be right. Wild Bill hired a country band. Still, the music beat through the walls. I drifted off to the sound of his voice in my ear.

"What a doll." Campbell stood to the side while Ella sat for the photo. She looked different. Older. And her hair was shorter.

"You're together," I said when Campbell looked at me. His dark eyes brightened.

"There's much to our story you don't know," he said.

"Tell me."

"Watch."

"Watch what?" I leaned toward him, but suddenly his attention shifted.

"Why am I doing this?" Ella asked Campbell while the photographer reloaded his camera with film.

"I told you in my letter," he said.

Ella looked at her hands in her lap. "You send me a lot of letters and packages when you're away on training missions. Your last package had the most beautiful set of ivory hairpins, and you mentioned good news."

"Okay," the photographer said. His assistant tucked a lock of Ella's bobbed black hair behind her ear and straightened the gray wool dress she wore. It had a modest V-neck and slender bodice that hugged her thin frame. A narrow black belt gathered her twenty-one-inch waist and pronounced the patterned skirt cut in flared panels that billowed out beneath her. Black satin sandals with lacy straps wrapped up her willowy legs.

"Why don't you stand for this one," the photographer said. "Turn sideways toward me."

Ella stood and shifted in Campbell's direction while the photographer snapped her picture.

"Beautiful," the photographer said.

Campbell shook his head.

"What?" she asked.

"You're missing something." Campbell walked to her. He reached into his pocket and withdrew a single strand of pearls that he gently draped around her neck. He fastened the gold clasp.

"Oh, Campbell." She gently touched the delicate gems. "They're magnificent."

"Nothing's too good for you, doll."

She smiled and the photographer adjusted his lighting.

"What was your news?" she asked.

"Wait," he said.

She rolled her eyes. "I have. I've waited a year."

She held her breath, certain he had finally passed his aircraft training and the necessary papers had been filed for him to take part in one overseas mission. After the mission, he'd be free and they could truly be together. He'd be through with the military, and they wouldn't be separated anymore.

"Actually, we have to push the wedding back by a month."

"That's the good news? Another month?" The light in Ella's violet eyes dimmed, and her smile faded. Another month seemed unimaginable, in light of her father. When Ella's father discovered his youngest daughter had been dating a man twelve years her senior, he hadn't approved. He made life for Ella unbearable.

Ella turned away from Campbell and brushed her cheek on her shoulder to hide her disappointment.

The photographer clicked the camera exactly as Ella looked lost in thought—or perhaps just lost.

The room suddenly faded to black, and Campbell appeared beside me on the couch.

"Come with me." He reached for my hand and led me from the private suite, down a narrow passageway that led to a back staircase.

"Where are we going?" I asked.

"To our suite."

"Our suite? I don't understand." I glanced at my shoes. "I can't climb stairs in these heels. I'll hurt my knee." He bent and unbuckled my shoes and placed them beside the wall in the passageway.

I followed behind in my stockings as we ascended an unfamiliar flight of stairs that opened to the sixth floor. The door to suite 632 was ajar. "I was supposed to stay there," I said, looking around.

Campbell pointed toward the small desk in front of the window where Ella sat. He stood beside her.

"What do you think of the photographer's proof sheet?" She handed him a glossy black-and-white photo sheet.

"Doll, you have the most beautiful neck. Look at those features, and the wave in your beautiful black hair brings out the violet in your eyes. I don't know what you're doing with an old goat like me."

She slightly smiled.

"I want that one to take with me." He pointed to the photo where she hadn't smiled. The photo that was taken after he told her they had to wait another month to be married. Her gaze was far off, as if in a dream.

"The photographer probably won't have them ready

before you leave," she said.

"Okay then." Campbell withdrew a small pocketknife from his pants, laid the photo sheet on the desk, and cut out the picture. He closed his knife and grabbed the pen in his front pocket. On the back of the photograph he wrote something.*

They were too far away, I couldn't see what he wrote, but when Ella did, she laughed.

"*I'll be back before you know it," he said, and suddenly the laughter between them dulled. More time away brought more uncertainty for Ella.*

I walked toward the desk, but they suddenly vanished. I sat in the chair, and the seat was still warm.

The door to the room swung open, and Ella placed a single piece of luggage beside the queen-sized bed.

Her bobbed hair was curled and pinned back in long, elegant spirals. She wore a simple ivory-colored dress, and in its simplicity, she absolutely shone. The pearls draped around her neck were a beautiful finishing touch. A short veil lay on top of her pillbox hat.

Oh my gosh, it's their wedding day! My stomach stirred with excitement.

"*Hello, doll." Campbell stood in the doorway to the suite.*

"*Hello, husband." Ella smiled at the man twelve years her senior. For more than a year they had snuck around, booking the same suite at the same hotel to be together until she turned eighteen and no longer needed her father's permission to marry the man she loved. Now she had. And she didn't have a care in the world.*

"Where's your bag?" She opened the closet and placed her luggage inside. He shut the room door and stood before her empty-handed.

"I can't stay," he replied quietly.

"What do you mean?" Confusion spread across her fair face. "It's our wedding night."

"My good news was finally confirmed. The last training mission went so well that the army asked me to re-up for another tour. So I did. There's not as much flying, but we'll have one overseas mission, and I've been placed in charge of a new air squadron in Casper."

"Casper?"

"It's home."

"It's your home," she said. "You reenlisted for another tour? I don't understand."

"Doll, this is my chance to really do something important in the war effort. I'm not a young flyboy. I'm one of the oldest men in the unit, so when they wanted me for another tour, it was an honor."

"Of course they'd want you for another tour. They want any able-bodied American they can get."

Hurt flashed across his face. "They moved the timing up for the next mission. I depart tonight."

"But it's our wedding night. My dress...," she began, and then quietly looked down at the simple ivory dress she wore. It wasn't what she would have chosen to be married in, but it was one of the few dresses she could afford with what she made as a secretary. She'd put off college and secured a

job in a local law firm when her father refused to support her choice to continue her courtship with Campbell. Ella's father had promised to feed his youngest daughter and put a roof over her head, but he wouldn't pay her the generous allowance he paid her four sisters. Ella willingly made these sacrifices to be with Campbell. Now they were married, and her husband had reenlisted for another two years and was already leaving. Where would she go? There wasn't housing for spouses on the base because of the POW camp. And her father had been clear—if she married Campbell, she was on her own—no housing, no food, nothing. Her new husband made no mention about a house or how he would take care of her in his absence. Had her husband even considered her in his decision?

Ella turned toward Campbell and looked at him. His face was worn, weathered by years in the sun and smoking. His dark eyes were beginning to favor a shade of gray that matched the color of his sideburns. He was only thirty, but the war had aged him. And now it would age him even more. She longed to be with him, and found herself torn between her desire for him and the security of her family.

"Campbell," she began, "I think we made a mistake." Her voice was steady and calm, surprising her. "I can file for an annulment."

His light, easygoing demeanor shifted.

"Just wait," he said in a voice that wasn't familiar to her; his words were a plea for her silence.

Their eyes connected, and the last year melted into an unspoken understanding that this would be their final evening together. She would file for an annulment with the attorney in her office, and no one would be the wiser of her marriage—especially her father.

It was 1944, and Campbell and Ella ended their marriage on the night it began. But before they parted ways, Campbell walked to the desk and turned on the radio.

The harmony of the Andrews Sisters singing about young lovers pledging their loyalty while one was away at war wasn't lost on Ella.

Still, she blushed when Campbell led her to the middle of the suite—not to make love, but to do the one thing they did so well—dance. His presence was disarmingly attractive and powerful to her. As he snapped his fingers to the music, she smiled, finding herself falling under the familiar spell of his charm.

He swung her away from him and grinned in her direction, so easily capturing her heart. The upbeat music was lively, cheerful, and buoyed Ella's drowning spirits, keeping any thoughts of tomorrow at bay. Campbell slowed his pace with the cadence of the music and held Ella close as he sang in her ear.

The words flowed from his mouth and into the depths of Ella's soul.

Tears rolled down her cheeks, and she lowered her head, resting it against his officer's jacket, which tonight had served as his wedding suit. Campbell tilted her chin toward him and wiped her eyes.

"This doesn't have to be goodbye," he said. "We can make it work. I'll be back before you know it. It's just two

years."

She nodded, her throat tightening and her lips trembling.

"Oh, Campbell," she muttered as he pulled her toward him and held her.

"Shh, doll," he whispered in her hair.

Ella ached. The love between them cried out for a different ending. But Ella couldn't wait another year or two while the military sent her husband on special missions where she couldn't go. She wouldn't be welcome at her home, and she wasn't welcomed by the army.

"Look at me." His voice again pleaded with her.

She looked up.

"Oh, doll, please stop your crying. It's breaking my heart." The song ended, and he checked his watch. "I've got to get back to the base. Don't do anything rash. Wait. We'll have our honeymoon as soon as I return."

He opened the door and stood in the doorway. "Goodbye, doll," he said, before walking away.

Ella went to the window like she had so many times before and watched Campbell drive off beneath the hazy cover of moonlight.

I looked at the moon from the window in front of the desk. Campbell would have said it was a quarter moon, maybe a half-dollar. I laid my head on the desk and gazed at the milky moon that hung in the autumn sky. My eyes felt heavy. *Just five more minutes.*

CHAPTER THIRTY-TWO

CODY

"Has anyone seen Reese?" The rooftop had cleared of princesses, zombies, and superheroes that were being shuttled to the off-site parking. Wild Bill had thought of everything, even hiring shuttle buses to ferry guests back and forth to the parking garage. And if they were too drunk to drive, the shuttle drove them home. Smart move.

Wild Bill had Millie tucked protectively beneath his arm. She was dressed as Catwoman, and wore black leather well. Wild Bill stood proud in what I imagined was a genuine headdress and buckskins.

"Like what you're wearing," I said.

"Likewise," he said.

"It was my granddad's."

"Same here. Represent." We bumped fists.

"So, Reese," I said.

"Last time I saw her, she was with you," Millie said.

"Uh, yeah, she wanted to show me something," I said.

"Have you gone to the love lounge to look for her?" a college kid dressed as Zorro asked.

I placed my hands on my hips, not sure how to defuse the bomb Zorro tossed into the conversation, but neither Wild Bill nor Millie seemed surprised. Wild Bill cocked his head toward the elevator. "We can go with you to check to see if she's still there."

"Sure. Thanks. I'm not sure about opening the bookshelf." *Great. I sound less like Shaft and more like Steve Urkel.* I shifted direction to Zorro. "If you see my partner, will you show him where we are?"

"Your partner?" Zorro looked confused.

"The other detective who's working with me tonight."

"Oh, snap. I thought you meant…."

"I know what you thought. His name is Dixon, and he's dressed like a Buffalo nickel."

"Copy that," Zorro said, and I shook my head.

"Yeah, no."

His mask couldn't hide his amusement. Never ceased to amaze me what college kids found funny.

I headed to the second floor, Wild Bill and Millie following closely behind.

CHAPTER **THIRTY-THREE**

"There's more to see."

His voice was in my ear. I tried to open my eyes, but I was so tired. I felt his hand on my shoulder.

"Please."

I nodded, slowly opened my eyes, and raised my head from the desk. "Where are we going?"

"I have to show you one more place."

"Where?"

He gently held my hand. "I'll take you there."

"Okay." I sleepily followed beside him.

Campbell was dressed in his khaki officer's uniform. I don't think I'd ever seen him in anything else. We stepped into one of the hotel ballrooms, and he led me to a collection of chairs in the corner. It was an old-fashioned sitting arrangement.

"Is this the parlor?" I asked.

He pointed my direction to the love seat and ottoman. A pinewood box was placed on the edge of an ottoman, which was positioned in front of the love seat. The two-person couch was upholstered in a rich paisley print that matched the chocolate-colored carpet. I sat off to the side and watched as Ella walked into the ballroom and toward the ottoman. She stopped before she reached the love seat.

"So, I'm curious," Campbell said, leaning out from behind the love seat.

Ella smiled at what seemed like a phantom of her past. A month had passed since their private civil ceremony, and Campbell was in Wyoming as he promised. But Ella didn't look happy. The box was too big for the annulment papers she'd mailed him. They had promised to meet one last time to exchange the signed papers.

"What's in the box?" she asked.

He tilted his head at her, as if to answer her question, but instead shrugged.

"I don't know," he said. "Why don't you find out?"

Ella followed him with her eyes as he nodded toward the wooden box. She stood, as if in a daydream, and watched him push the box in her direction. She sat on the edge of the ottoman, barely taking up a corner of the space. The box sat between them.

"May I?" she asked.

He looked at her, granting her permission.

She lifted the lid. "Is this a gun?" She carefully picked up the pistol.

Campbell waited for her reaction. When she said

nothing, he took the pistol from her.

"Doll, this isn't a gun. It's a custom-made, single-action revolving cylinder Colt revolver. The army calls it the 'Peacemaker' because it's the gun that won the west."

Ella stared at the pistol.

"It's your wedding gift. Nothing's as good as a Colt. It's the gold standard. And nothing's too good for my wife." He placed the revolver in the blue velvet-lined box.

My stomach sank. A pistol? He used to give her pearls. Ella looked as dazed as I felt. The couple who normally couldn't keep their hands off each other and were always excited to see each other, now found it hard to piece together a simple conversation.

"How'd your—"

"I read about our marriage in the newspaper," he cut her off. "And our private reception. The photo of you beside your father in your wedding gown was a nice touch." He reached into his jacket and threw the newspaper clipping on top of the wooden box.

"The attorney I worked for was a family friend. He told my father when I asked him to prepare the annulment paperwork. My father threatened to disown me if I didn't first publicly announce our wedding," she said.

"So instead, you fabricated how our wedding went? How do you think that made me feel? I know it wasn't the wedding you wanted or even deserved, but I thought being together was more important than appearances."

"You don't understand. My father was furious with me."

Campbell looked lost, like he was trying to decipher

what was happening. His dark eyes brimmed with tears. He wiped them away and tried to focus on Ella.

"You left," she said. "You left me. I had no one to turn to."

"I'm sorry to hear that," Campbell replied curtly.

"Sorry?" she said, reiterating his empty platitude.

"That must have been very hard on you." He softened, and for a moment, Ella reconnected with the familiarity of his voice.

"It was," she said. "We have no house together, and I can't be on the base."

"Our house is in Casper on my folks' place."

"Casper isn't home," she said.

He snorted. "And here I thought home was wherever we were together."

"That's not fair. You knew I wanted to live in Cheyenne by my sisters and family. I'm not in any position to buy a home here, nor would that be proper. But if you bought us a home...."

An exasperated sigh. "Why would I buy a home in Cheyenne?"

"So I have somewhere to go. As your wife, I could live alone in the home while you're overseas. My father couldn't say anything if we had our own house. We wouldn't have to annul our marriage. There are many married women living alone because their husbands are serving." Her voice was a plea to be heard, but he didn't. Or perhaps he didn't want to. They were both hurt. The loss hung in the room like the heavy drapery, shutting out any light.

"Well, you seem to be managing well." His tone returned to one of neutrality.

"I, uh...." Ella stammered.

"I won't sign the annulment papers. If your father was fine trumpeting our wedding announcement in the papers, then he'll learn to be fine with our marriage."

"The announcement was to keep appearances. If the attorney told my father, imagine who else he told? My father wanted to protect our reputation."

"Reputation? What about the Matthews' reputation? Did you ever consider me or my family?"

His tone was so sharp it felt like a slap. I looked at Campbell who sat with a steely look on his face.

"What happened to you?" Ella asked.

"The war! The goddamn war. I don't have the luxury of playing house or imagining playing house while Americans are dying."

"Luxury? I gave up college, my allowance, and went to work. I forfeited the house my father would have built for us if we had just taken our time and had a church wedding. Things have to be done a certain way."

He snorted. "Who are you kidding? Your father is too stingy to part with his lumber for a house."

"He built my other sisters their homes."

"That's because your other sisters married men he approved of—hell, he probably arranged each one."

Ella thought of the arranged weddings of her sisters and her stomach knotted.

She couldn't win. She loved her husband and her father,

and neither of them seemed to consider her. Or if they did, it was to protect their reputations. Campbell was also from money, so maybe his parents weren't pleased with his choice? Or maybe he just wanted to be the alpha to her father in some tug of war of egos? Whatever the reason, the distance between them was painful to watch.

"He did. Your father arranged your sisters' weddings, didn't he?"

She nodded, and Campbell smacked his hands together. "Told you!"

She stared at him in disbelief.

"So as long as you married someone he approved of, you'd get a house. But if you followed your heart, no house."

She said nothing. Was there ever a time, she wondered, when Campbell wasn't in control of the outcome?

I felt her sadness. It was a different time and era. Women didn't have the same sense of personal security as I did. Ella's security came from either her father or her husband, which created its own war. It wasn't a battle played out in the newspapers, but the war that raged inside her was as real to her as the war in which her husband fought so hard.

Ella looked at the newspaper photo resting on top of the Colt. Half smiles and a cautionary embrace, the photo was a reminder of broken promises and shattered dreams. She couldn't please her father or her husband. She gathered her purse and stood. She looked into Campbell's eyes and quietly walked away, leaving behind the pistol and the picture.

"Where'd she go?" I looked at Campbell, who said nothing.

I ran after Ella, and soon I realized Campbell had too.

Outside, the afternoon sun was bright and hurt Ella's eyes. She looked for a pay phone to call her father. He'd come get her. But so would Campbell, who found Ella just as she plunked a dime into the silver pay phone. She picked up the receiver, and he disconnected the call.

"Come back with me to our suite." The box was under his arm. He held out his hand, and when she refused to take it, his tone turned angry. "I won't sign the annulment papers, so if you want out of this marriage, you'll have to divorce me."

Divorce? Ella's heart sank to her stomach. A divorce would bring more dishonor to her family. A hasty marriage could be annulled and reasonably understood. She was young, people would say. But a divorce would leave a mark on her name she'd never be able to erase. She was trapped. There was no way out.

"Please, doll." His tone softened. "Things have changed. That's why I'm here."

She looked at him.

"D-day changed everything. My overseas mission was scrapped, and I've been assigned permanently to a desk job in Casper."

"What about being a war hero?" Ella looked lost. "You reenlisted and left on our wedding night so you could be heroic."

"Come to our suite" was all he said to her.

The light was so bright, I squinted. "Where are we?"

Campbell took me by the hand, leading me back to the hotel and suite 632.

"I left something for you in the bathroom," Campbell said to Ella, who blindly obeyed her husband's direction and disappeared into the suite's bathroom.

"Oh, it has a happy ending." I clapped. But then I saw Ella in the bathroom.

She dried her eyes on the sleeve of her silky pink peignoir and opened the wooden box. The Colt lay in blue velvet and shone brilliantly in the dim bathroom. Ella slowly withdrew it.

"What's she doing with the pistol?"

I waited for Campbell to answer, but when I looked for him, he had fallen asleep in bed waiting for his wife.

Ella slipped her feet into the matching slippers he'd bought her, so her feet didn't make a sound on the hardwood floors when she left the bathroom.

She stood at the foot of the hotel bed. It was the same bed in which they'd shared stolen moments together throughout the last year, but never consummated their marriage. She spoke so softly I could barely hear her.

"What happened to us?" Her eyes searched his face for an answer, but he was asleep. "I thought you wanted to fight the enemy and be a hero. What has this all been about? Now there's no heroic wartime duty, no dangerous flying mission, and no life as a wartime bride." Her shoulders shook, and she looked frail. "I've lost my inheritance, our house, and my reputation. Collectively, we have more than three strikes against us. And individually, you've left me with nothing but regret."

Tears filled her violet eyes. "When did I ever have a choice?

If I wasn't bending to please you, I bowed for my father and his wishes. And for what? Campbell, there's no glory in being married to an army paper pusher when my friends' husbands are actually overseas fighting." She reached into the pocket of her silky robe and looked at the newspaper announcement about her wedding. Her father stood beside her, not her husband. Her husband was MIA. "The only way for me to salvage this situation and my life is if you're out of the picture—permanently."

She aimed the pistol at his head.

"No!" I screamed. "No! You don't have to do this. Please. Don't. Ella, stop! You love him."

My cries weren't heard by anyone. Campbell was fast asleep, and I was with Ella in a dream memory.

"My father was so ashamed of me, he made sure everyone in town knew you left for your new assignment, before we could consummate our marriage. And I didn't correct him. I may not have had the wedding night I always imagined, but my father didn't need to know that long before our wedding, we had consummated our union. So, I let my father think his youngest daughter was a virgin, which allowed him to save face. Not that it made that big a difference. He was ashamed of me for running off to be with you. So, you won't die a war hero, but your suicide will return me to my father's grace and goodwill. Better still, I'll win the hearts of everyone in town. When they discover the virgin bride was widowed when her husband returned for a delayed honeymoon, but shot himself because he couldn't perform his husbandly duties, my unimaginable loss will win everyone over."

She slid seven silver bullets from her pocket into the rotating cylinder, gently reached for the extra bed pillow off the armchair, and placed it in front of the pistol with her left hand while her right hand steadily pressed the pistol into it. She swiftly pulled back the trigger and shot through the pillow just as Campbell opened his eyes. The bullet barely missed him.

"Ella!" He raised his hands in defense.

She threw the pillow at his head. Campbell instinctively caught it just as she discharged six more shots in rapid succession. She fired until the pillow turned red. When the last bullet left the pistol, she waited. When Campbell didn't move, she used the tip of the revolver to push the pillow away from his face. The hole in his head was smaller than she imagined. She carefully placed the revolver in her husband's hands and began to scream.

With blood seeping from the bed onto the hardwood floors, I ran out of the suite and toward the hidden staircase. I ran and ran until it felt like my legs couldn't take me any further. I found refuge in the passageway. I grabbed my shoes and walked aimlessly. *What just happened?*

CHAPTER THIRTY-FOUR

CODY

"Where the hell could she be?" The hidden room I had shared with Reese was neatly organized, but empty.

Wild Bill picked up her knee brace that had fallen off the far end of the couch. "She wouldn't leave this behind, would she?"

I shook my head. "No. Not at all."

"Maybe she got turned around leaving?" Millie said.

"That's probably what happened," Wild Bill agreed.

"Isn't there just one way in and out of here?" I asked.

"The tunnels are blocked, but if she turned left outside the suite instead of right, the passageway goes for a couple hundred feet before it dead-ends at the tunnel access, which was closed decades ago."

Something doesn't feel right. I grabbed my cell phone, but the signal inside the wall was shit. I withdrew my flashlight, turned it on, and held it in an overhand grip. The passageway was dark, and if I ran into anyone armed, they'd be more likely to shoot at the light in my left hand, and not at my right hand that held my Glock.

"Okay, I want you to take Millie and go find Dixon."

"The guy in the Buffalo nickel costume?" Millie said.

"Correct. Wild Bill, I want you to return him to this suite and tell him to secure the premises." I looked at Millie. "I need you to take the shuttle home."

"Why?" Her brown eyes reminded me of my sister, who would think she had done something wrong.

"I can't have the best server in Cheyenne trapped back here, or worse, have the rest of her Halloween night ruined," I said lightly. "There's still candy to be eaten."

"Ah, Cody, that's so sweet. I am kind of hungry."

"I bet," I said, smiling for her benefit. "You guys hosted a standup party." I glanced at Wild Bill, who followed my every move. "Okay, if you could make sure Millie gets in a shuttle, then find Dixon."

"Will do."

They exited to the right, and when they were well on their way to safety, I raised my flashlight and moved slowly to the left.

I glanced around quickly, conscious of a distinct feeling of dread. *Where the hell are you, Reese?*

CHAPTER THIRTY-FIVE

REESE

My knee felt like it was going to collapse. I leaned against the brick wall. The interior of the hotel was a honeycomb of secret passages, staircases, and hidden doors. I didn't know where I was or how I got here. I was turned around, lost, and certain no one would ever find me.

I was inching along, using the wall as a brace, when a light shone in my direction.

"Hello?" My voice sounded small, and I stood motionless, like I had been turned to stone, because I didn't know who or what was in the distance.

***

CODY

There was a haunted, almost desperate gleam in her eyes. Her mouth was drawn as she stared into the light.

"Reese, it's Cody. I'm here to help," I said.

Her eyes questioned me almost fiercely.

"I can't see you," she said, holding her arm above her eyes to block the glare.

I lowered the flashlight, and she stood for a moment as though waiting. For what or whom, I wasn't sure. Then she ran into my arms. "You found me!"

"Doll, I'll always find you."

Her body stiffened, and she thrust away from me. "Don't ever call me that again."

She crossed to the other side of the narrow passageway and stood for a moment, leaning against the turn-of-the-century bricks that even in the dim light showed signs of weathering and possible fire damage. I wasn't sure. I just knew I had to get Reese out of this archaic passageway.

"Did you see him?" she asked.

"Who?" My finger instinctively settled on the trigger of my Glock.

"Campbell. He visited me again."

"Okay." All I knew of Campbell was the legend. Wealthy cowboy and army officer who shot himself on his wedding night. Not the stuff of bedtime stories, but tormented ghosts usually weren't. But suddenly a thought crossed my mind. *Was he the uniformed man in the stairwell? And what's his hold on Reese?*

"He did. Campbell visited again. And now I know what happened to him." I wasn't sure if her smile was to assure me or herself.

"What happened to him?" I was sure the skepticism was

evident in my tone.

"Cody, he was murdered."

I made no response, but I did respond to the appeal in her eyes. I didn't know if it was for me to believe in her ghost story or get her to safety. I just knew the risk of staying in an antiquated, most likely unreliably built passageway that should have been sealed along with the tunnels was well beyond my comfort zone.

"Let's go somewhere warm." I held out my hand, and she slipped hers into it.

CHAPTER **THIRTY-SIX**

REESE

"Where are we going?" The question felt like déjà vu—as did wearing Cody's jacket. I still hadn't returned his other one.

"Well, we talked about breakfast," Cody said. "And Wild Bill said you're pretty crazy about the chef's breakfast burritos, so he put together a little breakfast basket for us to enjoy. I thought I'd take you somewhere I go after I've had a, uh, long night."

I sat beside him in his truck, which also felt familiar. "I'm okay. This isn't like last night when you found me in the boiler room. He didn't scare me."

Cody said nothing, but I could tell he wasn't closed to the subject.

"I must sound crazy to you," I said, testing the waters.

"No, actually." His green eyes were intense, but softened when he looked at me and spoke. "I want to know what happened. Wild Bill mentioned something about your dream last night. I didn't know that's what happened. When I found you...."

I reached across and placed my hand on his thigh. "I can't imagine what you thought. But just so you know, nothing happened. I took off my running clothes because it was *fucking* hot in the boiler room."

He laughed, and his effort to maintain control of the situation vanished. He pointed toward a freeway sign that read Curt Gowdy State Park.

"Well, speaking of haunts, this is one of my favorite ones in Wyoming," Cody said, taking the exit off the highway.

"Is it open?" I squinted at the entrance.

"It's open year-round. I try to get here between each season just to see the landscape. The change in season makes it unforgettable."

What was unforgettable was how easy it was to be with Cody.

Fall leaves in crimson, burnt orange, and mustard yellow littered the roadway and shone in his headlights. The truck's tires crunched the seasonal blanket of leaves.

"When we do get snow, this is a great place for tubing, sledding, and snowshoeing. You can even cross-county ski," he said.

"I'm pretty sure I can sled," I said with a laugh.

"Maybe we'll try our hand at ice fishing," he said, and I shook my head.

"No, I'm thinking, when winter hits, I'm going to sit my ass in front of a fireplace and finally read all those books I have packed in one of my boxes," I said. "And I believe the house corporate rented for me has an actual fireplace, and not one you turn on with a switch."

"Impressive."

"I'm a quick learner," I said.

The path through the park was curvy and ended in front of a mountainside of sheer rocks.

"This is Vedauwoo." He parked his truck in front of the towering rock formations that rose into the moonlight sky. "Hikers from all over the country come here."

"Veda who?"

"*Vee-Duh-Voo*," he said. "The Plains Indians named the area. It means 'Land of the Earthborn Spirits.' They believed it was a spiritual place, and I thought it might be the perfect place for you to tell me more about Campbell and what happened to him."

His sincerity made me feel safe and not judged. Aside from Wild Bill, I hadn't told anyone about Campbell's first visit—not even my sister.

We walked to a picnic table positioned in front of the most beautiful backdrop of rust- and white-colored rocks.

"This entire area was created by ice, wind, and water." Cody seemed to read my mind.

Dense pines covered the entrance to the ancient rock formations that reached high into the wide Wyoming sky. A sliver of moonlight cut through the trees, and I thought of Campbell.

"He didn't kill himself," I said, unwrapping the foil from my burrito. "I know that's what people think, but he wouldn't have done that."

Cody remained perfectly calm with a look of neutrality on his face.

"His wife did. She shot him in the head."

"What was her motive?" He bit into the flour-wrapped burrito. The smell of eggs, caramelized onions, and crisp, fresh bell peppers wafted in the night air.

I exhaled. "It's a long story, but from what I saw...." I paused. "God, I know this must sound insane, but twice now when I've fallen asleep in odd places at the hotel—like the boiler room and the hidden love lounge—I've dreamt about Campbell. Wild Bill calls them lost spirits and said that I was *visited* by Campbell's."

"What do you call it?"

"I don't know. But it's happened the two nights in a row and never before. And for the last two weeks, I've been a regular resident of the hotel. The only time I've been *visited* or dreamt about Campbell was in these random places."

"I wonder, though, if they are random. Or if they have something to do with the message this Campbell person appears to be conveying."

I raised my shoulders. "I don't know. Maybe."

Cody twisted off the lid to a bottled water and handed it to me.

"Last night, before I went to sleep at Wild Bill's, when he talked about these lost spirits, he said they stayed in this world, our world, until they could receive justice." I took a sip of water. "That sounds as crazy as it gets, doesn't it?"

"Stay focused on what happened tonight. I'm not here

to judge. I'm here to understand why these things keep happening to you," he said.

"Wild Bill thinks Campbell attached himself to me because he believes I can grant him the justice and peace he never got in his lifetime," I said. "And after tonight, that totally makes sense."

I gave a quick rundown of Ella and Campbell's love affair and how it ended in suite 632. I didn't delve into every detail, like the newspaper announcement, the Colt pistol, or the pillow she used to silence the gunfire, because they just didn't seem as important as the fact that Ella shot her husband on their honeymoon.

"So Campbell and Ella were lovers before they married," Cody said.

"Yes, they'd meet at the hotel. It became their rendezvous for romance. So the myth or legend that he killed himself because he couldn't perform his husbandly duties just doesn't fly."

"And so Ella's motive was to save her reputation and family name."

"And herself," I said. "She felt trapped. Or that's how it seemed. It was 1944. Granted, history isn't my strong suit, but it is my sister's, and she's always waffling on about the tremendous progress women have made in the last century. But for Ella, it had only just begun. She still lived in a patriarchal society where she was either tied to her father or her husband."

"Inequality sucks. Trust me, I know," Cody said. "But that doesn't give someone the right to kill someone."

"You're right, and I'm certainly not justifying her actions," I said. "But I do understand what drove her to murder."

"And being murdered would be the injustice that Wild Bill referenced," Cody said.

"Absolutely. Although I don't know how knowing this will help. Campbell was killed in 1944 when he was thirty and Ella was eighteen." I grabbed my cell phone and scrolled to my calculator. "This happened seventy-three years ago."

"That doesn't mean Ella's still not alive," Cody said.

"She'd be...." I rubbed my forehead.

"Ninety-one," Cody said. "On her eighteenth birthday, it would have been 1944 and World War II was still raging."

"I'm too tired to do the math that fast." I smiled. "But still, what are the odds of her still being alive?"

"You'd be surprised how long people are living," Cody said. "I just had a standoff, quite literally, with a woman who was...." His dark face paled in the moonlight.

"What?"

He shook his head. "Oh, I was thinking how this woman just celebrated her ninety-first birthday, but it's not the same person."

"Okay, so people live longer." I rose and stood for a moment, taking in the grandeur of the night. "But Ella? She was high-strung and stressed out at eighteen. I can't imagine she lived that long of a life, and if she did, I doubt it was happy."

I walked toward the edge of the rock formation with Cody beside me. The ground was covered in pine needles, and the rich scent of pine awakened me to something other than sorrow.

"I don't like how things ended—at all. It was the most awful thing I've ever experienced." I reached for Cody's hand. "I really don't know what you come across in your job, but if it's anything like what I saw, I couldn't do it."

"I happen to be selfish," he said, which took me off guard. "I can't bear the thought of what might happen to you or other women who are often preyed upon."

"Now that this is over, I don't consider myself in the slightest danger. Campbell was shot, and Ella is most likely long dead. It's a story as old as time."

"Along with the motive."

"Love?" I said.

"No, greed. From what you've told me, Ella was afraid of losing everything. Greed is so strong that people will even kill their own family or spouses for life insurance or inheritance money. It sounds like Ella would do anything to keep her wealth and reputation."

"I suppose. But it didn't feel greedy, it felt…." I gazed into the cloudless sky to the moon. "Desperate."

"Well sure, that's possible too. Women will kill their husbands if they feel there is no other way out of the relationship."

"He wouldn't buy her a house in Cheyenne, he wouldn't sign the annulment papers, so that only left her with divorce as an option, which apparently was a far worse sin than murder," I said.

"When a woman feels like she can't escape a bad

marriage, her safety and well-being often feel threatened. It doesn't mean that they are, but I've seen women who can't get a divorce due to religious or other reasons, but feel trapped. Sometimes, they snap and kill their spouse. Then they enter an entirely new prison for the rest of their life."

"God, that's awful."

"It's tragic, is what it is."

"Tragic and heartbreaking. When I saw her shoot her husband, I just couldn't make sense of it all. And I can't imagine that whatever happened to Ella afterward was good. Sure, she may have regained her reputation in society and with her father, but ultimately, she killed the man she loved. And there was no doubt they were *madly* in love with each other. That kind of loss stays with a person—don't you think?"

"For sure. Especially if they're the one who pulled the trigger."

I exhaled. The night patched together in a mosaic of pieces, from my sex fest with Cody to winding passageways that led to guns and remorse. Emotions somersaulted inside me. The only feeling that seemed to surface was, ironically, gratitude. "Thank you *again* for finding me."

"This time I had an ulterior motive," he said. "After you enticed me with the idea of breakfast, I had to find you."

"And who says chivalry is dead?"

"Not me," he said.

"So maybe you can explain why Campbell wouldn't buy his wife a house in Cheyenne? He had the money, and he was crazy about her."

"But from what you've told me, he wasn't crazy about her father?" Cody asked.

"That's true."

"Well, the male ego is a fragile thing. Campbell just basically got decommissioned by the army to travel overseas and fight in the actual war. He was relegated to a desk job. His pride was probably pretty badly wounded. When his new wife wouldn't uproot her life and move to Casper, he dug his feet in the ground—if for no other reason than to build and establish his ego as a man."

"That's crap."

"Agreed. I'm not defending him or his actions, but I've seen guys make shit decisions because they let pride and ego get in the way."

"Yeah, and Ella let reputation rule her."

"A woman's reputation was probably all she had as a commodity," he said.

I nodded. "It was a different time. It's just so sad." My chest ached for a different outcome than the one I witnessed.

"It is incredibly sad—and tragic because justice was never served for Campbell."

"Maybe I can do something at the hotel? You know, like a memorial?" I glanced at all the rocks and imagined a sculpture of Campbell. "Is that stupid?"

He laughed. "Tourists love memorials."

"I'll ask the staff, maybe they can help me come up with an idea."

With our hands interlaced, we walked toward his truck. It was so natural to be with Cody. Despite us not knowing each other, there was an ease and a connection greater than our physical attraction. The moon seemed to follow us, and my thoughts turned again to Campbell. Inside the truck, I leaned against Cody's broad shoulder and closed my eyes. The drive to the hotel for my car was quiet. The mystery of why Campbell haunted the hotel was resolved. Now, I could focus on creating new memories and possibly restoring Campbell's. Plus, I still had to find a way to save the hotel from the auction block.

CHAPTER THIRTY-SEVEN

REESE

A taco bar was stationed on a banquet table along the back wall in the employee break room. It was a Herculean effort to find a caterer, so I did the next best thing and asked another hotel to help out. In exchange, I'd loan them my kitchen staff for their year-end party. A galvanized bucket overflowed with sodas, energy drinks, and bottled water stuffed in ice. I eyed the chocolate iced brownies that looked worth the extra mile on the treadmill. I'd finally read the doctor's discharge papers, which curtailed running for six weeks. The paperwork didn't say I couldn't walk slowly on the hotel's treadmill in the onsite gym. When everyone had plates of food and drink in front of them, I began.

"Hey, guys. I thought I'd bring a little California to Wyoming. So, if you notice, there's sliced avocado *and* guacamole, because really, is there ever enough of the good green stuff?" The staff laughed.

"I wanted to thank everyone, especially Wild Bill and Toby, for putting in so much extra time and effort to make our annual costume ball last night such a *huge, huge* success."

At my request, the staff had gathered in the employee lunch room, where I had lunch catered by our neighboring hotel so even Chef and his kitchen crew could enjoy a respite from work. I'd extended a texted invitation to Cody and Dixon, but didn't see them sitting at any of the tables.

"We're heading into winter, or so I'm told. I haven't seen any snow yet." I was quickly interrupted by playful jeers.

"Shhh! Don't jinx us!" someone shouted.

"Now, we'll have snow in spring," another person said, laughing.

I slapped my forehead. "Damn! I'm sorry."

They laughed.

"Well, speaking of spring." I exhaled. "It'll be upon us before we know it." Dread settled in my stomach. *Stupid corporate.* "So, I was hoping to get your thoughts on what we could do to increase visibility for the hotel.

"I'm open to any and all suggestions, so don't be shy. With Toby's help, that little wooden box mounted on the wall"—I pointed to where my engineer stood beside a box that eerily reminded me of the box that had contained the Colt—"is there for you to drop me a line. I know many of you work the overnight shift and so our interaction may not be as frequent, but I'd love to hear from everyone. So, enjoy lunch and take a look at the employee bulletin board." I pointed behind me to the board positioned on the wall.

"The corporate office hired a photographer last night, who I don't think I ever saw! But he was there and he captured some great shots of the party. The governor, Zorro"—I nodded toward Zavi—"and the banquet and kitchen crew doing what they do so well. Wild Bill already loaded them to our social media page, so be sure to share our page with your friends. And thanks to Millie from the gift shop who decorated the bulletin board with some of the printed pics."

I paused and looked at their smiling faces. *How did I get so lucky*? I gently smiled in return. "I know I'm new and haven't probably made the best first impression. I mean, who gets locked in the boiler room? Look at my face."

When Wild Bill and Toby laughed, so did everyone else.

"But there's no place I'd rather be." My hand went to my heart. "I love Wyoming. There's so many hidden treasures here that I'm just discovering." I thought of Cody and the rocks at Curt Gowdy State Park. "If more people knew how much Wyoming had to offer, I think we wouldn't have a single room vacant. Who wouldn't want to be where the legend still lives?"

I raised an eyebrow and grinned. "And just in case there are rumors circulating about my interaction with our resident spirit, I think our days of Campbell haunting the hotel are gone."

When someone raised their hand, I nodded.

"Did you see him?"

I raised my shoulders. "I dreamt about him? Twice. And I think he just needed us to know his life and death were bigger than any of us could imagine." I paused. "I'd like to do something to honor him. So, if you can think of how we could do that…?" I volleyed my hands back and forth like I was weighing the options before us, when I didn't even know what they were.

"Anyway, that's something to think about, and thank you guys again. There's no way I could have even come close to pulling off what you all did. The rooftop didn't even look like there had been a tennis court. It was just wonderful. Thank you."

I visited with each table, and was headed back to my office when I spotted him in the hallway.

"Cody?"

He turned and iridescent green eyes shone from his face. "There you are." Yet when he reached me, he didn't seem sure what to do.

Kiss me? Hug me? Shake my hand? I watched his face wrinkle under the uncertainty, and it was sexy.

I leaned toward him until our lips were inches apart.

"You always smell like heaven," he said.

I chuckled. "What?"

"Heaven. My version is an endless field full of flowers—lavender, rose, and jasmine. That's what you smell like."

"But what do I taste like?"

His brow relaxed and his lips curved into a wonderful, bright smile. "You know, I'm not sure if I remember correctly. There was *a lot* going on last night. Maybe I should taste test it again?"

I nodded. "I think so."

"Can you leave?"

I shrugged. "I probably shouldn't, but I'm going to anyway. I figure, between getting locked in the boiler room and then corporate's location change for our party, I'm due a day off. Even if my staff did 99 percent of the work." I laughed. "Besides," I softly kissed him, "it's Sunday. Sundays are meant to be lazy."

"No argument there."

I grabbed my bag, slung it over my shoulder, and slipped my hand in Cody's.

CHAPTER THIRTY-EIGHT

CODY

The monthly maid service was due at my house sometime today. Sunday wasn't their normal cleaning day, but with the upcoming holiday, they had more houses to clean and less time to do it. I silently prayed they hadn't arrived. When no other car was parked in front of my house, I smiled at Reese.

"Is this your home?" she asked.

"This is it."

My 1930s red-and-blue Americana-style brick home was built on a small hill of grass. It made for a striking landscape, but was a bitch to mow. I didn't mind hiring a monthly maid service, but I drew the line at a gardener.

"Wow. This is nothing like my rental. This has real curb appeal. It's beautiful."

"Wait until you see inside."

After I gave Reese the Dixon-worth nickel tour, pointing out the arched doorways, original hardwood floors, and cedar-lined closets, we ended up in the kitchen.

"I think this is my favorite room," I said of the open floorplan. The kitchen extended into the dining room, which flowed into the living room.

"Mine too. It feels like the heart of the home," she said.

"Probably because I'm always eating." I chuckled. "And speaking of eating...." I lifted Reese and placed her on the granite countertop.

She sat on the edge of the counter in a pleated skirt, soft pink button-down, tights, and black closed-toe shoes that were nothing like her red heels, but in their plainness, they were sexy. Her tights did a good job of camouflaging her knee brace.

"I like this." I tugged on the hem of her skirt. "Makes you look like a naughty schoolgirl."

"Maybe I am." She playfully rolled her bony shoulders. "Eight years of Catholic school."

An overcast afternoon allowed our reflection to show like a mirror in the dining room window. I stood sandwiched between her thighs, and we looked good.

"God, you feel good." She pressed into me.

Her long red hair fell forward and softly brushed my face. As the sun disappeared behind clouds, the filter of light cast the kitchen in shadows.

Reese began to unbutton her blouse. Her fair skin was smooth and as untouched as first snow. Her breasts were ripe, full with a dot of crimson I couldn't stop staring at.

"Your body."

"Come here." She moved toward me.

I rubbed my smooth, stubble-free chin. "Where to begin."

Reese lifted my T-shirt and pressed herself against me. The heat between us was electric. I reached my hand up her skirt, but there was no garter. She seemed to read my thoughts because she grinned.

"Detective, you'll have to take me to a formal event for those goodies," she said.

I removed her brace, inched down her tights, slipped off her shoes, and tossed everything to the floor. She wrapped her lean legs around me, and I carried her to the couch. But before I could set her down, she slid out of my arms and playfully pushed me onto the couch.

"Jeans off," she said, and then giggled. "I'm not very good with belts and buttons."

I kicked off my shoes, slid out of my jeans and boxer briefs, and sat on the couch in nothing more than a smile, which seemed to please Reese.

She stood before me in a naughty schoolgirl skirt and open blouse.

"Bless me, Father, for I'm about to sin." She made the sign of the cross and winked, which was probably the most sacrilegious, naughty gesture ever.

She unzipped her skirt, which dropped to the floor, and walked back to the kitchen in her blouse and nothing else. She stood on her tiptoes and reached for the bottle of peppermint schnapps. Then she opened one cupboard after the other until she found what she wanted. She placed a dishtowel on the floor and stood on it.

"Stay there." I heard her giggle, and leaned forward just as she poured the thick, clear liquor over her body, basting herself in the syrupy alcohol. She then dusted herself with sugar. She reached into her purse for something, and it looked like she began drawing on the inside of her thighs. When she walked back toward me, granules of sugar sparkled like frost, showcasing her finest features. Her crimson areolas were circled in red, exaggerating their fullness. The red lip gloss mixed with the sugar and alcohol, staining her skin cherry. She was a neon-colored body cocktail, and looked delicious.

A sly grin slid across her face.

"Girl, what have you done?" I said.

She shrugged. "You make me feel like I can do anything."

It felt like my heart would explode. From the moment we crashed into each other, I'd always known she was a woman who knew what she wanted. I saw a boldness in her that turned me on, but it was her confidence that was the real aphrodisiac. Reese was sexually daring, which was different from the quiet reserve she presented to everyone else. When she was with me, I saw a confident, courageous, sexy woman.

"Want to taste?" She looked at me from beneath dark eyelashes and then spread apart her legs. My name was written on her inner thigh with an arrow pointing toward the origin of her pleasure.

"That's hot." I admired her bodywork.

"Lick," she instructed, and watched my resolve dissolve as quickly as the sugar and alcohol when my tongue traced the curves of her body. One look, and she had me. And she knew it.

"Minty," I said.

Reese enjoyed taunting me. With the tip of her tongue, she slowly traced the rim of my ear, gently sucking on my earlobe.

"You know you want me," she purred in my ear.

"I wanted you the first time I saw you." I licked the sugar off her shoulder, and then reached for my jeans and grabbed the condom I had stuffed in my wallet.

Her reddish eyebrow arched.

"Wishful thinking?" I ripped open the package. "I didn't know we'd end up back at my house. So, I came prepared." She watched as I slid the condom over my cock.

Reese gently placed her hand on my shoulder as she lowered herself onto me and wrapped her sugared legs around me. Braced against me, she tilted her head back and rocked us together. Her hair swayed like a red licorice rope that I held tightly.

"God, you feel good. Such a great ass." My hands sank into her. In the window behind us, our desire played against the glass.

Reese turned around and looked. "Not bad," she said with a grin.

"Your body is amazing," I said in her ear.

"So I've been told."

The woman knew what buttons to push, to push me further into her. "I don't want to know. You're mine." I thrust into her and she gasped.

"God, yes." She leaned back, and I cradled her body while she rubbed her clit against me and her swollen lips absorbed me.

Her pussy clamped around my cock, and I knew she was close to exploding. I increased my pace to come with her. She may have been on top, but I was manning the controls. I dug my hands into her ass, ground her against my cock, and my mind went blank just before I released my load into her. She screamed, I groaned, and we came together.

The front door suddenly opened, and Reese ducked.

"Hello, Mr. Pring?"

"It's my housekeeper, Ildy."

"Crappity, crap, crap." Reese pulled her blouse together, then grabbed her skirt and used it as a shield as she darted toward the kitchen.

"Ildy, hold up. Stay there. I'll be right with you."

I grabbed my jeans, pulled them on, then quickly went to the kitchen where I found Reese. She smiled mischievously, like we had just been caught by our parents. "Can I use your shower?" she whispered.

"Yeah, it's down the hall on the right."

The aroma and allure of her sexuality hung in the air. I cupped her face with my hand and gently, tenderly kissed her. It was a kiss meant to convey everything I felt that I didn't know how to put into words without sounding like a moron.

"Yeah, I like you too," she said, slipping into her skirt.

I chuckled. "Okay, yeah, you got me."

Reese glanced toward the front door and then looked

back at me. "Cover me." She made her best attempt at a dash down the hallway.

CHAPTER **THIRTY-NINE**

CODY

As soon as I walked into the clinic and the bells on the door chimed, dogs barked and cats yelped.

"I'm here to check on a dog I brought to Cal almost a month ago." The receptionist at the veterinarian clinic had some kind of blue-chested bird perched on her shoulder and a kitten in the corner of her desk. The black kitten kept reaching for the keyboard and the receptionist kept picking it up to place it back in the designated spot on her desk.

"What's the animal's name?" Her fingers remained poised on the keyboard.

"Oh. The dog didn't have a name. Maybe John Doe?" I laughed, but she didn't. What was it about my sense of humor that wasn't funny? I didn't get it. But Reese did, and that's all that mattered. Now that the business of Campbell visiting her was behind us, we spent most of our evenings and weekends together.

"There's no dog named John Doe in our system," she said.

"Maybe you could get Cal for me?"

She pushed out her chair and the legs scraped against the linoleum floor. A shiver went straight down my spine. Within moments, Cal Farmer appeared behind her, waving me into the back office.

"How's he doing?" I asked. I hadn't been able to visit the dog since bringing him to Cal on Halloween night, but I'd called every day for a progress report.

"I had the tox screens on his blood run a second time through the lab, and the results were the same." Cal was a tall, thin, white-haired man who wore silver wire-rimmed glasses that matched his moustache that hadn't whitened, but silvered with time.

"What'd they show?"

"Halothane."

I pulled out my notebook and wrote *Halothane*. "Okay, so what is that? And"—I shook my notepad at him—"dummy it down, Cal."

"Halothane is a very dangerous anesthetic. It's usually used to put down large game animals, like elephants."

"And the dog had it in his system?"

"There was a fair amount in his blood, which is why I had it retested. But it would explain why he survived."

"I don't understand." I glanced at the kennels, but his black-and-tan face wasn't one that looked back at me.

"Halothane is an oral anesthesia that dates back to the mid-fifties when I became a vet. Since it's inhaled,

Halothane was used in vaporizers on people who were difficult to intubate. However, what the medical community discovered was that overdosage was difficult to avoid."

"So why didn't the dog die?"

"Since Halothane reduces blood pressure, it decreased the blood loss for the dog. Whoever did this to him most likely first anesthetized him with it and then cut him open. He wouldn't have been able to fight back."

My gut tightened, and I gripped my notebook. *What kind of evil person hurts a dog?*

"But like I said, it may have inadvertently saved his life because he didn't bleed out and he maintained a low pulse rate, which helped keep him calm. He was fed the drug for at least a week, because the concentration in his bloodwork was consistent with long-term use."

"She didn't just torture the dog, she kept him anesthetized so he couldn't be found," I said.

"She?"

I shook my head. "I don't have any concrete evidence. Just operating on gut instinct."

"There were also trace amounts of muscle relaxants in his system, if that helps in your investigation."

"Why would she give him a muscle relaxant if she's already vaping him with anesthesia?"

"Muscle relaxants were used in conjunction with Halothane to maintain a lighter level of anesthesia. When overdosage with Halothane became an issue, anesthesiologists turned to using muscle relaxants to alter the depth of anesthesia," Cal said.

"So I'm looking for muscle relaxants or Halothane." I made another note.

"Cody, it's going to be hard to track down. Halothane may still be used in underdeveloped countries, but it's no longer FDA approved or commercially available in the US. There were too many issues with it."

"Copy that." I closed my notebook. "But I'm still going to be on the lookout."

"I know you will," Cal said.

"Can I see him?"

"The girls have taken to calling him Murray."

"Murray?"

"Like Bill Murray. Considering the condition in which he was brought in, the dog's got a lot of heart, and he's entertaining as hell."

"What does he do?"

"It's hard to explain. It's one of those things you just have to see to believe." Cal led me to a recovery room adjacent to the operating room. A viewing window allowed me to see Murray, whose eyes were closed while his ears were scratched by a vet tech.

"He's really the comeback kid," Cal said. "He's made tremendous progress. The massive incision has drained nicely, but he needs to stay in a cone so he doesn't lick it. He holds his tail low, since I think it hurts to lift it. He was pinned down so forcibly that it'll take a while for the bruising to heal. But his hind legs are braced, and he's gained weight, and as you can see, he's not lethargic."

"Can I go in?"

"From what Chief Wyman tells me, the renters disowned him, and the owner of the house where you found him refuses to accept any responsibility." Cal patted my shoulder. "We all just assumed Murray was your dog."

I looked at the rugged dog with a wolfish head, erect ears, and black-and-tan coloring, and smiled.

"He's a handsome dog, isn't he?"

Cal opened the door, and I walked inside. Murray looked up at me, and for having an injured tail, it wagged with vigor. The black marking across his face looked like a mask. My throat tightened, thinking of how I found him.

"Hey, buddy," I said.

He whined, and I knelt in front of the exam table, nose to nose with him. His tongue bathed my face, and I didn't care. I kissed his cheek, and his paw rested on my hand.

"You're the most courageous dog I've ever met," I said. "A lesser dog wouldn't have lasted."

And then he did the one thing I didn't expect—he winked.

I looked from the dog to Cal. "Did you see that?"

The young vet tech giggled. "Murray's a total flirt."

"Yeah, he is." I rubbed behind his ears. "Murray, when you're all better, you're coming home with me."

"Give us another week, maybe two, and he'll be ready," Cal said.

"Take all the time you need, and bill me," I said.

Cal shook his head. "Nope. This one's on me. As corny as it sounds, just knowing he's going to a good home is payment enough."

I swallowed. "Thanks, Cal."

I gently scratched behind Murray's ears and realized the timing of his discharge. "Murray, you'll be home in time for Christmas." His coat felt silky, he smelled clean, and life had returned to his eyes. "I can't wait for you to meet Reese."

His eyebrow seemed to rise.

"Yeah. I met a girl. I know," I said, gently rubbing his head. "There goes our bachelor pad."

The vet tech laughed, and Murray responded with a sideways smile.

CHAPTER FORTY

CODY

"Pring, Dixon, I'd like to see you in my office." Chief Wyman's head poked out of his office long enough to call us.

I grabbed my notepad and pen. "What'd you do now?"

"Me?" Dixon reached for the swamp-colored protein shake my sister now prepared for him daily. Her pregnancy had morphed into more oddities like cucumber-and-basil sandwiches and chunky drinks that had the consistency of that barium sulfate concoction they made you drink before a stomach X-ray. I half expected my partner to start glowing.

"Keep that shit away from me." I waved my hand, but it didn't diffuse the stink.

"I didn't do anything," Dixon said.

"Well, I just got back from Cal's, so I haven't been here," I said.

We walked into Chief's office, and he nodded toward

the door. "Close it."

"Fuck," I said under my breath to Dixon as I turned to close the door. "*What did you do?*"

His elbow landed into my ribs. I ground my teeth and took the seat beside him.

Before the chief began to talk, he started scratching the top of his head. "I wanted to wait to relay this until I knew it was concrete." He continued to scratch his head. "But this came from someone at DCI I trust."

"DCI? Did Dixon get the job?" I asked.

The chief's eyes widened. "Oh damn, sorry, Dixon, this isn't about the position. I don't have any updates on that. But from what I'm told, a lot of guys applied." He rubbed the bald part of his head.

"During the interview, they said it could take up to three months before they selected a candidate," Dixon said.

I felt like an asshole for asking.

"Actually, this is about the cyberattack, and more specifically, Gene Hanson." The chief stopped scratching his head and just laid his hand on the top of it while he talked. Usually when he did this, it was a tell that he was following orders from above, or he was in over his head.

Since all the chief's tics—tightening his tie, strumming his fingers across his Glock, and scratching his head—involved his hands, the detectives called these tells the chief's hand jobs. But now, I wasn't so sure. Was the chief in over his head or was he was following orders?

"What about Gene Hanson?" Dixon asked. "We've known he's the one that orchestrated the attack."

"What we didn't know was why," Chief said.

"I thought he had a beef with the governor because he was denied parole," I said.

"And that seemed probable," Chief said.

"But…?" I said.

"Pring, when you reported that one of the offices affected was Social Security, something about it didn't feel right," Chief said. "That's when I reached out to an old friend at DCI and he confirmed my suspicions. Hanson may have targeted the governor, but the office that was impacted the greatest wasn't the governor's office, but Social Security."

"What's the connection?" I asked.

"That's what I wanted to find out, but it took some digging. Hanson's records were hard to access," Chief said.

"Why? He's in the system. What would be hard about accessing his records?" Dixon asked.

"Unless he's well-connected," I said.

The chief slowly nodded and laid his hands on his desk. "Gene Hanson is the grandson of the late Ames Reed, which means he's the grandson of—"

"Estelle Reed." I cut off the chief, something I normally wouldn't do, but when it came to Estelle, I had no filter. "There's not even a single degree of separation between that woman and chaos." I thought about Murray, and my gut tightened.

"Agreed," Chief said.

"But if she's so well-connected, why is her grandson in prison?" Dixon asked.

"Apparently, Estelle was partially responsible for

placing him there. He stole something from her, and she filed charges," Chief said. "Combined with the other B&Es accrued on his jacket, the judge gave him a hefty sentence."

"Damn. I knew the woman was heartless, but I didn't know how deep her cruelty ran," I said.

"So, her grandson attacked Social Security because of his grandmother," Dixon said.

"Social Security was shut down the longest," Chief said. "It would have impacted her."

"Sure, if she collected Social Security, but come on, she's the heir to Ames Oil. She's not hurting," I said.

"That's what I thought," Chief said. "But apparently, it was a second wedding for both of them, and Ames required Estelle to sign a prenup. She had access to as much Ames Oil money as she wanted while he was alive, but as soon as he died, she received a modest part of his estate. The children and grandchildren inherited the bulk."

"Then how could she afford *that* lawyer?" I asked. I couldn't even say his name.

"Estelle may be collecting social security, but my sense is she hid a lot of her finances and assets before she filed for social security. She's no dummy. She's got money. It's just not on paper. And her renters made their checks out to her grandson, Gene. So that income wasn't in her name either."

"About those grandchildren, wouldn't that include Gene Hanson? And if so, why's the guy a petty crook if he's basically a trust-fund baby?" Dixon asked.

The chief drummed his fingers on the desk. It was a new tell. "Gene's continued legal troubles apparently put a large burden—both emotionally and physically—on Ames, and strained his relationship with his only daughter, Annie, Gene's mother. Ames apparently was very close with Annie, who died of uterine cancer. When she died, Ames was so devastated, he stopped bailing out his grandson. He figured, if Gene couldn't be there for his mother when she was dying, he wouldn't be there for him. So, of all his grandchildren, Gene was the only one Ames excluded from his will. Without Ames's influence, Gene served time for B&E, and when he was paroled, he lived with Estelle."

Chief rubbed his thumb across his coffee mug. "Apparently, Estelle took pity on Gene, who is technically her stepgrandchild. Ames and Estelle never had any children together. But Estelle allowed him to live with her, and he did odd jobs for her at the properties she owned. She undervalued the two homes she owns and no one at Social Security ever looked into it. Or, if they did, I suspect Gene may have known someone at Social Security who helped hide her assets or accept the devaluation of them. Anyway, it appeared to be going well, and Gene met weekly with his parole officer." The chief placed his hands back on his head. "Then he stopped showing up. That's about the time he stole something from Estelle."

I laced my hands over my head like the chief and placed them on my scalp. "So that's why Hanson launched his cyberattack on Social Security, because it would impact Estelle?"

"That's what DCI believes," Chief said.

"That's one jacked-up family tree," Dixon said.

"And rooted. It took considerable research and background checks to link all the limbs together, which is why it's taken so long," Chief said.

I leaned forward in my chair. "Chief, I think it's great that, together with DCI, all these dots were connected. Now we know what prompted Hanson's cyberattack on Cheyenne's capital, but it doesn't change the fact that Estelle did something so much more heinous to that dog—not to mention threaten a peace officer with a loaded gun—but thanks to her connection to Ames's lawyer, she won't ever be held accountable, while her grandson will spend another good chunk of time at Rawlins."

"It's frustrating, but we can keep Estelle on our radar," Chief said.

"So she's not off-limits?" I clarified.

"She's a person of interest in an ongoing investigation," Chief said.

"The renters who she threatened and locked out didn't file charges," Dixon said.

"Well, part of the reason was that her grandson, Gene, and not Estelle, was listed on the lease. But there's still the unresolved issue of animal cruelty," Chief said. "While both parties are blaming the other, that doesn't dissolve the issue that an animal was injected with, sprayed with, or inhaled anesthesia."

"Anesthesia?" Dixon leaned forward.

Chief looked at me. "I know Cal brought you up to speed today."

I glanced at Dixon. "I just found out."

"Dixon, Cal ran blood toxins on the dog, and found…." Chief referenced the yellow legal pad on his desk. "Halothane, which is an FDA-banned anesthesia. Wyoming may not have the strongest animal protection laws, but the introduction of a banned anesthesia raises the stakes from misdemeanor cruelty to animals to aggravated cruelty, which as you both know is a higher misdemeanor punishable by a year imprisonment, a five-thousand-dollar fine, or both." Chief drummed his fingers across the legal pad. "We're going for broke."

"What do you need us to do?" Dixon asked.

"Work your contacts in the field. Keep your eyes open, and find tangible proof that Estelle Reed injected or sprayed that dog with Halothane."

"Chances are this investigation may not yield anything, but Murray—" I smiled and looked at the Chief and then Dixon. "That's the dog's name. His suffering is something I haven't forgotten since the night I found him. And I don't think I'll ever forget it. But now, maybe his suffering won't have been in vain."

"That's what we're aiming for," Chief said, and nodded toward the door. "Keep me updated on your progress."

CHAPTER **FORTY-ONE**

REESE

White lights strung on the eaves of the hotel twinkled in the night sky. Boughs of holly hung from the windows, and the brass bell that Harvey, the doorman, rang ushered in the holiday season. Harvey opened both doors to allow me and my packages to enter the lobby.

"Thanks, Harv," I said.

"Anytime, Ms. Pemberton."

I stopped and turned on the heel of my snow-covered boot. "Harvey, it's Reese. Please. It's okay to call me Reese."

His cheeks were already ruddy from the cold, but they brightened. "Okay, well, if I don't see you next week when I'm on vacation, Merry Christmas, Reese."

"Oh, Merry Christmas, Harvey. Have a great holiday with your family." I practically skipped into the lobby, where Zavi was stationed behind the front desk. A twelve-foot Douglas fir tree rose toward the vaulted ceiling. Red ribbons were tied to the tips of the branches, and strands of popcorn were strung along the tree. Chunky, ceramic holiday bulbs in opaque green, blue, red, and yellow were draped on the limbs, giving the tree a vintage feel. It reminded me of my childhood.

"Millie and Wild Bill did such a good job on our tree."

Millie's blonde head popped out from behind the tree. "I'm still here, boss."

"Millie! Every time I see the tree, it just keeps getting better." I knelt and placed my wrapped packages beneath the tree on the red velvet skirt that wrapped around the base. I carefully scattered the gifts about.

"Boss, I thought we weren't placing real gifts under the tree, only wrapped empty boxes," Millie said.

I shrugged. "I did say that, didn't I?"

Zavi burst out laughing. "Yes, you did. I think you even put it in a memo."

I shook my head and held up a finger. "No. Memos aren't my thing. You've got me confused with corporate. Corporate *loves* memos." I gently tucked the last gift—a small jewelry-sized box—beneath the tree. "Speaking of corporate, I finally got the okay to have a painting commissioned of Campbell with a plaque beneath it for the front lobby."

"Oh, Reese, that's great," Zavi said.

"What's great?" Toby seemed to appear out of thin air, but I knew he had been in the walls behind the second-floor library. I wanted to ensure the love lounge was fully stocked with goodies for the staff during the holidays, and I had placed Toby in charge.

"Toviah," I said with a grin. "That's the Hebrew of Tobias."

He shook his head. "I'm not Jewish."

"Yeah, but it's the holidays, and I thought I should be politically correct and include all possible nicknames." I raised my eyebrows. "How'd the project turn out?"

"Santa's little helpers will be happy with all the fixings and the improved, ramped-up heating in the love lounge," Toby said. "And it's all to code."

"Excellent." I glanced from Zavi to Millie. "Okay guys, spread the word. The love lounge has better heat and more to eat." I slapped my thigh. "Ha! That rhymes."

My staff looked at each other and then laughed.

"Tobster, I just got the approval for a painting to be commissioned of Campbell, so if you want to ask your wife if she'd still like to paint it, we can proceed."

"Doc, that's wonderful. Ann will be so happy. You won't be disappointed. She's a great artist."

"I'm excited. It only took corporate a month and a half to agree to our suggestion to honor Campbell with a portrait in our lobby." I stood and wiped the pine needles off my jeans. "But I see it as our early Christmas gift."

"Did they say anything about our idea for the getaway promotion?" Zavi asked.

I tapped my teeth together. "Good question. I proposed both in the same email. But after I read the opening line giving us the okay for Campbell, I didn't finish reading the rest of the message." I grabbed my cell phone out of my back pocket, scrolled to the email, and read silently. I never knew what to expect from corporate, and I wasn't about to have them Scrooge the upcoming holiday with something nasty.

> *Reese,*
>
> *Happy Holidays! After discussing your proposal for a painting of army officer Campbell Matthews, we agreed it would be a wonderful, historic addition to the hotel. Please keep the total cost for the portrait and plaque to the suggested five hundred dollars.*

I'd suggested a thousand, knowing they'd cut it in half. Thankfully, Toby's wife had agreed to the commission. I skimmed the rest of the email.

> *The proposal for a Ghost of a Chance Rendezvous Weekend was also accepted. We'll tie this into the marketing plan you provided that will allow guests to rendezvous with the hotel's wonderful, historic past for a weekend. The horse-drawn carriage rides and campfire dinners at Curt Gowdy State Park were all well-received. Creative thinking. However, instead of offering the weekend package for three hundred, we propose that the all-inclusive weekend for two begin at five hundred to include the carriage ride and one campfire dinner. Extra amenities, such as a guided tour of Cheyenne, would be an additional cost.*

I smiled. "They agreed to five hundred for the weekend."

"That's what we wanted, right?" Millie said.

Millie, Wild Bill, Zavi, and Toby comprised my executive team. After reading the suggestions provided by the staff, which proposed that instead of shying away from the hotel's history, we tap into it, we did.

"Yup, Millie. We aimed for five hundred for the weekend to still turn a profit without overpricing the stay, so I wrote the proposal suggesting three hundred."

Toby laughed. "That's some clever thinking, Doc."

I tilted my head. "Tobias, not clever, I just know how corporate operates."

"Remember how you said we had a ghost of a chance to make this work?" Zavi raised an eyebrow. "Looks like we achieved the unlikely."

"Yes, we did. And fingers crossed when we market our Ghost of a Chance Rendezvous Weekend it'll be just as well-received." I clapped. "Okay, enough shop talk. Tonight is our staff holiday party, so everyone go home and get ready. I've got the phones and front desk covered. I want you all to enjoy yourselves."

As soon as my staff scurried away, I called Cody.

"So…."

"So…," he said.

"Come on, now. Don't make me beg."

"But I like it when you beg," he said.

"Cody Pring! Stop playing and please tell me that the newest addition to our family has arrived." No sooner had the word escaped my lips than I felt my neck burn with heat. *Family? WTF?*

"Our family?"

I cleared my throat. "Uh, I'm at the hotel. It's hotel talk. You know, like welcome to the family… of hotels."

His laughter broke the sweat on my forehead that threatened to drown me.

"So?" I asked again.

"Yes. The newest addition is home at last." As if on cue, I heard the sound of his bark. "That's a good boy, Murray," Cody said.

"When can I see him? What about tonight? At the Christmas party? He could come with you. You know we have dog amenities and we're a dog-friendly hotel."

"Reese, I really want to be at the party, and I know the Point is dog-friendly, but I don't know if Murray's party-ready yet. And I don't know about leaving him home alone."

"Sure. Of course. I understand." It was probably the first time I wasn't 100 percent with Cody. I did understand, but I wasn't thrilled. I wanted to share the surprises I had for the staff with him. *Maybe next year.*

When the grandfather clock in the foyer struck seven, I forwarded the phones to the telephone service I'd hired for the night, placed a sign on the front desk with my work cell number for guests, and took Otis to the sixth floor. I hadn't been in suite 632 since Halloween night. But something drew me back to Campbell and Ella's ill-fated honeymoon suite. Maybe it was the news from corporate that I'd finally be able to right his wrong, if only in a portrait to honor him, but Campbell's suite was where I planned to prepare for my first holiday party. I still couldn't believe I was GM of one of the greatest hotels with the best staff in one fantastic western city. Life was good. My master key opened the suite, where my green holiday dress hung in the closet.

"Nothing's as elegant as lace." I held the dress toward me, repeating what Sheridan had said when she helped me find the right shade of green. We instantly connected when Cody introduced us after Halloween, so when I needed a dress for tonight's holiday party, she was my first call. Leave it to "Peach," as Cody called her, to find the perfect green that complemented my red hair without making me look like the Joker. And at a thrift store, no less. The dress had a vintage feel that I wanted for the holiday party. Even on the hanger, the lace clung against me. It wasn't just elegant, it was alluring. And Cody wouldn't see me in it. *Bummer.*

I quickly texted a picture to Sheridan.

Me: It's everything. Thank you. Xo.

I pitched my cell on the bed and grabbed my overnight bag, where I found what I referred to as my heaven-scented bath bomb. I tossed it into the tub and turned the dial toward hot. The pastel pink-tiled bathroom in the suite reminded me of the one in my rental. I kicked off my boots, stepped out of my jeans, and tossed my sweater in the corner. The bomb fizzed as I stepped into swirls of shimmering silver and pink that tinted and softened the water. The sweet scent of lavender, the scintillating hint of jasmine, and the potent aroma of rose blended together into what Cody called heaven. I called it the most relaxing, indulgent soak ever. Winter had finally arrived, and my skin took a beating. My hands and lips were always chapped, but after one bath bomb, my skin felt silky and smooth. I turned off the water, grabbed a hand towel, and placed it beneath my head. I had an hour until I had to be in the grand ballroom to host my staff. I closed my eyes and let my senses come alive. The water lapped against the side of the tub, and his faint whistle sank me further into a state of relaxation and warmth.

"Hello, doll." Campbell held the car door open.

Snow fell on him, and I saw in Ella's eyes she was in love. She had that glow people get when they see the person they're crazy about.

"Where's your bag?" he asked when she approached him. She stood before him empty-handed.

"I can't go," she said quietly.

"What do you mean, doll?" He placed his hand on her shoulder as he guided her into the car.

I watched her try to resist his direction, but she instinctively followed his lead and sat in the front seat of the town car. A small American flag waved from the black hood, and his olive-colored army jacket draped across the seat. It was adorned with medals and stars, reminding her of his higher military rank.

"Now, what's this nonsense about not going?" He got into the car and started the engine. "Party jitters? I told you it's only an officers' Christmas party, nothing to worry about."

I studied Ella, who was lost in thought. What was she thinking?

"My father doesn't approve of our courtship."

Campbell slowly nodded. "He'll come around. It's only been six months. He's skeptical. I understand. It'll take time, but he'll come around."

I leaned toward Ella until her thoughts became my own.

Her parents were driving to her grandparents' home in Colorado, which was how she was able to sneak away. Campbell had planned an overnight getaway before he had to depart for another training mission, and she still hadn't told him she had to end their courtship that had moved at such a whirlwind pace she hadn't been able to think of anything but him and their future together. But her father was clear. Campbell was not right for her. Yet, despite the tension in her shoulders, she relaxed beside him and smiled.

"That's better," he said, rubbing her thigh. "Doll." He reached into the pocket of his white dress shirt. "This should cheer you up." He handed her a key.

"Campbell?" she stammered. "What? What is this?"

"It's a key to our suite. I worked out an arrangement with the front desk manager that you can access the suite anytime you want. So, while I'm away, if you need some time for yourself, the suite is yours to enjoy. We'll try your key out tonight."

"Tonight?"

He nodded and smiled.

"But I didn't pack—"

"Don't worry, doll. It's all taken care of."

I couldn't tell is his self-assuredness attracted her to him or not.

"First, we're going to a private dinner at the general's house, before the officers' cocktail party."

"But my dress…," she began, and then quietly looked down at the simple navy dress she was wearing. It wasn't what she would have chosen to wear to meet a general, but it was one of the few dresses she had that wouldn't have alarmed her sisters when she left. She'd told them she was meeting a friend for drinks. Her navy dress wasn't a holiday party dress. It was a dress that went unnoticed. Sadness washed over her.

"We've got time," Campbell said as they reached the back highway that led to the base. He accelerated, merging past a truck on the two-lane road. "There's a little boutique I know just past Cheyenne. We'll go find you something there."

A little boutique. The thought settled in her body. How would he know about a boutique? Had he done this before? Her sadness became heavier.

"Don't worry, doll, we've got time," he repeated, gently stroking the side of her face.

Ella turned toward his hand and looked up at him. She knew every line on his face and the way his thick, dark hair fell to the side when he didn't put enough pomade in it. His hands were large and made her feel small when he held her. She knew he splashed Old Spice on his face, which made him smell spicy and manly. But it was the dollop of shaving cream he always missed by his ear that drew him to her. She gently brushed it away. Everything Ella knew about Campbell, she cherished. It was the uncertainty of their future—sneaking around to be together—that kept her awake at night.

"Campbell," she began, "there's something I need to tell you." Her voice shook. He turned and looked at her.

"This isn't over. Doll, it'll never be over between us."

"I can't go to the hotel with you tonight," she said. "My father and mother will be home tomorrow. But my sisters are still here."

"That's okay. We have tonight, and we'll make the most of it."

He pulled into a parking lot covered in snow and walked around the car to open her door. The boutique owner opened his closed doors for them and discreetly fit Ella into an emerald green lace cocktail dress with matching shoes and handbag.

While Ella was fixing her hair in the mirror, Campbell reached into his shirt pocket and tucked something into her handbag. Was it the key? I thought he already gave it to her. I squinted, but I couldn't see what he put in her purse. I glanced at Ella, and the dress looked so familiar. Maybe it was the rich color that offset Ella's violet eyes and raven-colored hair, but I couldn't stop staring at the dress.

Intricate details like the scalloped hem and the formfitting yet flirty way the lace clung to her shape meant that Ella looked like a beautiful dream as they dined at the general's table.

Ella blushed when Campbell excused them and led her to the general's living room, where his daughter played the piano. When they walked into the room, the young girl changed the tune to a Bing Crosby holiday song. Campbell's presence in his officer's uniform was disarmingly attractive and powerful to her. As he snapped his fingers to the music, she smiled. This was the man she loved and always would.

The car ride home was quiet. The night concluded where it began, a block from her house.

"Doll, you looked beautiful tonight."

She nodded as her throat tightened and her lips trembled.

"Wear this on Christmas." He touched the bodice of her dress. "Stop hiding your happiness."

Ella hid her face as she dissolved into a mass of tears.

"Oh, Campbell," she muttered as he pulled her toward him and held her.

"Shh, doll," he whispered in her hair.

Ella ached for her father to understand and for Campbell to be patient.

"I won't be here to spend Christmas with you, but you'll always be here." He touched his heart. "Always."

She nodded, but the mere sound of his voice made her cry even harder.

Campbell pulled her near to him and kissed her. She relaxed and became calm, knowing it wasn't over between them and it never would be. Theirs was a love affair for the ages. And her father would just have to understand. It was Christmastime—magical things were supposed to happen.

"Goodbye, doll." He kissed her before getting into his car.

Snow fell as Ella walked back to her father's house alone.

It was cold, and I felt the chill. I wrapped my arms around myself, but my lips trembled.

The alarm on my cell phone in the other room jarred me out of my sleep. I jerked forward, and the air in the bathroom was cool. The bath water had chilled, and I hadn't turned on the bathroom heater. My escape into the tub for shimmering, glowing skin hadn't quite turned out. I was cold and my skin was goose pimpled. But as I stepped out of the tub, my thoughts returned to my dream. Ella and Campbell struggled before they ever got married. How could it have worked? Yet theirs was a love story that created a sadness in my body that was hard to shake. Why couldn't they have just made it work? Why didn't he give her a key to a home and not a hotel?

I wrapped a towel around me and reached for my phone. There was a text from Sheridan.

Sheridan: You're going to look beautiful tonight! Take lots of pics!

I half smiled. *Lots of pics by myself.* As I found myself slipping into self-pity, my thoughts returned to Ella. My dad would love Cody. My whole family would. I wasn't pitted between my family and the man I was falling for. *Nope. Not having Cody at tonight's holiday party is not a deal breaker.*

But what felt like a deal breaker was the back zipper that Sheridan had zipped me into at the thrift store. My arms weren't long enough to reach the middle of my back, where the zipper remained. I wiggled, but it didn't inch the zipper to the top of the high neckline. *Damn.*

I turned sideways and faced the full-length mirror hanging on the inside of the closet door and gasped. The silhouette of the sheer lace, scalloped hem, and flirty-yet-refined dress that hit me at the knee was exactly like Ella's Christmas dress.

"Is this her dress?" I tried to spy the back inside label, but despite what my brother said, my head didn't turn all the way around like a scene from *The Exorcist*.

This dress felt like it belonged to Ella. The similarities were eerie. I slipped my foot into the matching green shoes that Sheridan had found at the thrift store. I was only missing Ella's handbag and, of course, Campbell.

"Hey." I spoke toward the ceiling. "I got corporate to commission a portrait of you, so if there's a picture of you that you like, let me know and I'll have it painted to do you justice."

There was no response. I wasn't surprised. Campbell only revealed himself to me in my dreams. And I hadn't been visited by him since Halloween. Maybe that's why I'd returned to their suite. I missed their love story. I missed the happy times.

I smoothed the front of my dress. "If you were here, Campbell, I could really use an assist with my back zipper."

I glanced over my shoulder at my pale Irish skin that practically glowed in winter. Thankfully, my hair would cover the open back until I could find someone to zip me up.

"It's not Christmas yet, but if I don't get back to your suite, Merry Christmas, Campbell."

I turned off the lights in the suite and had grabbed the door handle when it twisted in my hand.

CHAPTER **FORTY-TWO**

CODY

Even in the dim light, her hazel eyes sparked. "Cody?"

I stepped into the suite and palmed the wall until the light glowed overhead. I stood before the most beautiful woman I'd ever seen. In a green dress that embraced every delicious curve of her body, she was a vision.

"Wow."

She slightly tilted her head, and ribbons of red, crimped hair fell forward, covering part of her face. I gently tucked a long lock behind her ear.

"You're missing something," I said.

Her eyes again flashed. "Oh! My zipper!"

She turned around, pulled her hair off her back, and looked over her shoulder at me from beneath those long, dark lashes that made me want to ravage her. "Zip me up?"

I grimaced. "You're really testing me here, Reese. I mean, why should I zip you up when I want to be unzipping you?"

"Please?"

"Could I ever say no to you?"

She shrugged with a happy grin while I carefully pulled the zipper up her slender back. I took a step back. "You look so beautiful, but you're still missing something."

Her smiled turned upside down.

I reached into my dinner jacket and withdrew a Tiffany blue box that was crowned with a white ribbon and placed it in the palm of her hand.

"What is this?" Her face flushed and my heart beat faster.

"It's a gift from Murray."

"Oh my gosh, where is he? I can't wait to meet him."

"He's being dog sat by Peach and Dixon."

Her hand went to her chest. "Oh, that's so sweet, but you didn't have to be here."

"Reese, there's no place I'd rather be."

Her eyes said everything. When Reese looked at me, all my tomorrows looked better. "Open it."

She untied the ribbon, lifted the lid off the box, and tilted her head. "Oh, Cody."

"Peach said you didn't have anything sparkly for your dress."

"They're beautiful."

"They're black diamonds." I laughed. "Which until now I didn't realize was either cheesy or apropos, I'm not sure."

"Definitely *not* cheesy." Her hand gently touched mine. "But very apropos. You're my black diamond." She placed the diamond studs in each ear. They shone like the rare gem she was.

"Do you like them?" They suddenly seemed so small for the price I paid. *Damn Tiffany.*

"Cody, I *love* them." She gently kissed me, and our lips lingered together. I could kiss Reese all night long.

"Oh, Cody, I love…." Her cheeks spiked crimson, and I smiled. "I love *Murray* for giving me such a thoughtful, beautiful, amazing Christmas gift."

"Nice save." I raised an eyebrow.

"No save. Just the truth. I love Murray. He's one dog with some *fine* taste."

"Murray for the win."

She smiled. "Exactly. Murray for the win." She put the jewelry box on the entry table in the suite. "Your gift's downstairs beneath the tree. I was planning on giving it to you tonight after the party, but I can't wait." She grabbed my hand and was headed toward the open door when she spotted my overnight bag in the hall.

"What's this?" Now she raised an arched eyebrow.

I shrugged. "Sheridan insists that Murray spend the night with them. So I was thinking…."

"That you know the GM of the best hotel in Cheyenne?"

"Know? Hell, I'm hooked up with the *hottest* GM at the best hotel in Wyoming."

She grinned widely. "Yeah, you are. Let's go celebrate!" She grabbed my bag and placed it in the closet beside hers. Our luggage looked like a perfect pair.

"I almost forgot, there's one more thing." I unzipped my bag and handed her an emerald purse that fit with her dress and shoes. "It's from Peach. She went back to the thrift store and found it in some bargain bin. She thought it'd match your outfit."

Reese's eyes misted. "It's a complete set." She opened the purse, dropped her master key inside, and before she placed her phone in the purse, she checked the time. "Party, then present?"

"Party, then present."

CHAPTER **FORTY-THREE**

"Doc, this is one of the best parties we've ever had." Toby and his wife, Ann, danced beside Cody and me.

"It's the Bee Gees, isn't it?" I swayed to the smooth sound of the Bee Gees. If I didn't look at the Wyoming-based band, I was okay. If I did, it ruined everything. The band I hired lived up to their reputation and sounded like carbon copies of the band of brothers. But they looked nothing like them. The banquet stage held a band of beer-belly rocker wannabes. They had all the costume clichés, and thankfully the singing talent, but their leather pants looked more like sausage casings, and half-open silk shirts exposed graying chest hair and barely covered their expansive stomachs. If anything, they looked like a Bee Gees cover band whose clothes barely covered them. But again, they could sing, and when they crooned about crying a river, it set the tone for a great dance night.

Cody was definitely in his element. The man had moves. *Damn.* The last time we danced was on Halloween, and we were both still learning our own dance. Months later, we melded into each other like we were one.

"I can't wait to see that dress on the floor," he whispered in my ear.

I closed my eyes and felt his breath on my neck. I imagined his hands roaming my body while he discovered new ways to bring me pleasure. Cody said I smelled like heaven, but he *was* heaven.

When the band kicked up the beat, he swirled me away from him, and on the return, his lips stopped me cold. I wrapped my arms around his neck, he placed his around my waist, and we slow grooved while the band sang that we should have been dancing.

"The sushi bar was a hit," Wild Bill said, dancing past us with Millie.

"Don't forget the sushi chef and sake," I chimed in.

"Wild Bill's already had *a lot* of sake," Millie said.

"That's okay. I knew the alcohol would be flowing freely, so I've got the shuttle service so everyone can enjoy the party," I said.

"Is there anything you didn't do for this party?" Wild Bill asked.

I playfully batted my eyes. "Oh, I don't know. Yummy dinner, dancing, and door prizes? I think I covered it all."

"Usually, company holiday parties are boring yawn fests or drunken, embarrassing exploits with really bad table dancing," Cody said with a grin as Wild Bill and Millie danced away. "Not that I know about the latter."

"Sure." I giggled. "I want this party to become the stuff of legends, but for the right reason."

"Why?" Cody's light green eyes honed in on me.

"Corporate's not going to reward these employees with gifts or bonuses, so I did."

"Because…."

I hesitated. Cody was persistent because he knew I was holding back. He pressed me into him.

"What aren't you telling me?"

It was his detective skills at work, his boyfriend radar. Cody just got me. He knew when I wasn't 100 percent.

"If the hotel doesn't turn a considerable profit by spring, it'll be put on the auction block and sold to the highest bidder," I said.

"For real."

I nodded.

"Reese, I didn't know."

I shrugged. "I came here with one objective—to learn how to be a GM in the hotel industry with a small property. Who knew I'd be placed at the beautiful, antiquated, Historic Wyoming Point Resort in Cheyenne that has one working elevator—and that's questionable—steam heat, a boiler that I never care to visit again, and a resident ghost. But this hotel gave me a chance. So when corporate revealed their plans, I began to think of ways to resurrect what was once a great phoenix in the hotel industry."

"Which is why you work all the time," Cody said.

"Yes, but so do you, so it's a good partnership."

"I prefer family," he said, and it felt like my heart melted in my chest.

"I really do love your dog," I said, which I hoped he knew was code for him.

"And he really loves you."

We lingered on the dance floor, kissing, until the beer-belly band needed a break. I grabbed my purse off the table and had opened it to check my cell phone when I noticed a small inside pocket. I opened it, hoping to find a blank cashier's check that was big enough to buy the hotel, but instead I found a black-and-white photo. The folded corners were yellow, but the image was clear. I sat down and turned the picture toward the light from the candle centerpiece. The flame illuminated the khaki officer's hat, dark eyes, and sideways smile.

"Oh my gosh." A chill crept down my spine.

"Did we miss a guest?" Wild Bill and Milly sat at the table beside Cody.

I shook my head. "No." I smiled. "I mean, maybe, many, many years ago."

"What?" Cody asked.

I turned the photo to face the table and Toby and his wife who had joined us. "This is Campbell."

"Our Campbell?" Millie said.

"Yes. Our Campbell." I passed the picture around.

"How'd you get that?" Toby asked.

"It was in my purse." I stared at the purse and knew it was Ella's. It had to be. I didn't know about the dress or shoes, but the purse had to be hers. "I can't believe it." I glanced at Cody. "I dreamt about them while I took a bath."

"You mean his spirit visited you again?" Wild Bill said.

I nodded. "Yeah, he did. And it was Christmastime. He bought Ella this beautiful dress and gave her a key to their suite. He worked something out with the front desk manager."

"I imagine," Wild Bill said. "Backdoor deals happened here all the time."

"It wasn't anything shady," I said. "I think it was just his way of having a place for Ella to go." I looked at Toby's wife and Millie. "Ella and Campbell loved each other, but Ella's family disapproved of their courtship, and even though it was the forties, she didn't have the same independence we do."

"I can only imagine," Ann said. "My grandmother came from money and so did my grandfather, but my mom has told me many times how my grandmother's money came with conditions. Thankfully, her parents liked my grandfather."

"Ella's father didn't, and so she suffered her father and the restrictions he placed on her. He put a roof over her head, but he cut her off emotionally. It was really hard on her," I said.

"It sounds like you're defending a woman who basically killed her husband," Toby said, "or at least from what you've told us of these visits."

"I'm not defending her actions, but even tonight I saw a different angle to their relationship," I said.

Ann held the photo. "This would make a great portrait."

I leaned against the back of my chair with a gentle awareness that somehow Campbell had gotten the photo to me. "You're right. That's the one." Tiny goose pimples rose on my arms and legs, but this time it wasn't from being cold. It was knowing Campbell had made contact with me in this world.

"I'll make a copy of this and return the original to you," Ann said. "If that's okay?"

I smiled. "That's perfect." I glanced around the table. "Well, combined with getting corporate's approval for our Ghost of a Chance Rendezvous Weekend, this has turned out to be a better holiday party than I hoped for." I placed my hand on Cody's knee. "I still have some Santa gifts to hand out, so if you'll excuse me...." I stood and guided Cody out of his seat and toward the lobby, where his smile turned upside down.

"What?"

"I thought we were going back to your suite," he said.

"Soon." I smiled and led him to the Christmas tree. He sat beside me on the velvet skirt that wrapped around the tree. I reached into the stack of real and fake presents until I found the small box.

"Close your eyes and hold out your hand, and you will get a very big surprise," I said.

"So we are going back to your suite."

"Don't be an idiot." I giggled. "Now, close your eyes."

Cody's beautiful eyes closed, and I placed the wrapped box in his hand. He opened his eyes and seemed to study the box.

"It's not a ring," I said, and relief visibly washed over him. I swatted his shoulder. "Oh my gosh! Did you really think I'd do that?"

"You remind me a lot of my sister—in a good, not creepy way—and she popped the question to Dixon, so yeah, anything's possible."

"Well, good for Sheridan, but no, this isn't a ring. It is, though"—I slyly smiled—"a proposal."

"Hmm." He ripped apart the red foil paper, popped the lid off the box, and picked up the circular silver charm. "Is this…?"

"I told you I loved your dog."

His eyes watered, and he wiped them on the sleeve of his jacket. "Reese, this is beautiful." He held the dog tag engraved with "Murray."

"Flip it over."

When he did, he didn't even try to hide the tear that ran down his cheek. His voice cracked when he read the inscription. "Always by my side, forever in my heart."

"I guess it's not a proposal as much as a promise," I said.

He leaned into me with the warmth, tenderness, and passion of a man in love. And I responded.

CHAPTER **FORTY-FOUR**

CODY

Damn. It was the most perfectly shaped side breast I'd ever seen. I'd spent every night with Reese since her holiday party, and I still couldn't get enough of her. Her thighs were toned, tapered, and added to the overall lean shape of her legs. Her knee was slightly propped up like she was lying out at the beach and not leaning against one of the oldest brick walls in Cheyenne.

Her toes were painted dark violet. I didn't have a foot fetish, but her toes could change that. They were as suckable as her side breast that kept poking out of her jog bra.

What is it about this woman that makes my palms sweat and my mouth get dry whenever I'm with her?

Her hair screamed to be released from whatever she had it trapped in. I reached toward her to do just that, but she swatted away my hand.

"No, sir. We're running." She covered her perfect piggies

with socks and stuffed them into her running shoe. "I've waited longer than the six weeks suggested, and I'm ready to finally test out this knee."

I pressed against her. "Do you really think you should push it? Maybe we should go back to my place. I know Murray misses you. We can start a fire"—I raised an eyebrow—"and do all that *reading* you claimed to want to do once the snow fell."

Her eyes widened. "Oh my gosh! Thanks for reminding me. When Toby moved me in, we were rushed so we just put boxes wherever we could find space. But I haven't been able to find my books. I finally asked him if he might know where they are, and he told me they're in the basement cellar. That's why I couldn't find them. I've been meaning to grab the box. Thanks for reminding me."

"Sure, think nothing of it."

When her running shoes were laced, she swayed her hips. "Cody, I get to run!"

I rolled my eyes. "Yippee. It's only ten degrees out."

"Yes, but the sun's out, and the streets are dry, so it's a good day to run."

"It's Sunday. Sundays are meant to be lazy, remember?"

"I do." She smiled.

"So let's go be lazy."

She shrugged. "If you're not into it, I'm sure I could find another running partner."

"Nuh-uh. That may have worked the first night we were together and every other time, but—"

"Cody, it's cool. I know not every man can keep up

with me." She lowered her sunglasses, tucked her earbuds into her ears, and raised one eyebrow. "But those guys who *can* keep up are *richly, deeply* rewarded." She hit the side of her cell phone that was wrapped around her arm, and I could hear the music.

Bruce Springsteen. Shit. Who didn't like the Boss?

She shot out of the alley like she was the Flash. *Damn, wild redhead's gonna get hit by a car if she's not careful.*

I followed behind her, not because I was slower, but I had a better view. *The girl's got a fine ass.* She turned on 17th Street and headed toward Carey. Estelle's house was on Carey. *There's no way she'll run all the way to 30th Street. It's too damn cold.* Still, I trailed closely behind her.

The closer we got to 30th Street, the more my heart rate increased. Ballistics hadn't been able to link crazy's Colt to any other crime. Not that I was surprised with a gun that old. The only hope we had of putting Estelle away—even for as little as a year—was if we could connect her to the Halothane used on Murray. I don't care how or where she hid her money, not even her pricey, five-hundred-dollar-an-hour attorney could get her out of that charge. There was no jury in Wyoming that would side with an animal abuser, not in the cowboy state.

I stared at the house in the distance. The roof on the corner house was covered with snow. A single strand of pathetic white holiday lights was strung haphazardly across the eaves. As I got closer, I noticed the front door had been replaced with an oak door, which was actually an improvement. Fake garland was draped over the doorframe, and red bows were tied to the outside trees and mailbox. If I didn't know the horrors hidden within, the house had a real Christmas feel to it—even though Christmas was like two weeks ago. Stupid bitch.

The house may look homey, but I knew. And Murray knew. I stared at the corner house.

"It's cute, right?" Reese jogged in place, waiting for me.

I nodded toward the stoplight up ahead. "Oh, hey, that's a long light. Let's get there by the time it turns green so we don't have to wait."

"Oh, I was just going to turn around and run the same way we came." She jogged toward me and had leaned in to kiss me when something silver flashed from one of the windows in Estelle's house. I whipped my head toward the house. But all I saw was tinsel hanging from the tops of trees like frosted cupcakes.

"You really like this house, too, don't you?"

I forced a smile. "Hey, what's this about turning around." I had to get Reese away from this house, but she seemed intent to linger. "What fun is that? Come on, let's make this count."

Reese smiled. "Sure. I'm all about making it count." And with that, she finally darted past Estelle's house of horrors. I stared at the house, and it looked like someone was standing in front of one of the upstairs windows. I squinted against the afternoon sun, but whatever I'd thought I saw wasn't there. My mind was playing tricks on me. *No one's watching us.*

CHAPTER FORTY-FIVE

REESE

"Hey, you okay?" I placed my hands in front of the heater in his truck. "You know I was just talking smack about finding someone else to run with, right?"

He nodded, but his thoughts were somewhere else. I unstrapped my iPhone from my arm and checked my messages. Nothing from the hotel, not that I expected it. The holidays were over and the hotel was quiet. But my landlord had texted that she needed to check the furnace today and asked what time would be good. I scanned the message to see when she'd sent the text. Must have been while I was running. I texted that I was on my way home and anytime would be fine.

"What do you say I prepare us something yummy for Sunday dinner?"

"Sure. Uh…." Instead of turning onto Evans, he headed up Warren. "Can we swing by my place first? I want to get

Murray. Do you think he could hang out with you? There's something I need to check at the office, and I don't want to leave him home alone any longer."

"Cody, you never have to ask. I love Murray."

Cody still had to help Murray into the truck, and it broke my heart. For all the energy Murray had, his hind legs just didn't seem to want to jump. Cody wouldn't tell me what had happened to the dog, or why, but it was clear by the scars on Murray's body he had been through hell.

"Hey, buddy," I said, and rubbed behind his ears. He sat between Cody and me and laid his head on my lap.

When Cody pulled alongside my rental, he carefully placed Murray on the sidewalk and handed me his leash. "What time? For dinner."

"My landlord texted while we were running and wants to come over and check the furnace, so how about we rendezvous at seven?"

Cody smiled. "Rendezvous, huh?"

I grinned.

He glanced at his cell. "Three hours? Is that enough time."

I laughed. "Yeah, I think even I can pull off dinner in three hours. Plus, it'll give me time to shower and grab my box of books in the basement cellar. Unless you want to shower with me?"

"I'd love to conserve water with you, but I really need to check something at the office."

His kiss was rushed. "I'll be back at seven."

He pulled away before I could say goodbye.

Steam rose above the pink porcelain tub and masked the mirrors in fog. A steady flow of water cascaded out of the copper pipe and washed over the Merlot-scented bath bomb Sheridan made for me for Christmas. She figured, since she couldn't drink the wine, she'd make bath bombs out of it. It worked, because the water had the scent of a good, woodsy Merlot and the feel of baby oil on my skin. I loved a quiet bath, and the absence of sound became more pronounced the further I sank into the warm abyss. Submerged, the tips of my breasts partially surfaced as they bobbed in and out of the silky water.

My hair swam freely. My body was energized from the run, and the warm water was a smoothing solace for my knee. Cocooned in heat, I occasionally came up for air to check on Murray, who lay on the cool tile. Then I'd reenter the white sound. *I love baths.*

Water trickled over the side of the tub and quietly landed on the pink tile. Murray's dark eyes looked at me from his mask.

"Sorry, buddy." I grabbed a towel and placed it between him and the tub. He laid his head on it and closed his eyes.

I slowly raised my head out of the water and rested it against the edge of the bathtub. "Murray, what should I make for dinner?" My fingers danced along the rim of the tub. All the pink reminded me of the extra salmon Chef sent me home with. I didn't have the heart or the guts to tell him

I thought fish was nasty.

But steak. Yum. "What about steak and salmon?"

Murray opened his eyes. "You can have the salmon, and we'll have steak."

His eyes looked sad. "I know it's not really a fair trade, but the vet did say fish was a good protein for you. So the next question is how to prepare them." I tapped my fingers on the tub. "I don't have a grill, but I have an oven. I could bake the steaks. That's a thing, right?"

Murray closed his eyes, and I leaned back and did the same thing. I mentally cataloged the contents of my refrigerator. Steak, bell pepper, onions, and beer. *Oh, fajitas.* "Murray." I opened my eyes and so did he. "I won't *bake* the steaks. I'll pan fry strips. Oh, that's a much better idea. Don't you think?"

I reached for my cell phone and texted Cody.

Me: Hey could you pick up tortillas, chips, and salsa?

His texted reply was instant.

Cody: Would you just like me to pick up takeout?

I rolled my head against the edge of the tub.

Me: No, no, no. I'm just missing a few things. See you at seven. And I've got fish for Murray.

While the steak gently sautéed on low heat with the onions and bell peppers, I slipped into a pair of jeans and soft University of Wyoming Cowboys sweatshirt, a gift from my staff. I towel dried my hair, grabbed my cell phone, and headed toward the basement cellar. Murray stood at the top of the stairs.

"Oh, buddy, I don't know if I can lift you." But the disheartened look on his face made me find Herculean strength. "Okay." I carefully scooped him into my arms and cradled him in my arms. The stairs that led to the basement cellar were concrete and unforgiving. *Please, do not fall.*

Murray nuzzled his wet, cold nose against my neck. When we safely reached the bottom stair, I slowly set him on the concrete and gently scratched behind his ear. Cody called it Murray's happy spot.

Murray lay beside me. I rubbed along his side and felt his ribs. "Oh, Murray. We've still got to fatten you up."

I placed my forehead on top of his head and softly spoke into his ear. "I don't know what happened to you, but it won't ever happen again." My throat tightened for this sweet dog. "I'm here. And so is Cody, who absolutely loves you."

Days were shorter in the winter, and moonlight cast its glow through a small basement window. Murray looked up at me. The dark mask around his face always made me smile. "I would have called you bandit, but that's just me.

"Okay, Murray, I'm looking for a box of books." The basement had the only overhead ceiling light, which made no sense. But after overseeing a hotel built in the 1900s, I realized there was no rhyme or reason to how things were built.

Behind where Murray lay was what I suspected was an electrical box mounted to the wall.

"Well, it's good to know where that is. If that's what it is." I scratched behind his ears. "Now if I could just find my box of books."

Murry laid his head on my knee.

"Okay? Can you stay here while I go look?" I gently moved his head off my knee and started to rise. Murray mirrored my movements and stood beside me. "I get it. You're going where I go. Understood."

I reached into my pocket and retrieved my cell phone. I activated the flashlight and shone it on the metal box mounted to the wall. It opened by a slide latch, which released nicely. The few utilities that fed into the electrical box were labeled: Kitchen, Master Bath, Guest Bath, Library, Master Bedroom.

"Yup, just what I thought." I was about to shut the door when my cell shone on something. It looked like an envelope. I picked it up.

What is this? Tucked inside the envelope was a folded paper. I sat on the concrete in front of the electrical box, with my back to the stairs, and unfolded the linen paper to find the letter was addressed to Ella.

> *Doll,*
>
> *Where do I begin? I had to write to explain these last couple of months. I never want you to doubt how I feel about you and what we have when we're together. You are in my every prayer, you are the breath that keeps me going, you are the only person I've ever wanted.*

I always knew chasing after you was wrong. You were on the verge of graduating, with college on the horizon. I understand your father's hesitancy toward me. I want to be able to provide a life for you, but I didn't realize that by reenlisting I was taking that away from you.

Doll, I've never met a person quite like you. You mean so much to me and to so many other people. That's why your father is protective. For the longest time, I blamed your father for us not being able to have an open courtship. But he did what he did for good reason. He knew I'd only hurt his youngest daughter. When I reenlisted, I did. Will you ever forgive me?

Whatever you decide, decide for yourself. Don't worry about your dad, or me, or anyone. And if you decide to remain married to me, or to be on your own, show the world who you really are. Show them the strong, fearless woman I fell in love with. Don't be afraid of your own power just because the men in your life are.

Doll, you are everything I've always wanted. I'm sorry I ever made you doubt yourself when I reenlisted. Don't doubt who you are or the love we have shared. Your courage, your spirit, your fearlessness—it's still there. And so am I. I will always be there for you.

When you look into the Wyoming sky—the first star you will see is mine for you. If I'm not

> *there to protect you, I will guard over you—*
> *now and forever. I love you—always.*
> *Campbell*

The letter fell to the floor. Murray nudged his wet nose against me. "Oh, Murray." Emotions blocked my throat. Again, our sweet dog nudged me.

"I don't understand?" My voice shook. "Why is this letter here?" I looked inside the envelope, and there was something stuck in the corner. I shone my cell phone and carefully retrieved it.

It was a photo of Ella. "What?" I flipped it over, and *Doll* was written on the backside. "I don't understand. Why is *this* here? This belongs to Ella and Campbell."

Murray slowly began to growl. His body tensed beside me, and his tail stiffened.

"What?" I lifted my head, and a pungent smell assaulted my senses. The last time I smelled something that bad was when I got keys to the house. I placed the photo in my back pocket just as Murray sprang to his feet, head and ears pulled back, brow furrowed, and his eyes rolled so the whites were visible even in the dim light. He intensely stared at someone or something behind me. A cold chill settled in the dank air. I knew I shouldn't have gone down here by myself.

I slowly stood, bracing my bare feet firmly on the concrete floor. A shiver ran down my neck as I turned around.

CHAPTER **FORTY-SIX**

CODY

The list on the dry-erase board in the chief's office was titled "Missing Evidence" and numbered. Questions were written next to each key piece of evidence listed. In the last hour, I had stared at the board. The one person who could answer a bulk of these questions was a dog. My dog.

I stared at the itemized list.

> 1. Halothane—Who knew? Where did banned Rx come from?

> 2. Serrated knife—Where is it? Was it used in any other crime against an animal?

> 3. Hanson—What does he know?

I reread each numbered piece of evidence: banned prescription drug, a knife, and an angry stepgrandson. Drugs, knife, burglar. Drugs, knife, burglar. Drugs, knife....

Burglar.

I hopped off the edge of Chief's desk and walked toward

the easel. Drugs, knife, burglar. *Hanson's a petty thief.*

I rushed to my computer and waited while it retrieved his arrest records.

"What are you doing in here?" Dixon tossed his jacket on his desk.

I looked up at my partner. "I think I may have a lead on the Reed case."

"Yeah?" Dixon walked to the coffeepot, which was empty.

"Yeah. We've been focused on how Estelle would have gotten the Halothane, when the answer may have been right in front of us."

Dixon placed a cup beneath the water cooler and filled it. "What's been right in front of us?"

"Her grandson's a thief," I said, and Dixon's blue eyes widened.

"Fuck. Have you been able to review the evidence list from his last arrest?" Dixon flipped on his computer.

"No, I'm waiting for the hamsters to stop spinning their wheels and toss me a breadcrumb," I said, and leaned back in my chair. "What the hell are you doing here on a Sunday?"

"DCI called. I didn't get the job," he said.

"Oh, man, I'm so sorry." I wanted to pat his back or something. I opted to tightly squeeze his shoulder. "I really thought you had it."

"Me too. I thought I'd catch up on some paperwork. Sheridan's in nesting mode, and if I'd stayed at the house, I'd only get caught up in one of her projects." His laughter didn't cover the disappointment on his face. His thumb brushed the rim of his cup. "You know what I was thinking?"

"That Cody's a fine name for a son?"

This made him genuinely smile. "No. But Chief mentioned that it was a second marriage for both Ames and Estelle."

"Yeah, that's right."

Dixon looked at me. "So maybe their first marriages could shed some light on this."

"That kind of thinking deserves an 'atta boy.'" I heartily whacked his back. "Nice catch, Detective."

He shook his head. "Listen, I don't know if it'll yield anything, but it's worth a look."

"Copy that. I'll work on Hanson's priors, you check vital records."

"Yeah, I was afraid of that. Estelle's ninety-one. This could take some time."

I glanced at my cell. It was five thirty. "As long as I'm at Reese's by seven, we're good."

"Dinner?" Dixon said, his back to me and his face turned to the monitor on his desk.

"You know it."

"Can she cook?"

"First real meal." I shrugged. "Can't be any worse than my sister."

Dixon's laughter filled the empty squad room.

CHAPTER FORTY-SEVEN

REESE

"Ms. Reed, you scared me!" My heart beat so loudly, I placed my hand over my chest. "Wow. That'll get the heart started."

Murray's steady growl grew louder.

"Shut that mutt up or I will." Her dark eyes zeroed in on me. "I was clear in the lease. No animals. I don't like animals."

"Oh, this isn't my dog. I mean, we kind of share him." I smiled. "But today I'm just dog sitting." I scratched behind Murray's ears, which remained tucked back.

Her stare hardened. "What are you doing down here?"

"Looking for my box of books. My engineer, you met him, Toby, he said he put some boxes down here."

"I thought my instructions were specific. My items were to be left alone." She tucked her graying hair behind her ear, and it reminded me of the photographer's assistant who did the same thing with Ella.

I shook my head. I hadn't thought about Campbell or Ella in weeks. I guess the letter unearthed my last dream in the bathtub.

"I haven't touched anything," I said.

She seemed to look past me. I turned behind me and the door to the electrical box was open.

"Oh." I closed it. "I checked to make sure it was the electrical box, and it is."

"You had no business opening that," she said. "Some things are better left in the past."

"What?" I swallowed hard, but it didn't dislodge the knot that tightened whenever Ms. Reed spoke. My body seemed to sense something I couldn't identify. Something was off about my landlord. I felt like I had been thrust into a fight-or-flight situation with her, and I didn't intend to flee. I hadn't lived in Wyoming very long, but long enough to know things were about to get western.

"The one survival tactic that hasn't failed me after all these years is denial," she said.

"Okay." I slowly nodded. "Denial? About what?"

"A past love."

Past love? My emotions flip-flopped inside me. I reached into my back pocket and withdrew the small photo. I held it up, looked at Ella, and then across at Ms. Reed. *Oh my God.* My hands shook and the photo fell to the floor.

CHAPTER **FORTY-EIGHT**

CODY

"Well, that's bullshit," I said. "The online evidence log is temporarily offline for maintenance."

"It is Sunday," Dixon said.

"How're you doing?" I wheeled my chair toward him.

"You wouldn't know it, but Estelle was a very popular name back in the day."

I glanced at the screen. "How far back in the day are you looking?"

"Well...." Dixon scrolled through Wyoming's vital records to the section that contained the registry of marriages.

The state-issued certificates were indexed on microfilm, which was a pain in the ass to wade through. My eyes hurt just looking at the stream of names in front of us.

"We know Estelle's ninety-one and she married Ames Reed in 1977. Her age listed on their marriage certificate is forty," Dixon said.

"How old was Ames?"

"Sixty."

"Robbing the cradle." I laughed and then cringed. "Actually, I can't imagine Estelle ever looking hot."

"Agreed. So, she married Ames when she was forty, so her first marriage would have happened, what, when she was twenty?"

"Probably."

"What was her maiden name?" I asked while Dixon scrolled through the registry by decades.

"Simone. Estelle Simone." Dixon stopped at the end of the fifties, and we began reading through page after page of entries.

"Fuck, how many marriages were there?" I said. "Was there some kind of special on mail-order brides?"

Dixon laughed. "No, that happened much earlier than the fifties."

"Go to the forties," I said.

The screen jumped to 1944. I leaned into Dixon's desk and stared at the list of records. My focus jumped to a record. I squinted. *That can't be right.* Suddenly, it felt like the blood drained from my body.

"Is that…?" I pointed to the row on the monitor. *May 5, 1944: Campbell Matthews (30), Estelle Simone (18), Cheyenne, Wyoming.*

"Is that Campbell Matthews—*the* Campbell Matthews that haunts the Point?" Dixon looked at me.

"*Haunted* the point," I corrected. "He hasn't shown up since he began visiting Reece in her dreams." I stated it as if it was the most normal thing to relate to my fellow officer.

"Sheridan told me about Reese's dreams. I thought it was strange, but not out of the realm of possible—not at that hotel."

"I'm with you. But remember how I found Reese wandering the back passageway in the wall on Halloween?"

Dixon nodded.

"Reese doesn't remember how she got there, but she was clear about the dream. Wild Bill calls them spiritual visits. But"—I shook my head—"she said in that dream on Halloween that Campbell had been murdered by his wife."

"You're fucking with me," Dixon said. "Sheridan didn't mention that."

"I'm not sure Reese would have shared it with Peach—not with her being pregnant. Reese wouldn't want to do anything to freak her out." I pointed to the vital record link on the computer screen. "Open that up."

Dixon clicked the link for the wedding certificate of Estelle Simone and Campbell Matthews.

"Do you have the marriage record for Estelle and Ames?" I asked.

"Yeah, I bookmarked it." Dixon minimized the window and opened the vital record tab with Estelle's second marriage.

"Print it. And then print this one."

"Okay."

"I want to compare the signatures," I said. "You mentioned there were a lot of Estelles. And Simone may have been a common last name."

"Copy that."

The printer hummed in the back of the squad room. I ran back, picked up the two black-and-white copies, and placed them side by side.

"Fuck," Dixon said beside me.

"Fuck is right," I said. "But all we have at this point is Reese's dream. We don't have any proof that Estelle killed Campbell."

"And the Colt was clean, right?"

I nodded.

Dixon returned to his computer. "Okay, she obviously kept her maiden name after her wedding, so she had to live somewhere in Cheyenne, because her marriage to Ames was in Cheyenne. So, it figures she probably never left Cheyenne."

"Right. Let's look at title records from, what, 1944 after her wedding to Campbell?" I said.

"Her short wedding to Campbell." Dixon pulled up Campbell's death certificate. "Campbell died on June 15, 1944."

CHAPTER **FORTY-NINE**

REESE

The photo fell to the floor and tears burned my eyes. "Ella?"

A disturbing smile spread across her aged face. "I haven't been called that in years."

You are Ella.

Wind whistled from a crack in the small basement window and reminded me of Campbell, who always whistled. The wind rattled the door to the electrical box, which hadn't shut completely. I slammed the metal door and heard the slide slip back behind the frame and seal it shut.

I picked up the folded letter from the basement floor. "He loved you."

She scoffed. "Love? Oh, sweet child. What has love ever gotten a woman but heartache and loss. Love should be ranked up there with the seven deadly sins. Love is corrosive, erodes the soul, and strips a person of their individuality."

"No." I shook my head. "Love isn't corrosive. It's not

always easy, but it's a lack of love that slowly erodes the soul. Campbell loved you, Ella."

"Ella? She hasn't been around for a *long* time. I'm Estelle."

"What happened to you?"

She tilted her head, as if she hadn't heard me, but when she spoke, her voice was terse with anger. "What happened to me?" She shook her head. "What happened to me was Ella. Campbell's Ella was young and foolish. It took me years to regain my father's trust. He built me this house." She glanced at the dingy basement walls. "But it was never as grand as my four sisters' homes. Ella practically ruined my life. But Estelle, Estelle resurrected it. I became someone. I married someone. And I pocketed everything I could so that I'd never be reliant on another man again."

"But Campbell wasn't just another man," I said.

Her once vibrant violet eyes were dark and menacing. "Campbell was a dreamer, and for a time, I allowed myself to get caught up in his dream. But I was a stupid, foolish girl."

"I saw you when you were with him. I watched your face the first time you danced with him at the Officers' Club. You had on a beautiful yellow dress, and he was in his uniform."

For a moment, her face softened.

"I felt your heart speed up any time he touched you, and I saw in your eyes that you loved him. You really loved him."

"Nonsense," she said. "Pure rubbish. I don't know where you get your information, but it's false."

"Campbell visited me. He showed me in my dreams the love you shared and how much he loved you. And how hard it was for you because you were torn between him and your father."

She shook her head. "No. My father was the only rational person. He had my best interest at heart." She cocked her head toward the walls in the basement cellar. "That's why he built me this house, so I'd have a home after Campbell died."

"Died?" My raised voice startled her, and her eyes narrowed their focus on me. "Campbell didn't die."

"This can go one of two ways." The edge to her tone matched the spite in her eyes. Her craggy hand reached into the pocket of her jacket and pulled out a gun. "You can give me the letter and picture and walk away, or…." She cocked the hammer. "You don't walk away at all and end up like my dear husband. I'll make sure, like I did with him, that your death is ruled a suicide."

The reality trickled slowly into me. *Oh my God. You really did kill Campbell.*

Her hands gripped the gun, which looked familiar. "It's a cheap county-issued weapon, like the one that cop of yours has. And, a Glock no less." She shook her head. "Glocks are *so* unreliable. But since you're dating that cop, using a Glock makes sense. I saw you two running together today. Interesting. I didn't take you for a Negro lover."

"Shut your mouth," I said.

"Tsk, tsk, if you're going to date a Negro, you're going to have to get used to people staring and saying nasty things."

"Sorry to break the news to you, but it's the twenty-first century. That backward thinking ended decades ago. Get with the times."

She waved the gun at me. "The times? Oh, I'm current with my news. In fact, did you know that just last week an officer's weapon—a Glock—accidentally discharged against a suspect? The officer was placed on administrative leave, but…." She shrugged. "Since the suspect died, there's no one to testify that it *wasn't* an accident. It's just a matter of time before the officer's cleared of any wrongdoing."

"You're crazy. No one will believe I shot myself. Or that Cody's gun accidentally discharged." I placed the letter in my back pocket beside my cell phone. I turned like I was checking on Murray as I quickly thumbed my phone awake. I hit the Voice Memos app, and when New Recording surfaced, I pressed the red button to record this crazy, confessing, murdering bitch. I pressed the side button to raise the volume and tucked it back in my jeans pocket. I silently prayed that it would record us. I didn't have a weapon, but the letter had enough ammunition to take the bitch down—for good. Or at least I hoped it did. I patted my thigh, and Murray responded to my cue and stood beside me. My pulse kept rhythm with my pounding heart. My body was on overdrive. *Keep it together. Just keep it together.*

Ella kept the gun aimed on me. "So, are we doing this the easy way? Or not?"

CHAPTER **FIFTY**

CODY

The title record search wasn't any faster than the marriage records. I jumped on my computer. "Okay, I'll take 1944 and you take 1945, and we'll work from there."

"Copy that."

On a sticky note, I had "Estelle Simone/Estelle Simone Matthews" written. I rubbed my eyes, but the microfilm blurred past me. I cracked my neck, but it didn't relieve the tension. Something just didn't sit right. Ever since we'd run past Estelle's house, something didn't click.

I leaned back in my chair. "The corner house on Carey and 30th Street, who's on title for that?"

Dixon switched screens. "The original title listed Ames Reed, who…" He paused. "Deeded it to Ella Simone, who then deeded it to Gene Hanson. That explains why she could collect SSI. She's not listed on the high-end house on Carey."

"Ella or Estelle?" I asked.

"Ella."

"Okay, let's look for Ella too." I kept thumbing the Page Down key, but nothing in 1944 surfaced under Estelle, Ella, or Campbell.

"I think I have something," Dixon leaned back. "In 1945, Ella Simone was placed on title as sole owner of a home at 21009 Evans Avenue."

My heartrate spiked, my mouth got dry, and I thought I was going to puke. "Give me that address again."

"21009 Evans Avenue."

"Has it been sold since 1945?" My palms began to sweat.

"Negative. Ella Simone's still on title. She didn't deed it to anyone. It's listed as her primary residence."

"Suit up." I grabbed my Kevlar vest.

"Copy that." Dixon didn't ask questions. He strapped on his vest, and we both mounted our mics to our bodies.

"I'll drive. Contact Connie or whoever's in dispatch. Tell them we have a suspected 10-32 at 21009 Evans Avenue."

"Copy that." Dixon was on the mic as we ran toward my truck. He was barely inside when I pulled out of the parking lot.

"That's Reese's house. The one she rents. And the landlord wanted to check on the furnace today," I said.

"Does a house that old still have a furnace? Wouldn't it have been upgraded to a heater? And if it did have a furnace, why would she need to check it? For what?"

"Copy that. I was so preoccupied with Estelle and what she did to Murray, I barely heard Reese when she said her landlord wanted to check the furnace."

"And you think a gun's involved?" Dixon asked, referring to the code 10-32, notifying dispatch that a weapon may be involved.

"It's Estelle" was all I said.

CHAPTER FIFTY-ONE

REESE

Ella pointed the Glock at me. Murray growled. When I didn't give her the letter, she aimed the gun at Murray.

"No!" I reached into my back pocket and took a tentative step toward her. "Don't hurt him."

"I already killed him." She nodded. "Look at how he whimpers."

"You hurt him?" I tightened my hold on the letter and practically tore the sides of the lined paper with my hand. I clenched my jaw. "How could you do that? How could you hurt an animal?"

She made a tisk, tisk sound that made me feel nauseous.

"You answered your own question. He's an animal."

"You're sick."

"That's one possibility," she said. "But he's the one who ingested all that poison."

"What?" I glanced at Murray, who looked like he was

ready to attack, and if I didn't think the bitch would shoot him, I'd let him rip off her ugly face.

"It was one of the few gifts from my grandson, Gene. He picked up the poison on one of his, let's say, outings."

"What? What poison?"

Her yellow teeth made my stomach tighten. "I guess your cop doesn't tell you everything."

"Shut up. There's things about his job that Cody can't tell me."

Her laughter made my skin spike with goose pimples.

"What that cop of yours didn't tell you was that the mutt was given enough Halothane to shut him up. He was always yapping and crying. I told those ingrates that, if they didn't take better care of their mutt, I would. And I did."

"Why? I don't understand. What did this dog do to you?" I thought about her history of violence and what I knew of it. "I get you felt trapped by Campbell, and I can almost understand how you saw his death as your only way out, and even how you played it off as suicide, but hurting a dog? That steps beyond an impulsive act that's covered up." I rubbed my forehead. "And Halothane? What the hell is that?" I shook my head and glanced at Murray, as if he could shed light on her rambling.

"I masked him, gassed him, and then sliced him." She seemed pleased with herself.

"Oh my God." Anger raged through me. "I really hate to shatter the perception you have of yourself, but while Ella may have been a little selfish, and even spoiled, Estelle is pure evil. Anyone who deliberately harms an animal with no remorse has crossed a line that no amount of mercy or clemency can make right."

"You're so much like her."

"Like who?" I raised my voice. *Ella or Estelle—whatever she called herself—the woman had cracked.*

"Ella."

"What? You think *I'm* like Ella? You're crazy. *You* are Ella!"

"Once. I was Ella once in my life, but Estelle saved me."

"You really have lost it."

She shrugged. "If that's what you need to believe. My attorney says mental illness is a wonderful defense." She held the Glock with the certainty of someone who had successfully killed before and had never been caught.

Shock numbed me. I didn't know what to do. Murray couldn't climb the stairs, and I wasn't going to leave him— ever. I glanced at the staircase, which looked engulfed in smoke, and my eyes began to burn. *Fuck, the steak.* If the house had a working fire alarm, which I doubted, I hadn't heard it. There was no way I could carry Murray up the stairs now.

"I don't know why you look so worried. Your Negro came and rescued the pathetic mutt. I suppose they're a perfect pair. Both are damaged goods."

"Listen, bitch, lower your Confederate flag and remove your swastika. Ignorant racists like you lost both wars, and no one likes to listen to losers. So, shut up or shoot me, because I've had more than my fill of that tired old bullshit."

CHAPTER **FIFTY-TWO**

CODY

I jumped the curb and parked my truck at an angle on the sidewalk in front of Reese's rental. Dixon and I were out within seconds and approached the two-story brick house quickly, but cautiously. Dixon flanked my right side as I took the porch stairs two at a time and pressed against the side of the house by the front door. I glanced into the front window. The curtains were drawn, and I couldn't see inside. *Fuck.*

I quietly grabbed the door handle and twisted. It opened, and Dixon and I entered—and were overtaken by smoke. I buried my face in the crook of my arm, but the smoke was thick.

I glanced at Dixon. We had a decision to make. We didn't have the proper equipment to protect us and address the threat of fire, but if I knew my partner, he'd feel as compelled as I did to take action because Reese was in danger. We could either stand by and wait for the fire department, or act to save a life. Dixon nodded toward the smoke, which was all I needed to take the lead. I didn't know if Reese and Murray were trapped or dead. My adrenaline was on overdrive, and the smoke in the house didn't help me catch my breath. But I'd walk through any fire to save Reese.

****

REESE

"Shooting you would be too easy, but putting down that mutt, now that would be poetic." She aimed the Glock at Murray. "Now be a good girl and hand me the letter."

The smoke from the stairs now hung above us in the basement like dense fog. I tossed the letter to Ella, who was about to pick it up when Cody's voice cut through the haze.

"Police! Let her go."

Ella spun on the thin heel of her boot. "She's trespassing."

I stared at Ella's slouchy boots that stopped at the hem of her black slacks. Her waiflike figure rested on the small heel.

"I found her trespassing," Ella said with the innocence of a child. "She was irate and crying over this dog. And…." She paused and looked at me, shaking her head. "I think she's been drinking."

That's it. That. Is. It.

I rushed her and kicked the side of her sensible black boots. She fell like a domino. Her gun flew in the air. I ducked, but Murray jumped in the air and was about to catch the barrel with his mouth when I screamed, "No!"

Murray stopped midair and the weapon fell between us and Ella, releasing a shot, but it happened so fast I couldn't see where the bullet went or what, if anything, it hit. But when blood began to seep on the cement floor, I looked for the source.

"No, no, no." I scrambled to Murray, who was beside Ella. Suddenly, blood was everywhere, and Murray's coat was splattered red. "No, no, no." I began feeling his body, but Murray spotted Cody and went to him.

"Whose blood is this?" I glanced at Ella. A gaping hole in the back of her head oozed. I tore off my sweatshirt and pressed it against the wound.

Blood soaked through my sweatshirt and clung to my hands. "Ella…."

Her violet eyes lightened, and she seemed to be staring at someone above me.

"Ella, I'm so sorry." Despite how crazy she acted, I felt like I knew who she was—before she had turned into Estelle.

Her thin lips curved into a beautiful smile, and years seemed to melt from her face. She kept staring above me. I leaned toward her mouth as she whispered, "Campbell," before she closed her eyes, and her body relaxed as if her soul had been spirited away back to him.

My chest ached and tears streamed down my face. "Oh, Ella. No."

I felt his hand on my back. "Reese… there's nothing you

can do."

I lowered my head and tears fell into my lap. "I didn't want it to end like this." *Campbell. Ella.* Their love story unfolded in moments in my mind. Ella's yellow dress. Campbell's uniform. Their first dance. Ella's photo. Christmas. Their wedding. *Doll.*

"They were in love." I shook with sorrow. "It wasn't just in my dreams. They loved each other. And somehow they lost their way." I looked at Cody. "They just lost their way."

"I know." His arms wrapped around me. "But now they're together."

Cody's loyal, sweet dog whimpered beside me. "Oh, Murray."

A sharp gasp came from Ella before her head fell to the side and she quit breathing. I covered my mouth, but it didn't stop the hurt from pouring out. I gently moved my sweatshirt off her blood-soaked head. Before I laid it over her face, I leaned forward. "Campbell never left you or stopped loving you. He's been waiting for you."

CHAPTER **FIFTY-THREE**

REESE

The daily paper was on the counter beside Cody's car keys. The headline didn't make me smile, but it did bring closure.

1944 Cold Case: 73 Years Later Justice Found for Cowboy Campbell Matthews

Cheyenne, WY: It was a death that mystified the Cheyenne community for decades. Army Officer Campbell Matthews's apparent suicide with the Colt pistol he bestowed on his wife on their delayed honeymoon left a community with one question—why?

Now, Cheyenne police say that the 30-year-old Matthews didn't kill himself but was murdered by his bride. Estelle Simone was 18 when the crime was committed. Simone died over the weekend as the result of a bullet that discharged accidentally from her weapon.

Cheyenne Police Chief Patrick Wyman says that a letter

and additional sources revealed that on the night of June 15, 1944, Simone, 18, and Matthews, 30, met at the Historic Wyoming Point Resort in Cheyenne, then the Wyoming Inn, for a delayed honeymoon. The newly married couple argued over Matthews's reenlistment in the war effort. Court records reveal Simone had filed to annul their May 10, 1944 marriage, but allegedly Matthews refused.

The Cheyenne Division of Forensics retrieved three bullet fragments in the wall of the hotel that align with original police reports that cite guests recalled hearing multiple shots fired.

"Officer Matthews was shot between the eyes while lying prone on the bed—not typical of a suicide, but certainly of a person murdered in their sleep," Wyman said. "Ballistics proved it was murder, but that skill set was not around in the 1940s. Plus guests recall multiple shots, which a dead man cannot do. Ms. Simone's claim in the initial report that it was a murder-suicide gone wrong just doesn't align with the discovery and location of the bullet fragments."

Simone claimed her husband killed himself because he couldn't perform his husbandly duties. However, old hotel records discovered in a footlocker in the boiler room reveal Matthews and Simone were frequent guests of the hotel.

Wyman said the 91-year-old Simone was a resident of Cheyenne her entire life.

Cody placed his hands on my shoulders and began to massage me. "She can't hurt anyone anymore. Nor will she be haunting anyone."

I leaned my head against his chest. "Promise?"

He kissed my forehead. "Promise." His green eyes were unwavering. "You and Murray don't have anything to worry about."

I softly smiled. "You don't know how right you are."

Cody grinned. "I'm always right." He paused. "But what exactly am I right about?"

"Remember how I told you that corporate had plans to put the hotel on the auction block in the spring?"

"Yeah."

"Ever since news leaked that Campbell had been murdered at the hotel, the reservation line hasn't stopped ringing. Who knew a decades-old cold case would be a source of endless fascination and generate so many room bookings?" I laughed. "Now corporate is looking to put more money into long-overdue renovation work. Like a new boiler and possibly even an elevator, if I can convince Toby we need another Otis."

"Your staff would follow you anywhere," Cody said.

"And what about you?" I asked, turning around in his arms. He brushed a strand of hair off my face.

"Always by your side, forever in my heart."

My chest swelled and my eyes watered. This man. This beautiful, beautiful man.

Cody leaned forward and kissed me. Slowly. Tenderly. Passionately. It was the kind of kiss that was the beginning of forever. And we would forever be together in mind, body, and spirit.

CHAPTER FIFTY-FOUR

REESE

It was a new year and new start for the hotel. The Historic Wyoming Point Resort was no longer in jeopardy of being sold at auction. I stood behind the front desk beside Zavi, who entered another reservation for suite 632.

"That suite is booked until August," he said.

The portrait of Campbell Matthews had replaced the portrait of Governor Campbell. I glanced up and smiled at my friendly spirit, who I hadn't dreamt of or felt since Ella died. The woman I encountered in the basement was Estelle, but the one who left our world peacefully in front of me was Ella.

"Everyone wants to come here now because of Campbell," Zavi said.

"I think the biggest draws are the daily tours Wild Bill arranged," I said.

"Yeah, he does a boss job. Plus, it doesn't hurt that he

believes in spirits," he said.

I tilted my head at Zavi. "And you don't?"

Zavi grinned. "I believe the hotel was haunted until you calmed Campbell down."

I rolled my eyes. "I didn't do anything."

"Not true." Toby walked into the lobby from the second floor, with Cody and Dixon beside him. "You solved the mystery."

"Thanks, Tobster, but it was a group effort," I said, nodding toward Cody and Dixon. "Cody came to my rescue more times than one man should. And if you"—I glanced at Toby—"and Wild Bill hadn't remembered that footlocker in the boiler room, we wouldn't have the archival documents to back up our story. By the way, I love the glass case you made to house the original hotel registry book." I glanced at the display case that welcomed guests when they entered the hotel. The registry was open to the page that contained Campbell and Ella's last entry as guests at the hotel. Every time I walked past it, I imagined their one last dance in their suite.

My engineer grinned. "Yeah, that protective glass and lock makes it look like we're housing the Constitution or something."

"And how's our other project coming along?" I raised an eyebrow at Toby. Cody stood with his arms crossed.

"Didn't we pass inspection?" I asked. Cody and Dixon had taken a preliminary look at the development project for safety issues, but we still had to pass a builder's inspection.

"The love lounge has been expanded—within code—to

host intimate murder mystery dinners," he said.

"I don't think you'll have any issues passing inspection," Cody said.

"Then why the long face?" I asked.

His voice lowered and a sheepish look crossed his masculine face. "I liked the love lounge."

I felt heat rush to my cheeks.

"Buddy, we all liked the love lounge," Zavi said, causing us to all laugh.

"I'm sure you'll find another hidden room in some wall and we'll have another love lounge for the staff," I said. "But in the meantime, we'll be able to host murder mystery dinners behind the library wall."

Zavi pumped his fist. "That is so badass."

I laughed. "We might as well capitalize on our selling points and having a haunted hotel—or formerly haunted hotel—is pure gold. Combined with the historical significance of the property, Wild Bill's come up with four different types of tours. Not bad for such an old hotel."

"Not bad at all," Toby said. "And to think it all started with one ghost. Or spirit."

"So, speaking of ghosts—what do you think makes a good ghost story?" Zavi looked at me.

I gently smiled and thought about Campbell and Ella, but it was Cody's warm eyes I stared into when I spoke. "The best ghost stories have a rich history, a little bit of mystery, a one-of-a-kind hotel and, of course—" I grinned. "—a wonderful love story."

THE END

ACKNOWLEDGEMENTS

There were myriad sources I discovered when researching the premise for *Spirited Away*.

Shawn Cook, a Cheyenne native, owns an HVAC shop. I met Shawn when we both appeared on an entrepreneurship panel at Laramie County Community College. During lunch, I picked his brain and Shawn patiently explained the difference between water and steam heat. He explained how a radiator worked, described how a boiler from the 1900s could and did function, and sent me in the direction of the historic mansions and other notable landmarks in Cheyenne. Thank you, Shawn for skipping lunch to talk to me.

Diane Edgar—another writing student who used to work police dispatch—gave me the "411" on all things code-related for Detective Cody Pring. And how officers and dispatch form relationships. Her helpfulness to answer my questions brought another dimension to my favorite Cheyenne Detective. Thank you so much, Diane!

Amiee Reese is my neighbor and friend. She's also

kickass at hosting big events in Cheyenne. So naturally, I sought her out on July 4 when we celebrated the holiday together. I was more interested in how my hotel GM could host a party on the rooftop tennis courts than eating dinner. Amiee researched how to winterize an outdoor tennis court to make my vision a reality. Thank you so much! And to your husband, Shawn, who put out my hair when it caught on fire later that night from a rogue sparkler. True story. You guys are the best!

To the Night Writers, who let me drop into the writing group on Monday nights at the library—Dave Lerner, Anna Lane, Rene Minder, Merissa Racine and John Schutlz— you were the best beta readers for this book. From Dave's suggestion I christen Wild Bill with the last name Goldstein, to John's P.Nus jokes—I left laughing and hopeful that I could bring the necessary humor to this story. Thank you, gang!

To my publisher, who believes in me and makes me feel valued, respected, and appreciated—thank you, Becky Johnson and Hot Tree Publishing. I had one goal this year: write three, full-length romance books and have them published. You made that goal a reality and in the process shaped my work as a writer. I am better because of your hard work and editing process. Thank you. I love this series and I look forward to growing it even more! xoxoxo

Olivia Ventura—Liv—I promised you a talking elevator when we rode one in Hot-lanta and laughed uncontrollably. I keep my promises so "Otis" was for you. So were the BeeGees. Thank you for knowing my voice and protecting it in the editing process. I have grown as a writer because of you! Xoxoxo

And to my family…

Super Cooper—When I needed a name for my attorney, you pulled two Coke bottles, which featured first and last names, from the vacation cooler and David Benjamin was born. Kid, you're genius. And a wonderfully talented writer. I love your stories and our time together. Life is #BetterTogether.

To my husband, Ron Gullberg, for making me laugh when I ask the most ridiculous questions about men. Every writer has their muse and when I met you, I knew I had found mine. I love you to the moon and back.

To my twin sons, Austin and Kyle, who patiently respond to my texts about millennials. Thank you for always making time for me. And sitting beside me at book signings. That means everything.

To my daughter, Ciara, you just make life better. In each of my heroines, I imagine you—strong, independent, and brave. The world is yours.

To my stepsons, Dylan and Max, thank you, gentleman, for always supporting me and welcoming me into your lives.

To my siblings, Suzanne Billiter Cragin, Stephen Billiter and Patrick Billiter, this book reminded me of Halloween, which Dad loved and Mom made so fun. Thank you for believing in me and always buying my book, which make great holiday gifts in case you need to buy more than just one…. Xoxoxo

And finally, to my readers—at each book signing I meet

someone new, which inspires me to move forward in my craft so I can meet even more readers. Thank you. It's an honor and privilege to write and be read. I truly appreciate each and every one of you.

ABOUT THE **AUTHOR**

Mary Billiter is a weekly newspaper columnist and fiction author. She also has novels published under the pen name, "Pumpkin Spice."

Mary resides in the Cowboy State with her unabashedly bald husband, their combined children, and runaway dog. She does her best writing (in her head) on her daily runs in wild, romantic, beautiful Wyoming.

Connect with Mary:

WWW.MARYBILLITER.COM

WWW.TWITTER.COM/MARYBILLITER

WWW.FACEBOOK.COM/MARYMBILLITER

ABOUT THE **PUBLISHER**

Hot Tree Publishing opened its doors in 2015 with an aspiration to bring quality fiction to the world of readers. With the initial focus on romance and a wide spread of romance sub-genres, we envision opening up to alternative genres in the near future.

Firmly seated in the industry as a leading editing provider to independent authors and small publishing houses, Hot Tree Publishing is the sister company to Hot Tree Editing, founded in 2012. Having established in-house editing and promotions, plus having a well-respected market presence, Hot Tree Publishing endeavors to be a leader in bringing quality stories to the world of readers.

Interested in discovering more amazing reads brought to you by Hot Tree Publishing or perhaps you're interested in submitting a manuscript and joining the HTPubs family? Either way, head over to the website for information:

WWW.HOTTREEPUBLISHING.COM